CARTERET

CONFIRMED BACHELORS BOOK 3

JENNY HAMBLY

This book is a work of fiction. Names, characters, places and events,
other than those clearly in the public domain, are either the product
of the author's imagination, or are used fictitiously. Any resemblance
to actual people, living or dead, are purely coincidental.

CHAPTER 1

Laurence Westerby, the fifth Viscount Carteret, stepped wearily down from the post chaise and four. He had been on the road for five days and it was with some relief that he entered what was, in his opinion, the most comfortable coaching inn that Stamford had to offer. He was well known at The George and although the inn was always busy, the landlord assured him that he had been holding a private parlour for him for the last two days in expectation of his arrival.

"Thank you, Skelton. Three days of incessant rain hindered my progress somewhat. Has Faden arrived with my curricle yet?"

"Yes, my lord," the landlord confirmed. "He arrived yesterday. If you would like to step up to your parlour, I'll bring you some refreshment whilst your valet unpacks your bag."

"A glass of claret would be most welcome," Laurence said with a gentle smile. "But send it up to my room along with some hot water, will you? I'll dine in an hour."

When he had washed and changed his raiment, Laurence made his way to the parlour set aside for his use. He was pleased to see a fire had been lit and the curtains drawn for August was fast approaching its end and an autumnal chill accompanied the approaching dusk. He stretched out his legs, crossed them at the ankles, and leant back, closing his eyes.

The small sigh that escaped him was not one of contentment. Although his wealth allowed him to indulge himself in any way he chose and his acquaintance was large, he had begun to feel dissatisfied with his lot. If anyone had suggested to him five years ago that he would be the last of his particular friends to marry he would have been incredulous.

Whilst he had thought himself madly in love with a young, gentle lady of quality, his friends had been chasing females of a quite different stamp. It was fortunate that his calf love, Diana Ramshorn, had turned him down. He had been attracted to a lively but fragile beauty who had aroused all his chivalrous instincts and had wished for nothing more than to shield her from every ill wind that blew. When she had rejected him for a man of higher rank after offering him every encouragement to believe his suit would prosper, he had turned cynical. Meeting Diana again this season, he had realised that they would never have suited and had finally let go any bitterness he felt towards her.

He smiled wryly. He had for several years considered himself the most sensible of fellows and had long ago banished any foolish romantic fancies, yet he had recently been caught up in two eminently romantic episodes. Admittedly, neither had concerned his own heart but had culminated in his closest friend, Allerdale, and that gentleman's cousin, Charles Bassington, becoming tenants for life.

Neither episode had left him untouched, however. Witnessing the palpable bond that had arced between Allerdale and Miss Edgcott had unsettled him. He had been delighted for his friend but had felt a pang of something that had been strangely akin to envy. He had been aware of it again when he had attended the wedding of Charles and his bride, Lady Selena.

He shook his head ruefully. In helping Charles come to a realisation of his true feelings for the young woman he had known since she had been a child, he had played a dangerous game. His attentions to Lady Selena had been marked enough to rouse Charles' jealousy but had also perhaps given her cause to think that he might offer for her. Laurence's lips twisted. There was no perhaps about it, as had been made clear to him when she had given him the broadest hint that she would welcome his proposal.

You once told me that you had been disappointed in love, Lord Carteret. I hope that this circumstance will not prevent you seeking happiness with another. Perhaps someone who has also suffered in such a way and would therefore be willing to settle for liking and respect.

Laurence opened his eyes and reached for the wine glass at his elbow. He would have been in the briars if Charles had not come up to scratch; his sense of honour might well have prompted him to offer for Lady Selena, and although he quite agreed in principle that liking and respect were solid foundations on which to build a marriage, they must have been seriously undermined by the knowledge that his bride was deeply in love with another.

He rose to his feet as the door opened and two servants hurried in carrying various platters. As the aroma of roast meat reached him, he nodded his thanks, crossed the room to the dining table set before the window, and reached for the carving knife. He cut two thick slices of beef, a slight frown marring his brow.

He had advised Lady Selena not to settle just yet, trusting that Allerdale would be able to drum some sense into his cousin. He was thankful that he had, but the exuberant, unadulterated happiness that had marked Charles and Selena's short engagement, and the more restrained but powerful connection between Allerdale and his new bride had made him question his own willingness to settle. His twenty-ninth birthday was imminent, however, and he knew it behoved him to think seriously about marrying. Perhaps next season he would meet a lady who could pierce his famous reserve.

He paused in the act of raising his fork to his mouth as the door opened. A lady in a black cloak, the hood drawn up, whisked into the room, shutting the door behind her with exaggerated care. She leant her ear against it for a moment and then gave a low chuckle, turning on the pleasant sound.

Laurence stood and offered her a bow.

"How can I be of service, ma'am?"

She stilled and pulled her hood a little further forward so that her face remained in shadow.

"Forgive me, sir. I heard no sound when I listened at the door and assumed this room was empty."

Her voice was as low and as melodic as her chuckle.

The ghost of a smile touched Laurence's lips. "Are you in the habit of listening at keyholes?"

"I should think not, sir. I am far too tall; it would be most uncomfortable," she said lightly.

His mysterious visitor was indeed tall, he realised. He was a little above average height for a man, but he judged her to be only a head shorter, if that.

"I will leave you to your dinner." She turned on the words and cracked open the door, poking her head through the gap. Laurence could not help but be intrigued by her furtive behaviour.

"Are you sure there is nothing I can do for you, ma'am?"

Her head whipped back so fast that her hood slipped from it, revealing a mass of glossy hair the colour of polished mahogany. She gently pushed the door closed and drew up her hood again before turning. Laurence felt a twinge of disappointment; he had hoped to see if her face was as beguiling as her voice.

She stood looking at him for a few moments and although he could not see her eyes, he felt them assessing him. As he raised an enquiring eyebrow, she nodded and came towards him, her movements swift and her stride long and graceful.

"I shall trust you, sir. If you truly wish to be of service, I would ask you to deny that you have seen me."

As he had not, in fact, seen her, this request was not an onerous one.

She carried on past him, opened the curtains and sat on the window seat. Swivelling sideways she brought her feet up before her and pulled her cloak close. "Draw them behind me, if you will."

He looked down at her for a moment, his fingers itching to pull back the offending hood.

"Hurry," she murmured, her tone urgent but calm.

As voices sounded in the corridor, he pulled the curtains closed, quickly sat down, and picked up his fork wondering what he was getting himself mixed up in. His hooded lady did not appear to be afraid, but she seemed very keen to avoid someone.

The landlord's harassed voice penetrated the closed door. "Bow Street Runner or not, you have no right to disturb my guests. This parlour is reserved for Viscount Carteret, and I know for a fact that he is alone and eating his dinner. He will not wish to be disturbed."

Laurence slowly chewed a morsel of beef. She was not a criminal, surely? He had only glimpsed a few inches of her dark green, cambric dress and although it had been a trifle muddied at the hem, as had her jean half-boots, there was no doubting the quality of them or her well-modulated voice.

The runner's reply was calm but intransigent. "There's no need for you to fatch yourself; if all is as you say, then I won't keep him above a moment."

Skelton's voice rose another notch. "I tell you he is a very correct gentleman and would never dine alone with a lady in his private parlour unless she was a relative of his."

"And I tell you I saw her disappear into this room as I reached the head of the stairs."

The voices fell silent, and Laurence heard a low rumble issue from behind the curtains. Being pursued by a runner had not apparently affected his fugitive's appetite. Whilst he admired her insouciance, he could not help but feel that such a prosaic response showed a remarkable want of proper feeling.

The door was suddenly flung wide, and the two men staggered through it locked in an embrace. The landlord was the taller of the two and well-muscled, but the runner was a barrel of a man and determined. Laurence watched his unprepossessing face redden as he planted his legs and resisted the landlord's attempt to pull him back out of the room.

"Enough." The words, though softly spoken, caused the men to immediately break apart. He regarded them with a cold, disinterested stare as they caught their breath. "I hope there is a very good reason for this interruption; your food is excellent, Skelton, but it is rapidly cooling."

"I'll have some more sent up, sir. I tried to stop him——"

"So I heard." His gaze dwelled on the runner for a moment. His blue coat had seen better days and was caked in mud. It hung open revealing a yellow waistcoat that strained over an impressive girth. Above it, he sported a grubby neckcloth whose ends wilted sadly. "I believe you have come from Bow Street?"

The runner reached for his hat. The felt was discoloured in places and one edge curled up like a desiccated autumn leaf. It fit him ill, almost covering his small, sharp eyes. He removed it and bowed.

"That's it, sir. I am apprehendin' a lady and thought I saw her enter this room."

Laurence caught a spear of asparagus on his fork and said casually, "As you see, you are mistaken. Might I ask why you are apprehending this lady? Is she dangerous?"

He bit into the succulent vegetable as the runner's eyes scanned every corner of the room, a confused frown wrinkling his glistening brow. He pulled a handkerchief from the pocket of his coat and mopped it.

"As to that, sir, I couldn't say, but her relative thinks she has run mad, and she is certainly cunning. Who knows what an unhinged female might do?"

The lady had not seemed mad to Laurence but unusually composed, and he did not like the look of the man standing before him. "I have no idea what such a one might do," he said, "nor do I wish to know. What I do wish is that you will go away and continue your search. I hope, however, that you will do so in a less clumsy fashion. Why did you not simply show Skelton your warrant?"

"Because he don't have one," the landlord said, folding his arms and looking at the uninvited guest as if he were a cockroach. "I caught him coming up the back stairs."

Laurence frowned. "How very irregular. What is your name? I am well acquainted with Sir Nathaniel Conant and will ask him when next I see him how it is a man cannot enjoy a hot meal after a long day without being rudely interrupted by one of his special constables, one, furthermore, who has no authority to disturb anyone."

He had, in fact, never had occasion to meet the magistrate but as he had hoped, his words pierced the runner's thick skin. The interloper began to fidget with his hat, twisting it round by the rim.

"The thing is, your lordship, I am working in a private capacity—"

"So, you have not come from Bow Street," Laurence said coldly. "Are you even a runner?"

The man began backing towards the door. "Not any longer, I works for meself now."

"Then you are an imposter and a liar, and you still have not given me your name."

"There's no need for any unpleasantness, sir. It is in the public interest that I find this woman— "

"You mean it is in *your* interests to find her, if she even exists. I am inclined to think she is a figment of your imagination and suspect that you are foxed, sir."

"Now, that I am not!" the man protested.

"Either way, you will leave both this room and this inn or I will have you arrested for disturbing the peace and assaulting Skelton."

The man cast one last glance about the room. "Very well, sir, but don't blame me if you are murdered in your bed."

"Content yourself with the knowledge that if such is to be my fate, I could hardly do so."

The man stomped from the room, almost colliding with a maid carrying a tray. Skelton stepped forward and took it from her as a damson tart, a jug of wine, and a glass threatened to slide from it.

"Off you go, Milly. Bring his lordship some hot—"

"That will not be necessary," Laurence said. "I have suffered enough interruptions and would ask that I remain undisturbed for the rest of the evening. You may send someone to clear the table in the morning."

Skelton began to unload the tray. "As you wish, milord."

"Thank you, and make sure that encroaching fellow leaves the premises, will you?"

The landlord grinned. "It will be my pleasure, sir. I'll have two of my boys throw him out if he is foolish enough to hang around."

"Yes, I think that will be best," Laurence concurred. "He lowers the tone of your fine establishment."

He waited until the landlord had been gone for a minute or two, and then stood, saying softly, "I think it is safe to come out now, my lady."

The cloaked figure slipped from the window seat, drawing the curtains behind her. Her stomach rumbled again as she did so.

"I think you had better join me for dinner," he said wryly.

When she did not reply, he added, "That rascal looked like a sneaky fellow. I hope I have done enough to discourage him, but I would not hazard any large sum on the chance. I suggest you give him time to grow tired of skulking in the shadows before you leave."

His intruder seemed to come to a sudden decision. She walked to the fireplace and retrieved a reticule from the pocket of her cloak before shedding it and casting it over the back of a chair. She wore a high-necked, long-sleeved gown. This modest garment made no concession to fashion; no ribbons, frills or furbelows decorated it and it was unusually wide in the skirt. It could not completely hide her shapely form, however.

"In truth, I am extremely hungry as the unladylike noises issuing from my stomach can attest. But please, give me a moment to tame my unruly hair." She rummaged in her reticule and withdrew a few pins before regarding herself in the mirror, a look of humorous dismay coming into her eyes. "Oh dear, I look quite wild."

Laurence's gaze rested on the thick tendrils that had escaped. They reached almost to her waist. "Do not dress it on my account, you have beautiful hair." He felt a spurt of surprise as he heard his thoughts issue from his lips.

"Yes," she agreed, her tone matter of fact, as she began to twist the strands into the large knot at the back of her head. "It is quite my best feature." A smile lurked in the eyes that met his in the mirror. "It seems the landlord does not know you as well as he thinks, sir. Not only have you invited me to dine with you, but you would have me sit at table looking like a hoyden, and yet I believe I heard you described as a very correct gentleman."

"I am thought to be so," he admitted, watching her attempts to restrain her wayward tresses. "But I find myself in uncharted territory."

Her gaze slid away from his. "As do I, sir."

He was acutely aware of the intimacy of the situation and realising that he was staring in a most ungentlemanly fashion, dragged his eyes away from the striking woman before him. She was not ethereally beautiful as Diana had been, nor had she the vulnerability of Lady Selena, in fact, she had none of the attributes that had hitherto attracted him. There was nothing at all delicate about her features; her lips were plumper than was the fashion, her cheekbones prominent casting a shadow into the hollows beneath, and her chin decided. Rather than curving delicately, her eyebrows winged upwards above chestnut brown eyes framed by thick black lashes. It was a strong, characterful face and disturbingly sensuous.

"There," she said, "that will have to do."

Laurence pulled out a chair before expertly carving her a slice of beef. He placed it, along with some vegetables on the plate that had been brought for his dessert.

"Thank you," she said, a small smile tugging at her lips. "Are you not afraid to be alone with a madwoman?"

"No more than you appear to be at the prospect of dining alone with a complete stranger," he countered.

"Ah," she said, hastily swallowing a mouthful of food, "but your actions speak of your character, sir. You are calm, resourceful, and truly the gentleman. You handled Mr Chubb masterfully." She gave a low laugh. "He is aptly named, don't you think?"

"If that is indeed his name, certainly," he murmured. "Might I know your name, ma'am?"

Her smile turned rueful. "You have earned my trust, sir, but I find myself reluctant to give it. Besides, I doubt very much we shall meet again and so it is entirely unnecessary."

"I would like to know it, nevertheless," he said quietly. "You have the advantage of me, I believe, as Skelton mentioned my title to Mr Chubb before they came into the room."

He poured some wine into the fresh glass the maid

had brought and passed it to her. She took a thoughtful sip.

"I did not catch it," she said, "but we will compromise. Do not furnish me with your title but only your given name, and I shall tell you mine. It will be shockingly forward of us, of course, but we have already consigned convention to the devil, after all."

Laurence accepted her unladylike language without a blink; it seemed to suit her somehow. "Everyone refers to me by my title, even my closest friends,"

"Everyone?" she said, an amused challenge in her eyes. "Even your mother and siblings?"

"My mother did not, of course, and neither do my sisters. They are some five years older than I and can never be made to understand the respect that is due to me now that I am head of the family," he said, his plaintive tone belied by his fond smile. "However, if anyone other than them so errs, Anne is most put out. Everyone else does call me by my title, however."

"Very well," she said, shrugging, "sir and ma'am, it shall be."

"Laurence," he found himself saying, suddenly wondering what his name would sound like on her lips.

"Laurence," she repeated slowly.

As her warm, rich tones wrapped around each syllable, he felt his heart beat a little faster. Not trusting his voice to have its usual level calmness he merely quirked an eyebrow.

"Cassandra," she said.

CHAPTER 2

assandra pulled a face. "I have never liked the name but now positively detest it. My fate seems to be mirroring that of my namesake."

She was not surprised when her very correct gentleman choked on a mouthful of peas and was forced to spit them out. The faint colour that brushed his cheeks hinted at his mortification. She realised she was not playing fair, but the temptation to provoke him out of his calm was irresistible.

"I don't mean literally, of course," she said, taking pity on him. "I have not broken any promises or had my virtue ripped from me, and I certainly cannot predict the future, more's the pity, but it is just that no one will believe what I say, or if they do, they think that I am mad."

Her rescuer regained his equanimity with disappointing swiftness.

"You are well read in the classics, I see. What is it

that they don't believe? And why has Mr Chubb been set on to find you?"

Cassandra sighed. "I am not sure I should tell you; I do not like the role of damsel in distress and would rather remain a lady of mystery."

She pulled the damson tart towards her, cut a slice, and bit into it.

"Oh," she said, closing her eyes, "this is delicious. You must try it."

"I do not enjoy sweet food. Now, stop prevaricating!"

Her eyes sprang open at his exasperated words. "It is not sweet but delightfully sour. I feel sure you will enjoy it."

His lips quivered. "Do you not think I deserve some sort of explanation?"

The tart might not have been sweet but the smile that accompanied these words certainly was. It surprised her and threw her a little off balance. As her rescuer brushed at a few stray locks that had fallen across his brow, she realised for the first time that his hair was at variance with his elegant dress and dignified bearing; it was a little long and apparently left to fall where it would. She found the incongruity intriguing.

If the truth be told, she had known a moment's alarm when she had realised that the parlour was occupied by a gentleman, but it had quickly faded when she had taken his measure. His calm, unruffled acceptance of her intrusion had impressed her. His manners had been excellent if a little stiff, and his gaze direct. She had listened with great appreciation as he had quickly and efficiently stripped Mr Chubb of his pretensions. The only time he had given her reason to doubt him was when he had complimented her on her hair, but she had immediately realised that he was more surprised than she and had been amused. He had no doubt been thrown a little more off-kilter by finding himself alone with a strange female of quality than he cared to show.

Laurence seemed to take her silence for acquiescence. He stood and refilled their glasses. "Shall we retire to the fire where we can be comfortable?"

When they were both seated in the deep armchairs, he sipped at the ruby liquid in his glass, waiting patiently for her to enlighten him. An expectant silence stretched between them, only broken by the occasional crackle and spit of the fire. Finding herself under the regard of a pair of cool, penetrating eyes, she dropped her gaze whilst she considered what she might say. She did feel herself to be under some sort of obligation to him but was reluctant to share her tale with a stranger; one moreover, who might not approve of her actions, or believe her. She hardly believed it herself.

"Very well," she said lightly. "Mr Chubb has been promised a handsome reward by the villain of the piece if he can find me and return me to my family home."

"I gathered as much. Where is your home, Cassandra?"

"Some way from here," she said evasively.

He frowned. "Will you at least tell me who it is you are fleeing from and why they think you mad? It may be that I can aid you further or at least offer you some advice."

It was her turn to feel a moment's exasperation; was her grandfather the only man to have walked this earth who thought a woman perfectly able to make her own decisions? She quickly quashed her impatience aware that she was being unreasonable and he very kind. It was not Laurence's fault that recent experiences had sorely tested her naturally cheerful nature.

"That is most thoughtful of you, Laurence, but I don't suppose they truly think I am mad, and I have quite had my fill of advice. I'm perfectly capable of ordering my own affairs, you know."

He put down his glass and crossed his legs, offering that sweet smile again. "Then satisfy my curiosity."

It was quite ridiculous, she reflected, that a woman of her age could be so affected by a smile. "My story is tedious, although I am unexpectedly enjoying my little adventure." She chuckled. "There is something quite invigorating about pitting your wits against another, but I do not intend to allow Mr Chubb to find me again."

Her companion's smile vanished, his eyes narrowed and his lips tightened. "You meant him to find you?"

"To follow me; I was acting as a decoy whilst my maid carried out my orders."

"You are reckless, Cassandra."

She did not know why she felt disappointed; she had expected his disapproval, after all. She stood and reached for her cloak, saying coolly, "I had not thought myself to be, but I must admit to a feeling of exhilaration, so perhaps I am. You would think so, of course."

Laurence rose to his feet, his gaze gentling. He

took the cloak from her but did not help her into it. "I apologise; it is not my place to judge you on so short an acquaintance. Please, sit. I shall endeavour not to be quite so fusty."

The rueful twist of his lips and the self-mockery she saw in his eyes persuaded her to do so.

"I accept your apology. I realise that my behaviour must seem extraordinary but so are my circumstances."

"Perhaps you would explain them to me a little more clearly."

Deciding she may as well be hung for a sheep as a lamb, she went straight to the heart of the matter. "My cousin wishes to marry me, although why is a mystery; I am not particularly wealthy or beautiful, and I have certainly given him no encouragement, indeed, he disapproves of me prodigiously."

"You surprise me."

She laughed, for this time his words were uttered with gentle humour.

"You are escaping an unwanted suitor, then," he continued. "Why was it necessary for you to run away? Could you not simply have refused him? You cannot be forced into marriage, after all."

"No, I cannot," she said firmly, "but the impertinent dog tried his best to force my hand. When I refused his offer, with far more tact than I am generally credited with I might add, he had the audacity to force a kiss on me just as his mother came into the room."

"Ah, he is your Ajax," Laurence murmured. "What a contemptible fellow. That must have been awkward."

18

"It was extremely awkward," she said dryly. "His mother gave a trill of almost hysterical delight and began to congratulate us."

"May I ask how you extricated yourself from the situation?"

Her voice took on a hard edge. "I told her that nothing would ever persuade me to marry her sorry excuse for a son, that he was a mawworm, a poltroon, a cabbage head, oh, and a host of other things."

"What an extraordinary vocabulary you have, Cassandra," he said, a small smile playing about his lips.

"It was perhaps not very well done of me," she said, "although I meant every word. But Mrs Fenton is not like her son; she is an extremely nervous woman and always anxious to please him. However, the words were out before I had mastered myself enough to moderate my response. My grandfather brought me up," she explained, her tone softening. "He was a very plain-spoken man."

"You were fond of him, I think."

"I loved him," she said simply. "I was only six when my parents and brother drowned in a boating accident, and he was like a father to me."

His eyes left hers and wandered over her features ruminatively. "I suspect you are only a few years younger than me, and yet I am sure I have never met you in Town."

"I have never been to London. By the time I was old enough to have a season, grandfather had suffered his first turn and although he recovered, I knew that if I was not there to watch over him, he would not heed the doctor's strictures and take things more gently."

She raised her glass to her lips and was surprised to discover it was empty. Laurence leant forwards and refilled it.

"I assume, then, that the cousin who wishes to marry you is his successor as he has driven you from your home?"

"Yes, he is a distant cousin. My grandfather only set enquiries afoot to discover the next in line when he became bedridden. Until then, he could never be brought to believe that he was seriously ill. It was discovered that his heir was one of a pair of twins. Fortunately, the only one who could be found was the eldest by half an hour. He was the overseer of a plantation in Jamaica." She sighed. "Grandfather was fading fast when we discovered it, but he was glad when he received a letter from F… my cousin, with a miniature enclosed. His words were respectful and his image pleasing." She gave a dry laugh. "The artist had made a competent likeness but had imbued his face with a benevolence that he does not possess; there is rather a hard, implacable set to his features. Whether this was from a lack of skill or to please his sitter I do not know, but I am inclined to think it is the former." She leant a little forward, her eyes suddenly lit from within. "It takes great precision of eye and a delicate touch to portray someone's character in a miniature portrait."

Her companion smiled enigmatically. "Are you merely a critic or do you have some skill in that direction yourself?"

She laughed a little self-consciously. "Well, I do not like to brag, but as it is the only real accomplishment I possess, I shall not dissemble. I am thought quite gifted in the art." Rising to her feet, she reached for her reticule which still lay on the mantelshelf and withdrew something from it, clasping her hand around it. "I could not leave this behind; it is all I now have to remember my grandfather." She held out her hand and slowly uncurled her fingers, revealing a portrait of a white-haired gentleman set within an oval, silver frame.

Laurence uncrossed his legs and sat up, taking it from her. His fingers tickled her palm as he did so, causing a pleasant tingling sensation. Cassandra sat on the edge of her chair, watching his face as he observed the portrait closely with a quiet intensity that unnerved her a little. She was not accustomed to feeling unsure of herself, but at that moment doubt assailed her. Could her grandfather and governess have been wrong? Perhaps to a man of the world, who moved in the first circles, her work would seem amateur in the extreme. She drew in a breath as he raised his eyes to hers. His expression was shuttered but his voice when he spoke, was sincere.

"A fine old gentleman with a mischievous side judging by the twinkle in his eyes, yet the set of his jaw suggests a stubborn streak. You are indeed talented, Cassandra. It is exquisite."

She felt absurdly pleased by his praise, but she had never known how to accept compliments gracefully and rushed into a speech that deflected his attention to her failings.

"Thank you, although you cannot know it, it does capture him before he became worn to a thread. I must admit, however, that I somehow fall short when attempting a landscape. I can accurately depict what is in front of me, but I am never pleased with the result. I can portray the scene but not the atmosphere I wish to capture. It is most vexing."

"Perhaps you are more interested in people than scenery," Laurence suggested.

"No!" she protested, throwing up her hands. "That is the most perplexing thing of all. I *am* interested in people, of course, but generally the ones it is… was… my duty to protect. I have always felt an affinity with nature. Perhaps it is because I have lived year round in the country." She coloured, a little embarrassed by this revelation, and her eyes dropped to the fire. She did not know what it was about the self-contained man in front of her that made her reveal far more about herself than was her wont.

"Forgive me, I digress. My grandfather thought that if my cousin was used to running a plantation, he would have the skills necessary to ensure the continued prosperity of D… of our estate. I admit he hoped for a match between us." She took a sip of her wine. "Grandfather died six months before my cousin arrived, and I am glad of it."

"You think he would have been disappointed in him?"

She glanced up. "Without a doubt. I tried to show him our ways; I had worked closely with our bailiff for years, after all, but he would not take the advice of a mere female seriously. He claimed he was very happy to support me, that he had promised my grandfather he would do so, but that I must confine my interests to the house and leave the estate to him."

"It was not an unreasonable request," Laurence said with an apologetic smile.

"I know it." She gave a ragged laugh. "Suffice it to say that I do not approve of his methods or manners concerning myself, the estate, or the house."

"It must indeed have been difficult to cede control after being so long in charge, but it is understandable that your grandfather wished for the match. It would be very advantageous to you; your future would be secured, and you would remain mistress of your own house."

"Advantages that my cousin, his mother, the vicar, and his wife have all been at great pains to point out to me, repeatedly," she said wearily.

"If the vicar approves of him, he can't be all bad."

She gave a wan smile, thinking how a touch of humour warmed his eyes. "Can he not? I might have considered the union if he had proved himself to be a man of integrity, but he isn't. At first, I gave him the benefit of the doubt. After all, the upheaval to his life was almost as great as to my own. I made allowances for his uncertain temper and his ignorance, but then he made life so difficult for both our butler and house-keeper that they were forced to leave. They had intended to retire but they should have been allowed to go at a moment of their own choosing and not because their every move was questioned, and their accounts constantly checked as if he suspected them of lining their own pockets at his expense.

"I was surrounded by strange servants, and I do not believe I would have remained mistress of anything. He may have charmed the vicar and his wife, presenting to them only his pleasant side, but the other is cold, humourless, and tyrannical. He seems both fascinated and repelled by me. I am too lively, my opinions are too strongly expressed, my stride is mannish, and my levity excessive."

Laurence's lips twisted into something half-smile, half-grimace. "And yet despite this comprehensive list of your failings, he wishes to marry you?"

A glimmer of amusement sparked in her eyes. "He makes allowances for my motherless upbringing and feels sure that his own, if allowed to guide me, will temper the grave faults of my character. He is happy to relieve me of the burdens that should never have been placed upon my shoulders and feels sure that once I am married and immersed in domestic duties and motherhood, my femininity and the delicate sensibilities that should govern me, will emerge."

"Good God! Do not tell me this is how he proposed to you?"

A gurgle of laughter escaped her. "I do not know how I prevented myself going into whoops; his proposal was too ridiculous for words. It was only when he laid hands upon my person and kissed me that I flew out at him."

She took another sip of her wine. "I begin to think it is my cousin who is unhinged. I only hope Mr Chubb is discreet. My grandfather would not have liked any hint of scandal to be attached to our name."

Her gaze returned to the fire. "I have no close relatives and had been wondering where I could go for some days, and then I received a letter from my old governess, an excellent woman. I am very fond of her; she stayed on as my companion when I outgrew the schoolroom. She reluctantly left me three years ago to live with her ailing, widowed sister."

She glanced up, her eyes darkening. "That was a

terrible business. Her sister's husband had been murdered in the street by a common thief." She gave an involuntary shudder. "His throat had been cut in the most vicious manner and so it is hardly surprising that the shock sent the poor woman into a deep decline from which she never recovered. Louisa said in her letter that the lady had died some three months ago and left her the house they lived in. The timing of her missive seemed propitious.

"I had come to cuffs with my cousin again that morning because he informed me that I was to no longer ride out alone, not even on the estate. When I told him that I would not brook such interference, he coldly told me that he would be forced to let go whichever of the stable hands allowed me to do so if I went against his will. He said the same fate would befall any who allowed me to go anywhere in the carriage without his or his mother's chaperonage. It was intolerable."

"I quite agree," Laurence said, a thread of steel winding through his soft tones. "Outrageous. Did he give you a reason for this unreasonable behaviour?"

"He said he had a duty of care to me and that he must consider my safety, though I am not a green girl but a woman of six and twenty."

Laurence rested his chin on one hand, his eyes thoughtful. "Had you given him any inkling of your intention to leave?"

"Yes, a few days before. He informed me over the breakfast table that a house could not have two mistresses and that his mother would give her orders to the housekeeper from now on. I would act as companion to her until I married him when the reins of the household would revert to me. I informed him that I would never marry him and quite agreed that a house could not have two mistresses and that as I am quite capable of supporting myself if I am not extravagant, that I would begin to look about me for somewhere else to live."

She suddenly sat up with a jerk. "Oh, that is why he tried to practically make me a prisoner; he did not wish me to have the opportunity to make any arrangements. I wondered why Mr Penwith, my lawyer, had not replied to my letter asking him to visit me, but it would be in keeping with all the rest if my cousin had intercepted it. I had not put two and two together but only knew that I could not spend another night under the same roof as him. My cousin had taken his mother shopping when the letter arrived from my governess, and my maid and I hastily packed and slipped out of a side door. We walked four miles to the nearest inn and hired a chaise. Mr Chubb caught up with us this afternoon at Grantham."

Laurence's eyes had hardened. "Your cousin, Cassandra, disgraces the name of gentleman."

"He is despicable." A look of bemusement crossed her face. "Why is he so determined to have me? He cannot want a wife who despises him."

"He seems to think he can bend you to his will." A harsh note crept into Laurence's voice. "Some men enjoy exercising their power over others."

"He has no power over me. When I have reached the safety of my governess, I shall write to my lawyer and fully explain the situation. I will ask him to arrange for the rest of my things to be sent to me. He is an honest man and will render me every assistance,

I know." She glanced at the clock on the mantlepiece. "Now, you have my story, and I must go."

Laurence held up a hand to detain her. "Not quite all your story. I am curious as to how you escaped Mr Chubb when he first caught up with you."

Wrath kindled in her eyes. "We had intended to carry on our journey by stagecoach and had stepped out for a walk to stretch our legs before being shut up again in a closed carriage. When we returned to the inn, we found him waiting for us in the private parlour I had hired. He did us the *honour* of introducing himself before brandishing a pistol at us, saying that if we followed his orders, he would not harm us. He said that my cousin was so worried for me that he had offered a generous reward for my safe return.

"I was quite dumbfounded that my cousin would go so far, and Mr Chubb took my stupefaction for maidenly fear, I think. He had a carriage waiting for us but by the time we stepped up to it, I had recovered my wits. I grabbed my maid's hand, and we simply ran away. He was hardly going to shoot me, after all. Where would be the profit in that? Besides, there were too many witnesses."

Laurence regarded her, a small frown between his eyes. "Did he give chase?"

"Oh, yes, but it was market day, and the roads were jammed with carts and livestock. His coach was no use to him and so he was forced to follow us on foot. My maid gasped out that she had an uncle who had an inn not far from here and that I might be assured he would keep us safe. I sent her back to get our things and told her I would meet her there." Her anger faded and amusement took its place. "Meanwhile, I led Mr Chubb a merry dance."

"I almost begin to feel sorry for the man," Laurence murmured.

Cassandra chuckled. "As well you might. I am thankful that my stride *is* manly—"

"I do not find it so," he said, his voice expressionless. "You move with grace."

She choked on her wine and was grateful when he offered her a handkerchief to wipe her streaming eyes. "We are even," she said when she had recovered. "But joking aside, I always have my gowns made wider than is fashionable so that I do not trip over every step, and today I had reason to be thankful for it. Mr Chubb can move with surprising swiftness for one so portly, but I had no trouble staying ahead of him. I hired a horse, and he came tearing into the stable yard, his face puce and his chest heaving, just as I trotted out of it. He too hired a horse, of course."

A faint smile touched Laurence's lips. "I would have given something to see it."

"Y-yes," she gasped. "I don't know if I felt sorrier for him or his horse!"

"His steed got the better of him, I think," he said dryly, "judging by the mud on his coat."

Cassandra again wiped at her eyes with the handkerchief. "I could not resist the temptation," she said unsteadily, "I led him a short way cross country, and he fell at the first hedge."

"I imagine he might. Were you not afraid you might kill him?"

"No, I chose a particularly low hedge. I left him wallowing in the mud and made my way back to the road, arranged for the return of the horse at an inn, and came the rest of the way to Stamford by stage-coach as I had at first planned."

Laurence's expression sobered. "You have been playing with fire, Cassandra. Do not underestimate Mr Chubb; he may have grown sadly stout, but he was a Bow Street Runner and used to apprehending far more dangerous persons than you. If this room had been empty as you supposed and he had discovered you here alone, you would not have escaped again so easily."

"Perhaps not," she conceded. "I admit I did not expect him to come upon me so quickly. I had intended to walk the last few miles to our place of rendezvous, cutting across the fields to lessen the chance that anyone would see me, but then I saw him coming up the street behind me and slipped into this inn."

Laurence rose to his feet decisively. "I believe it will be best if I escort you to your maid. I am quite sure that Mr Chubb will be lurking somewhere hereabouts."

"Very likely," she said ruefully, "he does seem very determined."

"Then you will accept my escort?" he said, holding out her cloak for her.

She smiled gratefully. "Yes, thank you. I am tired of this game of cat and mouse."

CHAPTER 3

As Laurence began to wrap the cloak about Cassandra, he thought better of it and drew it off her again. She glanced over her shoulder, a question in her intelligent eyes.

"I think I must temporarily part you from your cloak," he said. "I shall ask my groom to don it and go for a walk. Let us hope that Mr Chubb is drowning his sorrows in one of the many taprooms to be found in this town, but if he *is* still hovering nearby, it would be better if we drew him off before we leave."

She turned, an approving smile on her generous lips. "A sensible idea." She laughed softly. "What a surprise he will receive if he does accost your man."

"He will get more than he bargains for, certainly, knowing Fadon," he said dryly, folding the cloak over his arm. "I will not be above a few minutes; promise me you will not disappear whilst my back is turned."

"I promise," she said, "word of a gentlewoman. Now I have supped and sat by the fire, I feel quite soporific, and the prospect of tramping a few miles across muddy fields by the light of the moon holds little allure."

Unlike her, he mused as he ran lightly down the back stairs to the stable yard, although she seemed to have little awareness of it. He certainly found her alluring and could easily understand her relative's attraction to her. He could not approve his desire to dominate her, however, or to subdue the animation in her mobile face and forever extinguish her spirit It was not her striking features that rendered her beautiful but the vitality that lit them. If her cousin had his way, he would turn her into a living sculpture; the angles and planes of her face would still draw the eye, but the essence of the woman would be lost. That such a thing should be allowed to happen was unthinkable.

The evening was now considerably advanced and the only signs of activity in the stables came from the rooms above them. Light flickered in the windows and a low rumble of conversation drifted down the stairs. Fortune favoured him and he found his groom checking on the horses one last time before turning in for the night.

Fadon quickly and efficiently made the curricle ready and brought it out into the yard, but his lips thinned, and his expression turned dour as his master passed him the cloak and explained what he wished him to do. He reluctantly donned it and fastened the clasp. He was a slight, wiry man, who was a good deal shorter than Cassandra, and the garment dragged along the cobbles.

"It is not ideal," Laurence admitted, "but if you

stick to the shadows, any discrepancies will hopefully go unnoticed."

The groom shook his head despondently. "I've watched you grow from boy to man, milord, and I've never yet known you to be caught up in anything havey-cavey."

An odd smile flickered on Laurence's lips. "I've always been a dashed dull dog, haven't I?"

"What you've always been, sir, is an honourable man and a fine master. I'm sure it's no business of mine what fix you're in, but this cloak belongs to a female, and if anything were going to get you into trouble, it'd be one of them!"

Laurence had no idea how his groom had arrived at this conclusion, nor did he have the time or inclination to find out. "I am not in any trouble, Fadon, now put up the hood; your sour face is giving me indigestion." His clipped tones informed the groom that he had gone his length. "Walk into town and disappear down a few side streets so that you are well away from the main thoroughfare. If you are followed, I would prefer you did not allow yourself to be caught, but if you are, be careful; the man pursuing you will have a pistol."

The groom's eyes narrowed, and his lip curled. "That puts things in a different light. I don't hold with violence against women, however troublesome they are. He won't catch me, of that you may be sure, and if he goes a threatenin' me, he will be sorry."

"Good man," Laurence said, beginning to stride across the yard.

"Milord!" Fadon called softly. "At least tell me where you are going."

Laurence glanced back, grinning ruefully. "I cannot; I do not know myself! Now, go!"

The groom pulled up the hood of the cloak and hastened from the yard, muttering under his breath all the while.

Laurence took the back stairs two at a time, his hurry not precipitated by fear that Cassandra might have broken her word and fled – he felt certain she would not – but by his eagerness to have her away from the inn and Mr Chubb. He had believed her story, the more so because she had been reluctant to share it. She had spoken in a measured way, her words occasionally punctuated by amusement, anger or exasperation but attended by none of the hysteria that might be expected of a woman in her situation. But her courage might yet be her undoing; he did not think she fully appreciated the danger she was in.

He could think of only two reasons for her cousin's behaviour; he had developed an unhealthy obsession for her, or the marriage must bring him some advantage as yet unclear to Laurence. Either way, he did not think he would easily give up the chase and so it was vital that as few people as possible set eyes on his fugitive. It might be true that Cassandra could not by law be forced into such a union, but if her cousin had her in his power, who knew what pressures he would bring to bear on her, especially in a household that had been stripped of servants who might owe her their loyalty.

He did not immediately go to the parlour but went to his room to inform Salop, his valet, that he was going to visit a friend and did not wish him to wait up for him.

"Very good, my lord," the slightly plump, round-faced gentleman said, his eyes flicking cursorily over his master's raiment. Seemingly satisfied with what he saw, he continued laying out a small pile of neckcloths ready for the morning.

Unlike Fadon, Salop had not known him since he was set astride his first pony, and Laurence had never appreciated the man's disinterest in his activities more.

As he stepped into the parlour, the reassuring smile he had donned slid from his lips. He halted just inside the door, disappointment smothering the rather pleasant feeling of anticipation he had felt at the prospect of being in Cassandra's enlivening company again. The room was empty. The word of a gentlewoman apparently meant nothing. His lips curved in a mocking half-smile and a cynical gleam sharpened his eyes.

"You fool!" he muttered, thinking that it had been a long time since a woman, however attractive, had duped him, although in this case, it was only herself she was likely to injure. Even if Cassandra escaped Mr Chubb, tramping miles in the damp, cool air without her cloak would expose her to the risk of illness. He was about to spin on his heel and go after her when the curtains twitched open.

"You are unkind, sir!" Cassandra said, rising fluidly from the seat and striding towards him. "I thought it only wise to conceal myself until you returned."

"It was," he said, feeling a measure of relief that was out of all proportion to the length of his acquaintance with her. "I was not referring to you but to myself."

She came to a stop before him, her eyes flashing

as she realised the import of his words. "You are indeed a fool if you thought I would break my word."

Her indignation brought a wry smile to his lips. "I did not think it until I saw the room was empty. I should have guessed you were behind the curtains, of course."

"Well, I do think that you might have considered the chance, at all events," she said more gently. Her anger fled and dismay shone in her expressive eyes. "Oh, what a vixen I am. You do not know me, after all, and have been so kind to offer me your help. Grandfather always used to say that my pride would trip me up if I was not careful. It would serve me right if you abandoned me to my fate." She put out an impulsive hand. "Forgive me."

What a mercurial creature she was, Laurence thought as he took her long, tapering fingers in a light clasp before laying her hand on his arm. "There is nothing to forgive. Now, come. I should not have left the horses so long."

They reached the yard without being seen. He handed her up into the curricle before springing lightly up himself and retrieving a blanket from under the seat. "Wrap yourself in this. You will not wish to catch a chill."

She took it from him, saying softly, "Thank you. I will do so to please you, but I am never ill, you know."

He could well believe it. Even after the trials and excitement of her day, her face showed no signs of pallor, on the contrary, a soft, rosy tint infused her cheeks.

"Where to?" he said lightly.

"The Red Lion at West Deeping. Do you know it?"

Laurence walked his horses through the archway and turned onto the road. "I have never visited the inn, but the village is some five miles east of here. It is a sleepy little place and will serve you well for tonight."

They crossed the bridge that spanned the River Welland and turned left onto a smaller road, soon leaving the town behind. The moon was almost full and easily lit the way.

"You have light hands," Cassandra said approvingly. "My grandfather was a fine whip in his day."

"And are you also a fine whip?" Laurence asked, slowing his horses as they came to a sharp bend.

"I would rather say competent. I generally prefer to ride; it is more practical and efficient in the country." She sighed. "I shall miss Blaze, my mare."

Laurence heard the wistful note in her voice. "When you write to your lawyer and ask him to send your things, why not ask him to also send your horse?"

"Perhaps I will," she said brightening. "But I have no idea if there will be stabling enough for her, or how long I shall stay. Louisa mentioned that another of her sisters had come to live with her and I am not at all sure how much room she has, although the widowed sister who died was married to a wine and spirit merchant so I imagine it will be of a reasonable size." She smiled fondly. "But even if it is not, I am confident of a warm welcome."

"Did she stand in place of a mother to you?" Laurence asked gently.

Cassandra looked up at him quickly, her white teeth gleaming in the darkness as she laughed. "Oh, no. She came to us when I was fourteen and is only seven years older than I. She is a dear friend, and I am very much looking forward to seeing her again."

Laurence thought he understood her. "I expect you have missed female company and am surprised you did not engage another companion after she left you."

"I did not see the necessity," she said. "We never entertained a great deal. There are very few families in the immediate neighbourhood, and after my grandfather became very ill, there was no question of it. By the time he died, I knew my cousin's mother was coming to live at the manor to lend me respectability. Besides, I have never enjoyed the inconsequential chatter that most ladies I have met enjoy, and I certainly could not have borne being subjected to it when I was... well, not quite myself."

Not quite myself. It was such a moderate way to describe the grief she must have been subject to when the man who had stood as father to her had died. Somehow it touched him much more than any outpouring of emotion could have. "Were you not lonely?"

"A little," she admitted, "but I always had so much to do, and it was only after dinner that I would especially feel my grandfather's loss." The wistful note crept back into her voice. "We used to play chess, backgammon or cards when he was well enough or discuss estate matters; if he was not, I would read to him."

It seemed a very dreary life for a young lady of intelligence and humour. Something of Laurence's thoughts must have shown on his face for she said, "I am sure it must all seem very dull to you, but I was not unhappy."

He noted that she denied *unhappiness* rather than claimed *happiness*. The difference might have been subtle, but it was one he understood all too well.

He glanced at her quizzically. "Were there *no* young bucks who tried to win your favour?"

She said, her tone droll, "The young curate seemed very enamoured with me when he first came some five years ago and might have tried to do so, but the poor man developed a terrible stammer whenever he was in my presence and so it is hard to tell." She gave a gurgle of mirth. "But it is Mr Rutherford who most nearly fits your description. He thought himself a very fine beau."

His attention returned to the road as they passed out of the small village of Tallington and came to another bend. "An opinion not shared by you, Cassandra?"

"I thought he looked like a peacock; he wore the most startling waistcoats under a very tight-fitting blue coat, which I will admit fitted his shoulders admirably, but the effect was quite ruined by his spindly legs and odd, spiky hair."

"I think," Laurence said, glancing down at her as the road straightened, "that he was sporting the style known as the frightened owl or perhaps the windswept." He smiled as Cassandra's lips parted in a gasp of surprise. "Either of which would have taken him or his valet a great deal of effort and time."

"I have no patience with such nonsense," she said with some severity. "Why on earth would someone wish to look like a frightened owl or as if they had been out in a gale?"

"I must admit that I have never been tempted to sport either style," Laurence said, his eyes dancing. "But I believe young men who wish to hint at a tortured soul, or a rebellious nature generally favour such a disordered appearance."

"That he was tortured, I can well believe," Cassandra said dryly. "He minced along as if he was in pain but the rebellious nature I cannot allow; as soon as his parents became aware of his interest, they forbade him to come near me." She grinned. "I was excessively grateful to them."

He quirked a brow. "And did this young arbiter of fashion tamely submit to their decree?"

"Oh, yes. The family had not long been in the neighbourhood; his father is a nabob and he bought Mr Ripley's manor when he died. He was a bachelor and a good friend of grandpapa's, but his relatives did not choose to live in Derbyshire and so sold the estate. Mr Rutherford made his son a very generous allowance. I can quite see why the threat of its suspension would act so powerfully upon him; his wardrobe alone must have cost him a small fortune and how would he maintain it without funds?"

Her words were thick with irony, which Laurence interpreted as indicating scorn for such frippery concerns rather than any chagrin at being so promptly abandoned. "May I enquire why they deemed you unsuitable? It is not uncommon for a family that has made their fortune in trade to wish to establish their son as a gentleman by marrying him to a lady of gentility, after all."

"Yes, but not at the tender age of nineteen to a female three years his senior with only a modest dowry and no pretension to fashion or any important connections. I cannot blame them for their dismay but only for their assumption that I might be tempted by a young pup still wet behind the ears with a predilection for penning execrable poetry."

As Laurence had been just as guilty of this apparently heinous crime when he had thought himself in love with Diana, he could not help but feel some sympathy for the young Mr Rutherford. He had never, however, been foolish enough to bring his amateur scribblings to Diana's notice. With hindsight, he realised that she would probably have enjoyed them and could only be glad that his modesty and natural reserve had prevented him from doing so. It might have tipped the balance in his favour, and he would now be leg-shackled to a pretty widgeon who needed a steady stream of adoration if she were not to go into a decline.

The lady sitting beside him was in stark contrast to her; indeed, she was the other extreme. She laughed off compliments as if they were a great joke, partly because she didn't believe them, and partly because she did not wish for them. They were unimportant to her as she did not define herself by such trivial parameters as beauty.

"I assume you were the subject of his creative endeavours?"

Her ready laughter sprang to her eyes. "I have been compared to Aphrodite, Athena, and Artemis; not in the same poem you understand."

The young cub had not been completely without

sense then. He may have spouted poetry to a woman who clearly had no appetite for it, but he had at least chosen strong women for his comparisons rather than delicate flowers or natural elements such as the sun or stars. As he passed these three goddesses and their spheres of influence under review, Laurence could quite understand the young man's thinking; she had elements of all of them and was as untouchable. Her confidence surrounded her like a shield, and it would be a brave man indeed who would try to broach her defences.

"It would have been an impressive feat indeed if he could have pulled it off," he murmured.

"It would have been even more of a hopeless tangle of nonsense than his usual efforts!"

Laurence thought her rather hard, and she seemed to divine it for she said more gently, "You need not think that I ripped his efforts to shreds for I did not. I was amused and exasperated by turns and had enough female vanity that I was glad he was persuaded to relinquish his interest before he discovered that I had feet of clay." She smiled ruefully. "The truth is I do not think I am at all suited to the wedded state; I would ride roughshod over any gentle soul and fight from cockcrow to sunset with anyone of a domineering disposition."

Laurence tended to agree with her. He could not imagine Cassandra tamely submitting to her husband's wishes if they did not accord with her own. Her grandfather had seemingly allowed her spirited nature free rein and encouraged in her a level of independence that she had relished. It had not perhaps, been wise of him. She was used to living life on her own terms but had not been left sufficiently well off to continue to do so, at least not in the style to which she had been accustomed. The old man had clearly realised it at the end, but to pin his hopes on a distant relative they neither of them had met as a suitable husband, had been clutching at straws.

They took a fork in the road and found themselves in West Deeping. Limestone cottages lined the deserted street, and The Red Lion soon hove into view. It was a modest-sized establishment with a barn attached. The ground floor was in darkness, but a dim light could be perceived behind the drawn curtains of the first floor.

"Oh," Cassandra exclaimed, surprised, "we are here already, and you have learned much of me, but I nothing at all of you."

"My history is unremarkable and my future predictable," Laurence said with a twisted smile, "unlike yours."

He turned into a small yard. There was stabling enough for a few horses and a carriage but no more. This was all to the good for it suggested that the inn did not generally accommodate overnight travellers.

Cassandra eyed him speculatively. "I think there is more to you than meets the eye, Laurence, but if you do not wish to partake in a fair exchange that is your prerogative."

He heard the pique in her voice. "I shall return tomorrow morning with your cloak and escort you and your maid to your destination. You may ask me anything you wish then."

Her eyes glinted with mischief under their raised

brows. "You are generous to grant me such a wide scope."

"I may have given you leave to ask questions, Cassandra, but I have not promised to answer them," he said softly.

A door that gave onto the yard was suddenly thrown open and a pretty, young woman rushed through it, her cap askew and her blue eyes wide.

"Oh, Miss Cassandra," she cried, "you are safe! You were so long coming I thought that fat jobberknoll had managed to catch you!"

Cassandra cast off her blanket, climbed down from the curricle without difficulty, and clasped the maid's hands in her own. "Have you so little faith in me, Grace?"

"Oh, no, miss," she said, looking up at her mistress with adoring eyes. "I know you are equal to anything!"

Laurence was surprised both by the informality of this greeting and the young lady who he assumed to be her maid. Having grown up in a household with three women, Laurence had some experience of ladies' maids. They generally took pride in both their own and their employer's appearance and necessarily were excellent needlewomen. Grace wore a dress of sprigged muslin that had been altered by inexpert fingers. The uneven hem dragged a little on the floor, the full-length sleeves had been shortened a little too much so that they stopped some two inches above her wrists, and the maid kept tugging at the dress where it repeatedly slipped a little off her plump shoulders. Had Cassandra's cousin disposed of her personal maid as well, forcing her to take on one of the housemaids? Laurence was aware of a growing desire to meet him.

A tall man with a dignified bearing now came through the door in a more leisurely fashion, a lantern held before him. He was followed by a very neat lady of middle years. He bowed before Cassandra and said with deferential civility, "Welcome to my humble abode, Miss Fenton. It is my pleasure and privilege to offer you shelter for the night."

The lady beside him dipped her head. "Although we do not generally accommodate guests, you may be assured that we can offer you every comfort, ma'am."

"This is my uncle and aunt," Grace said with simple pride, "Mr and Mrs Blinksop. They used to be butler and housekeeper at one of the big houses around here and so you will feel right at home, miss."

If Cassandra felt any irritation that her name had been revealed she did not show it but said with a warm smile, "I do apologise for descending on you in such a scrambling way and cannot thank you enough for your hospitality."

"It is we who must thank you, madam," Mr Blinksop said, "for taking good care of my niece." He smiled wryly. "We could not be prouder that she has risen to the position of lady's maid but are well aware that she has not yet acquired all of the skills generally deemed necessary for such an exalted position."

Grace had blushed rosily at the first part of this speech but glanced down at her gown in some dismay at the conclusion of it.

"I deem a stout heart and loyalty of far more importance than an aptitude with needle and thread.

The last accomplishment can generally be learned, the first two qualities cannot."

"Very true, ma'am," he agreed.

"Who did you work for?" Laurence asked, thinking that Mr Blinksop looked vaguely familiar.

The man glanced up at the curricle and raised his lantern the better to see its occupant. He bowed. "Lord Carteret, what a pleasure it is to see you again."

His years as a butler stood Mr Blinksop in good stead and not a trace of surprise or undue inquisitiveness marked his face. He appeared to have the advantage over Laurence.

"I am not surprised you do not remember me, sir. I believe you only visited us once. My former master was Sir Marcus Trent. I believe it was two years ago that you attended a hunting party at Frognall Hall."

"Of course," Laurence said, "I am sorry I did not remember you."

"Why should you? I pride myself on never forgetting a face, sir, an attribute to be expected in any good butler, but you can hardly be expected to remember every servant who crosses your path. As you probably know, Sir Marcus came to grief over a rasper a year after your visit, after which sad event I decided to retire from service and finally marry Mrs Blinksop." He cast her a fond glance. "I would have done so sooner, but Sir Marcus did not approve of his household staff marrying."

Mrs Blinksop came a little forward. "I am afraid we have no more rooms to spare, sir, but I can wake up the stable boy to look after your horses and offer you some refreshment."

The manners and mien of the proprietors of the

inn were better than Laurence could have hoped for, and he had no compunction in leaving Cassandra in their care. "Thank you, Mrs Blinksop, but now I have delivered my passenger, I must return to Stamford. I shall return in the morning, but in the meantime feel certain I am leaving Miss Fenton in safe hands."

Cassandra came back to the curricle. "Thank you for all you have done for me this evening, Lord Carteret. I am really very grateful."

Laurence discovered that he preferred the sound of his given name on her lips. He leaned down and took the hand she held out to him, a trace of mockery in his eyes. "I have ever been a soft touch for a damsel in distress."

CHAPTER 4

C assandra watched Laurence turn his curricle neatly in the yard, no mean feat in so confined a space, an amused smile playing about her lips. Damsel in distress, indeed! But when he trotted briskly out onto the road, a soft sigh escaped her. Perhaps it was because they had addressed each other by their first names which caused her to feel as if she was losing a friend. She hardly knew the man, yet somehow felt as if she did, but the truth was, beyond knowing that he had sisters, she knew little apart from that he was quick-witted, gentlemanly, and had a cool head upon his broad shoulders. She did not doubt for a moment that she could trust him or that she would enjoy encountering him again but knew that she would not do so.

She was not as reckless as he supposed, and now that she had had time to think about all that had happened that day and over the past few months, she realised that her cousin was playing a deep game. What his purpose in wishing to marry her was she did not fully understand, but that he had one she did not doubt. If he was prepared to make her a prisoner in her own home, never mind send Mr Chubb after her, he was more dangerous than she had at first supposed. She felt certain that Laurence would not intentionally betray her, but he might unwittingly lead Mr Chubb to her. She would not wait for him to escort her in the morning but leave at an early hour leaving behind a note of apology.

Mrs Blinksop brought her out of her reverie. "Come in out of the cold, ma'am. I've sent Grace to make some tea and there's a nice fire in the parlour."

She followed her hosts up a flight of stairs and into a cosy room. The chairs were upholstered in floral chintz as were the curtains, the table polished until it gleamed, and the floor largely covered by a thick Aubusson rug.

"What a pretty room," she said, going to the fire and warming her hands.

Mrs Blinksop smiled, clearly gratified. "Thank you. Sir Christopher Trent was very generous to us when he came into the baronetcy. He insisted we take some of the bits and pieces that had been languishing in the attics for years."

"I am happy that he repaid your years of service with gratitude and generosity." She turned from the fire. "I do not know how much Grace has told you—"

"Do not disturb yourself with explanations that must be painful to you, Miss Fenton," Mr Blinksop said gravely. "Grace has shared as much as she thought fit and we have a tolerable understanding of your plight. You may be sure of both our assistance and discretion."

"You are very kind," Cassandra said, relieved by his tact.

"It is you who are kind, ma'am. Grace informed us that you employed her as your personal maid after Sir Francis had arrived at the conclusion that there were too many servants at Darley Manor and had decided her services were no longer necessary."

"Maids come and go," Cassandra said, "but Grace has been with us since she was orphaned as a girl. I never felt the need for a personal maid, but if I did require assistance to dress, it was Grace I would call upon. I could not allow her to be so summarily dismissed. Honesty and loyalty deserve their reward."

"She is certainly loyal," Mrs Blinksop said. "We wrote to her last year and offered her a home with us, but she would not leave you, ma'am, in your time of grief."

"I did not know it," Cassandra said, surprised. "Perhaps she would be happier here."

"I'll not leave you, miss. Not at a time like this," Grace said, coming through the door with the tea tray, a stubborn set to her chin.

"Quite right," her uncle said. "You stay with Miss Fenton, at least until she is settled."

"Very well," Cassandra said, "but we will discuss it again when the future is more certain."

It was not until arrangements had been made for the morning and Mrs Blinksop had personally tucked her up in a very comfortable bed that Cassandra's thoughts drifted again to Laurence. His reserve was not like that of her cousin's, ice cold with a patronising edge, but that of a man who was very much upon his dignity, not, she felt sure, because he was overly proud but because he had learned to keep his feelings and thoughts very much to himself. And yet there had been moments when she had glimpsed a very different man, and his cool, grey eyes had lit with amusement and turned from the dull colour of a wintry morning to that of a lake when a beam of sunlight broke through the clouds and shimmered across its surface.

And then there was his smile. He had many. Sometimes his firm lips twisted in irony, sometimes they tilted up by the smallest degree in a wry fashion, but every now and then they curved in the gentlest of ways, and at those moments she thought it would be difficult to deny him anything. It was not like her to be so susceptible to male charm, although she had to admit that she had not had much experience of it. Her grandfather had been a rather bluff man, good humoured but brusque, and her male acquaintances few.

She sighed and stretched; she had had a long day and tomorrow would be another. She should put him out of her mind. He had a chivalrous streak that suggested he would be drawn by a woman who needed his protection, and she an independent spirit that would not be tamed. They were completely incompatible, and if she had felt unusually feminine when he had insisted she wrap herself in the blanket to protect her from the chill evening air, she knew that such solicitousness would soon exasperate her, just as her lack of appreciation for it would dismay him. This conclusion having been reached, she turned onto her side and fell into a fitful sleep.

Grace bustled into the room just after six with a round dress of lavender hue draped over her arm.

"I've brushed the mud off your other gown, miss, but thought you might prefer to wear this one today."

"Yes," Cassandra said sleepily, "with my purple spencer. It would be wise to change my appearance."

"My uncle has already gone into Market Deeping to hire us a chaise."

By the time they had breakfasted, the chaise was waiting in the yard below. Mr Blinksop came into the parlour.

"I've sent our stable lad off on an errand, Miss Fenton, but he won't be long, so you had best come down now."

"Certainly," she said, rising from the table. "Everything is ready."

"I've given your name as Miss Tatler, just tell the postillion where he is to go."

Cassandra came forward and held out her hand. He lifted a brow but took it.

"Mr Blinksop, you have been a Trojan! If you would like me to tell you our destination, I will."

"No, no," he said quickly, "it's best that you don't. I can't tell anyone what I don't know. Grace will write to me when you are safe, I'm sure."

The maid came forwards and startled her uncle by giving him a big hug. He stiffened for a moment and then awkwardly patted her back.

"You be a good girl, Grace. There's a home for you here if you ever need it. Mrs Blinksop can always do with a hand about the place."

"That I can," she said, coming into the room, a basket on her arm. "Take this, Grace, then you will not have to stop for refreshments on the way."

Grace took the basket and kissed her aunt's cheek.

Cassandra could see that however much the maid wished to stay with her, she was happy to know her family.

It took them ten hours to complete their journey. They relieved their aching limbs twice at towns along the way, moving to a different inn and hiring another chaise each time. It was approaching five o'clock when they turned into the driveway of Tremlow House, just outside the village of Thornham in Norfolk. It was an attractively proportioned building of three storeys, built in the traditional style of many of the cottages nearby. The roof glowed red in the afternoon sun and reflected off the rounded flint that made up the body of the house.

"It's like something out of a fairy tale," Grace said.

"A happy one I hope," Cassandra said dryly.

It was certainly happiness Cassandra felt when the front door opened, and Miss Louisa Thorpe stepped into the small porch. Of average height, she wore her black hair swept back in a severe style. Her dark brown dress was rather drab, and her features pleasant. They would have been easily forgettable if it were not for her rather piercing green eyes. They widened as she saw Cassandra's head poking through the open window of the carriage, surprise and delight chasing swiftly through them.

As she came quickly forwards, Cassandra pushed open the door of the chaise and all but tumbled into her arms. Never prey to an excess of sensibility, she was surprised to discover a lump in her throat and tears in her eyes.

"Louisa," she murmured into her friend's ear.

"How glad I am to see you. Forgive me for descending on you without any warning."

"My love," Miss Thorpe said, "you are most welcome. I wish I could have come to you when Sir Thomas died, only Clara's illness prevented me, and then you wrote that you were expecting your cousin and his mother at any moment."

Her calm voice steadied Cassandra. "I have so much to tell you, my dear friend."

"Yes," Louisa said, taking her hands and giving her a penetrating look, "but there will be time enough for that when you have rested. You look unusually tired."

"I am a trifle fagged," she admitted.

Grace had climbed down from the carriage behind her and was reaching into it to retrieve their bags. "I expect you have the headache, miss," she said. "It would be a miracle if you did not after being jolted about all day over the most shocking roads." She turned and nearly overbalanced, the curtsy she attempted to offer Miss Thorpe hindered by her over-long dress.

"Ah, Grace," Louisa said, "I am happy to see you again." As the chaise swept off, she glanced at the portmanteau and cloak bag the maid carried and then at Cassandra. "Is this all your luggage, my dear?"

"It is all we could carry," Grace explained when her mistress did not immediately reply.

"I see," she said calmly.

"You do not, of course," Cassandra said, sighing.

Her friend took her arm and led her towards the house.

"Whilst my maid makes up a bed for you and

Grace unpacks your things, you shall lie down in my room. You have half an hour before dinner and there is no need to change your gown."

Cassandra was not in the habit of resting during the day but now that she and Grace had safely reached their destination, she felt intensely weary. She hardly took in her surroundings as Louisa led her into a cool hallway and up a set of stairs to the first floor. A strange buzzing had started in her ears through which she vaguely heard her friend directing Grace to another room further along the corridor.

"Here we are, my dear," the distant voice said, "lie down and be quiet and you will soon find yourself restored."

She obediently lay back on the bed she had been led to and listened absently to Louisa's voice as she moved over to the window and drew the curtains. She found she could not concentrate on what she was saying but, nonetheless, found her gentle tones restful. Her eyes suddenly burnt with tiredness, and her heavy lids closed.

When she awoke, no trace of light filtered through the curtains. She turned her head and saw that a fire had been lit in the grate and Louisa sat beside it hemming Grace's dress by the light of a candle.

"You will strain your eyes," she murmured sleepily.

Louisa glanced up, a smile in her eyes. "Better that than Grace breaks her neck tripping over it."

Cassandra swung her feet to the floor and chuckled. "She is most unhandy with a needle, but it is not for want of trying. What time is it?"

"About nine."

Cassandra looked startled. "So late? You should have woken me."

"Nonsense. Your adventure had caught up with you, my dear. Come, sit with me."

She removed a muslin cloth from a plate set on the table beside her, revealing some bread and butter, a thick slice of ham and a honey cake. As Cassandra tucked into her supper with appreciation, Louisa crossed the room to a silver tray that sat atop a clothes press and poured them both a glass of wine.

"Now, we can have a quiet cose. Grace has already explained the general gist of your story, but I think her undoubted devotion to you may have led her to exaggerate a little."

However, when Cassandra had finished her tale, she was forced to revise this opinion.

"Sir Francis' behaviour is quite unaccountable unless he has fallen desperately in love with you or you have something that he wants," she said thoughtfully. "If it is the first, he has gone about attaching your affection in the strangest way, and if it is the second, I cannot think what it can be. A dowry of five thousand pounds, whilst not paltry, is surely not enough to explain the lengths he has gone to. He has inherited a profitable estate, largely thanks to you, my love, and so cannot have need of it."

"If he is in love with me, it is against his will," Cassandra said with some asperity. "Everything I am he wishes to change, and I cannot think of anything I possess which he would covet."

"It is most perplexing," Louisa agreed. "If only Sir Thomas had listened to me when I begged him to let me take you to Bath or Brighton so you might have had some chance of enlarging your acquaintance and meeting a respectable gentleman." She sighed. "He loved you dearly, but he was most selfish in that respect. He could not bear to be parted from you."

"Nor I from him," Cassandra said firmly. "How could I leave him when I was all he had?"

"Your feelings do you credit, my dear, but look where your self-sacrifice has left you."

"Louisa!" Cassandra protested. "I wonder you dare talk to me so when you refused an offer of marriage before you came to me and then devoted yourself to your sister! It is the outside of enough!"

"Very true. And I was quite in disgrace for refusing Mr Brampton. It was thought that as a vicar's daughter, I would be perfectly suited to marry a clergyman. I suppose I might have become accustomed to his bulbous nose in time," she said ruminatively, "and his protuberant eyes whilst a little alarming were not an insurmountable obstacle, but although you may say it was shallow of me, the wart on his chin was not."

Cassandra's indignation was forgotten, and she went into peals of laughter. "Oh, Louisa, how I have missed you. Was he really that ugly?"

"Oh yes," she said, a twinkle in her eyes. "A man cannot help his looks, of course, and if he has a handsome character and a good heart such defects in his appearance might be overlooked, but Mr Brampton had an overweening pride in his position and a prosy attitude to boot. He was the most objectional man and as it turns out, I have not ended my life as a drudge as my father predicted but am now mistress of my own establishment thanks to Clara."

Cassandra leaned forwards and took her friend's

hand. "Dear Louisa, I have not even offered you my condolences on her loss. Forgive me."

"There is nothing to forgive," that lady said promptly. "I do not want them. To you, at least, I need not pretend an affection for her that I did not feel. Her death was a release for both of us. She was a difficult woman, but I would not have wished such a painful, lingering end on my worst enemy." Her hand returned Cassandra's comforting grip. "You are much more to be pitied for you lost someone very dear to you and have now lost your home also."

Cassandra never could bear to have her wounds touched upon and withdrew her hand saying brusquely, "I do not need anyone's pity. Like you, I thought my grandfather's death a merciful release; his last stroke rendered him completely helpless. Besides, my case is not desperate. I am not destitute and if I like it here, I shall perhaps rent a house in the vicinity."

"Only if you wish to deeply offend me," Louisa said, her eyes offering a challenge.

"I cannot impose on you indefinitely," Cassandra protested.

"Impose on me? It will be no such thing. Although I have my eldest sister Emma residing with me, she is profoundly deaf and sometimes very much in her own world. I am so happy to be able to offer her a home for I love her dearly. My sister, Jane, was very good to her, but her family has increased so much she could not afford to keep her. Your company will be most welcome for both of us, I assure you. You may consider Tremlow House your home for as long as you wish, and as a sop to your pride, I shall even let you contribute to its upkeep."

"Thank you," Cassandra said. "I shall make myself useful, of course. If there is anything I can do for you, you must not hesitate to inform me of it."

"There is something, now I come to think of it," Louisa said, her eyes sharpening even as a small, mischievous smile flickered across her lips. "You have told me much of your cousin, and drawn a colourful, even amusing portrait of Mr Chubb, but you have said nothing at all of the gentleman who drove you to West Deeping. You may satisfy my curiosity if you wish to please me."

Cassandra knew a moment's consternation. She had omitted this episode of her history, not because she feared her friend's disapproval – one of the reasons she and Louisa had always rubbed along well together was her seeming inability to be shocked by anything – but because she possessed an uncanny ability to divine one's unspoken thoughts.

Louisa was the youngest of four girls born to a vicar of moderate means. She had been an unexpected addition to the family, arriving at a time when her parents had neither the inclination nor energy to raise another child. Her eldest sister had been twenty when she was born and had earned her keep by caring for her. Louisa had never mentioned before that Emma was deaf, but perhaps this explained her friend's knack of understanding what was left unsaid. Not that she had anything to hide, of course, but she had very much enjoyed her time with Laurence and for some reason wished to hoard their clandestine meeting to herself. She certainly did not wish Louisa to imbue it with romantic overtones that were both nonsensical and uncalled for, but it had to be said that for all her calm sense, Louisa could not be brought to believe that Cassandra neither had the desire nor temperament to marry.

Louisa's amused voice broke into her reverie. "I must tell you, my dear, that it is useless to prevaricate. Grace did mention him, you see. She could not recall his name but referred to him as a smart swell who was bang up to the echo "

Cassandra smiled. "Lord Carteret is certainly smart but in a restrained, dignified sort of way. I would not have called him a swell. Everything about him is neat without being ostentatious, well, almost everything; his hair is a little untidy, but it suits him somehow. He is intelligent and very gentlemanly, if a little reserved, although when he lets down his guard, he can be both amusing and charming."

"Ah, so he let down his guard with you. Very promising."

"It is not promising at all, Louisa," Cassandra said a little sharply. "I believe that when we weren't rubbing each other up the wrong way, we got along tolerably well, but it is highly unlikely we shall see each other again. Although I almost wish that we would; I left my cloak in his possession and as I could not fit a pelisse into my bag, I only have my spencer with me. It is perfectly adequate for a fine day, of course, but as I intend to explore this area on foot, I could wish that I still had it. He ordered his groom to wear it to draw Mr Chubb away from the inn, you see, and then kindly drove me to West Deeping."

"You may borrow something of mine, of course,

but surely Lord Carteret will return it to you when he has the opportunity?"

"He can't," Cassandra said. "He does not know where I am and so I would be amazed if I he should do so."

Her friend smiled enigmatically. "But then so many amazing things have recently happened to you, my love, that I would not be at all surprised by the advent of another."

CHAPTER 5

When Laurence returned to The George, he discovered that Fadon had been followed by Mr Chubb but had successfully eluded him.

"He was waiting in a doorway across the road, but if he wished to remain undetected, he should have known better than to wear a yellow waistcoat," the groom said scathingly.

"I fear Mr Chubb may have been parted from his luggage earlier in the day. Have you the cloak?"

"I'll just fetch it for you, sir."

The groom disappeared into the stables, returning moments later. Laurence frowned as he saw mud and heaven knew what else generously coating the bottom few inches of the woollen garment.

"It couldn't be helped," Fadon said. "There's been so much rain of late that the back lanes are filthy."

"Do what you can to clean it up, will you? We shall be returning it to its owner in the morning."

"Very well, sir."

The groom's expressionless tone and suddenly wooden countenance informed Laurence that he did not approve of this course of action.

"We really must do so, you know," he said gently.

"I suppose so," Fadon said grudgingly, "but I must admit that I had hoped your part in this smoky business was finished, milord. If you will give me the lady's direction, I can deliver it for you first thing in the morning."

The inflexion he put on the word lady suggested he thought her anything but.

"This *business* might be smoky, Fadon, but the lady of quality concerned most certainly is not. I would ask you to remember it."

The thread of steel in these softly uttered words silenced the groom.

"And my part in it," he added, "will be finished when I am certain that she is safe."

"Yes, sir," he said meekly. "At what time shall I have the curricle ready?"

"Eight o'clock. Goodnight, Fadon."

"Goodnight, sir," the groom murmured watching his master stride away, a frown between his brows. After a moment he turned back to the stables muttering to himself, "If it's a lady of quality he's driving about in the dead of night, we are in the basket."

A greater disparity of feeling than that which existed between master and groom on their way to West Deeping the following morning would have been difficult to find. Whilst Fadon was consumed with the melancholy reflection that his master was about to put his head in a noose from which there would be no escaping, Laurence was aware of a fizz of exhilaration coursing through his veins.

A soft laugh escaped him as he realised that such excitement was more fitting to a callow youth than to a man of nine and twenty. He had not felt so drawn to a woman since he had fallen for the angelic face of Diana, and the sensible side of him knew that Cassandra was no more suitable a bride for him than she had been. The two women were as different as night and day, but it would be just as wearing to be constantly challenged and teased as it would to pander to the needs of a woman permanently in need of his approbation and adoration.

It was not his sensible side that was in the ascendency at that moment, however, and he could not help but look forward to spending a little more time in Cassandra's company.

Mr Blinksop had clearly been on the lookout for him as no sooner did he pull up his horses at the inn than he came into the yard and invited him to step into the coffee room for a moment.

The stable boy, a young lad with a fresh face that held a look that hovered somewhere between surprise and awe had run out of the stables and stood by the horses' heads as if uncertain of what to do. Waiting only to quietly adjure Fadon not to breathe a whisper of their errand, he climbed down and followed Mr Blinksop into the inn.

"It might be best, Mr Blinksop, if you could contrive a way to be rid of your stablehand until we have departed the premises."

"There will be no need for that, Lord Carteret,"

the man said gravely, leading him into a coffee room that was empty of customers.

"I am sure he is a good lad," Laurence said gently, "but I think it would be prudent to do so. The fewer people who see Miss Fenton the better."

Mr Blinksop cast him a wary look. "I quite agree. And I did indeed send him on an errand before Miss Fenton and my niece departed some one and a half hours ago."

Disappointment and an odd sense of betrayal vied for supremacy in Laurence's breast. "Departed?" he said blankly. "But how is this? Miss Fenton knew I intended to see her safely to her old governess."

"That is true, sir, and I admit I would be easier in my mind if she had waited for you to do so, but she was quite adamant that she had troubled you enough."

"I see," he said, his voice flat and hard.

It seemed the attraction had been on his side alone. He should consign Cassandra to the devil and go on his way. But even as this unaccountably angry thought flitted through his mind, he found himself saying, "Wither has she gone? If it is not too far out of my way, I would like to satisfy myself that she has arrived."

"It is to your credit, sir, but I do not know where she has gone."

Laurence looked sceptical and said coolly, "Do you expect me to believe that you have no knowledge of your niece's destination?"

Mr Blinksop might have taken objection to his tone had not the suspicion that the viscount was deeply smitten suddenly crossed his mind. He had arrived at the inn with a spring in his step and an aura of anticipation hanging about him. Mr Blinksop did not wonder at it; Miss Fenton was a most unusual lady. Without being at all high in the instep, she commanded respect. Her easy manners and confidence spoke of her quality, and her looks, whilst not conventionally beautiful, drew the eye and held it.

He suspected that, as a true gentleman, which Lord Carteret most surely was, he would have helped any lady in need of his assistance, but there was something about the stiff way he was holding himself and the intent look in his eyes that suggested he was exercising considerable restraint, as if he was rigidly suppressing some strong emotion. These reflections allowed Mr Blinksop to answer in a milder tone than he might otherwise have done.

"I do, sir, for it is the truth. Grace will, in due course, write to inform me of it, however, which reminds me, Miss Fenton asked me to deliver a letter into your hands. If you will excuse me for a moment, I shall fetch it."

By the time Mr Blinksop returned with the letter, Laurence had mastered his disappointment and managed to offer the man a distant smile.

"Thank you," he said, pocketing the missive and retrieving his card case. "Here is my direction. Perhaps you would oblige me by sending word when you have heard from your niece. Having interested myself in Miss Fenton's affairs, I would be easier in my mind if I knew they had reached a satisfactory conclusion."

"Certainly, sir."

Laurence nodded curtly and strode towards the door but paused when he reached it. "Miss Fenton has exercised a cautiousness I had not credited her with, and which is even to be applauded, but I can see no reason why you should not inform me of where it is she hails from."

Mr Blinksop gave a relieved smile. "Now in that, at least, I can oblige you. Darley Manor lies a few miles north of Matlock, in Derbyshire. Sir Thomas Fenton was by all accounts a good man, and it is a great pity that the same cannot apparently be said of his successor, Sir Francis Fenton."

Laurence drove on to Market Deeping in a mood of deep abstraction. He stopped there for breakfast and sent Fadon off to make some discreet enquiries of Miss Fenton. However half-heartedly he accepted this task, Laurence knew that if there was some news of her, he would discover it.

Although the letter was burning a hole in his pocket, he finished his repast before drawing it out and slowly unfolding it.

Laurence,

Are you very cross with me? I expect you are, but you really shouldn't be, you know. It did me a great deal of good to talk things over with you, and I hope you will be pleased that I have taken your advice concerning Mr Chubb to heart. I will not make the mistake of underestimating him again. Whilst I feel it was most chivalrous of you to offer your escort for the remainder of my journey, I believe it will be best if I refuse it. It has occurred to me that if anyone happened to see me drive off with you in your curricle, you might unwittingly lead him to me and that would be a most tiresome occurrence.

I shall always appreciate the hand of friendship that you held out to me; if I was not precisely a damsel in distress, I was certainly a lady in a hobble.

I am aware that in writing to you at all I am breaching the
bounds of propriety yet again, but I felt some explanation was
due to you. I suspect that once you have recovered from the pique
of your wishes being thwarted, you will be very glad to be rid of
me. I, on the other hand, must regret losing the chance of asking
you all manner of questions you may or may not have answered.
Cassandra

His lips twisted in a wry smile at this last sally.
He was not glad to be rid of her but as Fadon's
enquiries drew a blank, he was forced to accept that
he would have to rely on Mr Blinksop's promise to
write when he had some news. He continued his
journey feeling strangely flat, but the wide, open
skies and gently undulating landscape of his home
county of Norfolk could not help but lift his spirits a
little.

It was nearing six o'clock when he turned into the
gates of Westerby. The house had been Elizabethan in
origin but had been transformed into a Palladian
mansion by his grandfather, and little of the original
house remained. His father had, in turn, enlarged the
entrance hall, raising the ceiling and adding a series of
marble columns calculated to inspire any visitors with
the requisite amount of awe and respect. Whilst his
father had been extremely satisfied with the huge
space, Laurence had always found it rather oppressive
and whenever possible entered the house by a lesser
entrance.

He would have driven his curricle around to the
stables as usual had he not seen that the huge oak
doors were wide open and the steps leading up to the
colonnaded terrace lined with servants waiting to greet
him. He raised a brow in faint surprise. His father may

have enjoyed such displays, but he did not, as Needham, his butler, knew full well.

Fadon had maintained a respectful silence for most of the day, knowing better than to attempt to jolly his master out of his abstraction, but he now said gruffly, "Don't you go riding grub, sir. If you do not know what is due to you on your birthday, there's others that do."

"Apparently so," Laurence murmured, drawing his horses to a halt and handing the reins over to the groom.

He could not help but reflect that he had a great many servants for a house that he only visited at irregular intervals, preferring to spend his time in Town or visiting friends. He had briefly considered swathing it in Holland covers and reducing the staff after his mother had died three years before but had decided against it. It would have been the perfect revenge on his father, of course. A large part of his life and a great deal of money had been ploughed into making Westerby as grand as he could make it. He may have only been a viscount, but he had seemed determined to make his residence and grounds as grand as that of any duke. He had not done it at the expense of his fortune, however. He understood the value of his land and having been acquainted with Coke of Holkham, had made sure that his stewards had been kept apprised of all the latest farming methods.

Laurence had not taken such a petty revenge, however. This was partly due to his awareness that employment was not easily obtained in the district, and partly because his sisters had a fondness for their family home. Consequently, they had an open invitation to visit Westerby whenever the fancy took them whether he was present or not. They frequently did so, especially in the summer months as they wished their children to enjoy the vast grounds and sea air.

As he jumped down from the curricle, the white-haired butler came forwards, a small smile of welcome on his lips.

"We were hoping you would arrive this evening, my lord, and were sure of it when your valet arrived with your luggage an hour ago. I hope you enjoyed your stay in Northumberland?"

"I did, very much," Laurence said with his gentle smile. "I am pleased to see you looking so well, Needham." He turned to his housekeeper. "Mrs Webb, I must apologise for not having been able to send more precise information about the time of my arrival."

The housekeeper had a forbidding exterior that might have kept the housemaids in firm order, but Laurence knew to cover a kind heart, at least towards him. He had always inspired an affection in the servants that he could not feel he fully deserved. Perhaps it was because he never failed to thank them for any service they rendered him no matter how trivial, unlike his father, who had barely noticed them unless he was displeased.

Mrs Webb offered him a curtsy, the stiffness of which he knew to be due to a touch of arthritis and not meant as a reproof to him.

"Of course you could not, sir," she said, her eyes softening. "Our country may be superior to most others by all I can discover, but it cannot be denied that the weather and the state of the roads are unpredictable."

"Just so," Laurence murmured, leaning a little closer to her. "It is not to my credit, Mrs Webb, but I am afraid that I cannot quite remember all the names of the maids waiting to greet me."

"That, my lord, is hardly surprising. At least three of them are new, and if the others had drawn themselves to your attention, I would want to know why." Her severe tone gentled as she offered him a conspiratorial smile. "Do not worry, sir, I shall introduce them all to you."

He was escorted up the steps and by the time he had accepted the felicitations of the maids, footmen, the gardeners, and the stable staff, not failing to address some general enquiry to each of them, some fifteen minutes had passed. Only the kitchen staff were absent, Mrs Webb explaining that they would be mortified if they burnt his lordship's dinner. He could only be grateful for their diligence.

He, at last, entered the hall breathing a sigh of relief, his eyes fixed on the pink-tinged marble tiles. Perhaps now he could relax. The prospect of spending his birthday alone within the gracious apartments of his family seat held little attraction for him. He would ask for his dinner to be served in the modest parlour that was part of his suite of rooms and invite his cousin and steward, Alfred Westerby, to join him if he were in. In his father's day, it had been a characterless anteroom positioned next to a small private study, with uncomfortable chairs ranged around the edge and dour-faced relatives looking down from dark portraits lining the walls. This uninspiring scheme had been calculated to make anyone unfortunate enough to have been summoned to a private audience quake with trepidation, of course.

Laurence had consigned those relatives to the attic without a qualm of conscience, replaced them with landscapes of the local area by artists of the Norfolk School of Painters, covered the floor with a colourful carpet, and furnished it with comfortable sofas and a table designed to feed no more than four people. As a cleverly concealed door in one corner gave on to some service stairs that came out in a corridor very close to the kitchens, he need not fear that his meal would arrive cold.

He was halfway across the hall, his footsteps echoing in the cavernous chamber when the pianoforte that crouched in one corner suddenly burst into life causing him to start. He quickly glanced up and discovered that a small party was gathered about it.

Two ladies in their mid-thirties, with hair of an unremarkable shade of brown, detached themselves from the group. Both were rather short in stature and their features identical.

"Laurie! We had almost given you up!" one said.

"Cecy," he said, taking the hands offered to him and smiling down at her with real affection. "Is it you I have to thank for my welcoming committee?"

"No, dear brother," the other lady said, her eyes as sharp as her sister's were vague. "You know full well that Cecy is far too shatterbrained to organise such a reception."

"Perhaps," he agreed, releasing Cecy's hands and obediently kissing the cheek offered to him. The smile remained in his eyes, but he added dryly, "And far too good-natured."

"I told you he might not like it, Anne," she said, her brow puckering. "He has never liked the cold magnificence of the hall."

"Oh, stop fretting, sister," Anne said, but not impatiently, her eyes quizzing Laurence. "It would be most ungracious of him to complain when we have gone to so much trouble to make it a little less imposing." She put a hand on her brother's arm and made a sweeping gesture with the other. "Look, Laurie."

A slow, incredulous smile dawned as he looked about him properly for the first time. The huge, fluted columns had been wreathed in greenery and the classical statues that were placed at intervals about the room had been dressed in modern clothing. A caped driving coat hung over one and a beaver hat had been placed on his brow, another wore a muslin gown and a straw bonnet wreathed in flowers, but he thought his favourite was the one sporting a woollen cap, rough shirt, and buff breeches in the style of a gardener. A hoe rested in the crook of his arm.

His eyes involuntarily went to the portrait hanging over the door to the west wing. His father's proud stare seemed to bore into him. He offered him a small bow and a cynical smile.

"He would be appalled, of course," Cecy said, her voice a little anxious.

"Quite apoplectic," Anne said, "but there is no need for you to look so worried, Cecy; his portrait can hardly remonstrate with us." She turned rueful eyes on her brother. "Not that he ever did remonstrate with us; we were of no interest to him, and I am very thankful for it. It was you who bore the brunt of his capricious-ness. Do you remember, Laurie, that when he had been particularly beastly to you, you were twelve, I think, you said that you would like to paint black mustachios on all his precious statues?"

"No, did I?" he said, his soft tones faintly appalled. "I can only be glad I did not give in to the impulse. They may only be reproductions, but they are very fine ones."

"Oh, you would never have done so, of course," Anne said, "and neither would we. But I did not think you would mind our little joke."

"I don't," he said. "I have a mind to leave them as they are."

"Laurie," Cecy said, giggling, "you don't mean it?"

Anne was not so amused. "He had better not. I would not have suggested it if I thought he might. You can't mean it, brother!"

"No, I don't suppose I do," he said a little regret-fully. "If any of our neighbours came to call, it would give them a very odd opinion of me."

Anne looked relieved. The sisters each took an arm and led him towards the piano, and his amuse-ment faded as he saw a pretty stranger playing it. She was very young and could not long have emerged from the schoolroom. Dusky curls framed a heart-shaped face and when she briefly lifted her eyes to his, he saw they were large and of a soft, brown hue. She smiled tremulously and then bit her lip as she stumbled over a note, her eyes dropping back to the keys.

"There is no need for you to poker up," Anne murmured. "I am not matchmaking; we did not even know you were coming home until your letter arrived.

Miss Reynolds is some sort of cousin to my husband and has come to stay with us for a few weeks. She is a sweet girl."

Three gentlemen were clustered about the piano, but two of them now came forward to shake his hand. Lord Malmsy, husband to Anne, was in his early forties. He was not handsome; his nose was rather thin and pointed, but his lips were nicely moulded, and his eyes held a great deal of lurking humour. Her father had felt that in catching an earl, Anne had excelled herself.

He had not had any such ambitions for Cecelia. He had always been used to say that Anne had all the brains whilst Cecelia only had her good nature to recommend her. He had not hesitated to accept the offer made for her by Mr Trevor Pellow. His lack of title was regrettable but his family and fortune respectable. As neither of the girls had any marked degree of beauty, he had felt a certain amount of pride that they had secured husbands in their first season. This pride had been rooted in his own conse-quence, however, rather than any paternal feeling towards them.

Mr Pellow, a quiet, bookish man, now in his late forties, was considerably older than Cecy, and if this had concerned Lady Carteret a little, she had soon realised that such a union might be wise for a girl who was not only forgetful but who seemed to lack any degree of worldliness.

"Good evening, Carteret," Lord Malmsy said. "Your sisters and the children have had great fun preparing for your arrival, whilst Pellow and I have been denuding the lake of trout."

"I am glad that you have all been so well entertained," Laurence said, shaking the hand offered before turning to Mr Pellow.

As this gentleman was not known for his sporting proclivities, Laurence might have felt some surprise at his spending the afternoon fishing, but a long, if not intimate acquaintance with him, furnished him with the answer to this conundrum.

"Distancing yourself from the scene of the crime?" he said, with a faint, amused smile.

"Indeed," Mr Pellow acknowledged, his own smile wry. "I must admit to some qualms at such fine representations of antiquity being so disrespected." He looked kindly at his wife, who was looking a little shame-faced. "There is no need to look so worried, my dear. If your brother is amused, what have I to say to the matter? And at least it is Dionysus who has been garbed as a gardener. Very apt."

Although there was no marked resemblance between Laurence and his sisters, Cecy shared the same sweet smile. She bestowed it on her husband saying, "Well, that is what I thought. I could not remember who he was meant to be, but the bunch of grapes he is holding seemed to suggest a connection to the earth."

"And wine," the third gentleman said, now coming up to them and holding out a glass to Laurence.

Mr Alfred Westerby was in his late thirties and the cast of his countenance was aquiline. A second cousin of Laurence's, he looked very much like their great-grandfather. Alfred's father and grandfather had gone into the church, but not having any desire himself to preach, or any military bent, he had gone into the law.

His intention, however, had always been to eventually manage some gentleman's estate. In his mind, it was the next best thing to having his own.

As he had never met the fourth Viscount Carteret before he had applied for the position as his steward, he had thought himself very fortunate to have attained the position at Westerby, the seat of his ancestors, even though his father had never spoken well of his cousin. However, if the viscount had been an exacting master, he had, at least, not been at all clutch-fisted and had paid him very well for his work, as well as giving him a set of rooms at the back of the house on the ground floor of the west wing, next to the main offices.

Laurence had always treated Alfred with a consideration that his father had never approved of. That gentleman had felt that as the head of his house he was being very generous in providing his cousin's child with a means of earning his living, not that he would have continued to do so if he had not soon realised his capabilities and been sure that no one might better look after his interests than a Westerby, but he was far too high in the instep to treat him as anything other than a poor relation.

Laurence had been in his last year at Oxford when Alfred had attained the position of steward and had thought it deplorable to treat someone with the same blood as he running through his veins and who, moreover, was eight years his senior as a mere employee rather than a member of the family. He raised a haughty brow and said in arctic tones, "Well, Westerby, and what do you mean by allowing such vandalism? I thought you were supposed to look after my assets?"

Mr Westerby grinned. "And so I do, as I am looking forward to showing you… in great detail."

"Yes, but not tomorrow or even the day after," Anne said firmly. "We must insist on having Laurie to ourselves for a little while, Alfred." Her eyes swept past him and saw Miss Reynolds hovering a little uncertainly by the pianoforte.

"Come here, child," she said.

Laurence observed that she was slender and delicate in appearance, seeming to float over the tiles rather than tread upon them, and he thought her a little older than he had first supposed. He was not quite sure what had drawn him to this conclusion, perhaps it was that although she seemed extremely shy – her eyes even now were downcast – she held herself well and moved confidently.

"Here is Lord Carteret, my brother, Miss Reynolds."

She sank into a deep curtsy and looked up at him through long, curling lashes. "My lord."

"Miss Reynolds," he said, taking her hand and helping her to rise. "I am only a viscount, you know, there is no need to treat me like royalty."

She coloured delightfully, and stammered, "Oh, n-no, it is just that your home is so fine, so grand—"

He smiled gently at her. "You would not think so if you had ever been to Carlton House or the Pavilion in Brighton."

She seemed to regain her composure. "Then I am glad I have not visited either place, sir. I think I would be quite overwhelmed."

"Then you would not be alone," he assured her. "I have known more than one lady to faint from the heat.

The Prince Regent is terrified of catching a chill and so will not countenance a window being opened, no matter how many people crowd his rooms."

A hint of mischief came into her eyes. "Or his statues to be dressed?"

A soft laugh escaped him. "Certainly not."

CHAPTER 6

Cassandra was delighted to discover that Tremlow House possessed stables of a reasonable size. As they were currently only occupied by two horses, a gig, and a carriage, she wasted no time in writing to Mr Penwith, asking him to arrange for her clothes and horse to be sent to her, and to make the necessary arrangements for it to be possible for her to draw any funds she might need from a bank in King's Lynn. She then settled into a comfortable routine at Tremlow House.

She would rise early and go for a walk, each day exploring a new direction. The large back garden of the house gave onto a creek that fed into an estuary. A wooden bridge spanned the creek and on the other side of it, slightly raised, narrow tracks led either to a small harbour, sand dunes and secluded beaches or meandered through saltmarsh that at first glance appeared rather desolate but on closer examination revealed a wide variety of birdlife. Sheep and the occasional cow grazed it, seemingly content with the rather sparse vegetation. Whichever way she walked, Cassandra was aware of a feeling of openness, of vast skies stretching in all directions and felt as if she could breathe freely for the first time in months.

When she returned to the house, she would breakfast with Louisa and her sister. Emma was a petite woman with white hair and an absent air, but when she turned her attention on Cassandra, she would stare intently, her gaze frequently focusing on her lips.

She had soon discovered that Emma had a remarkable gift; she could understand a great deal of what a person said by the movement of their lips. She had not been born deaf but had become so after a severe case of measles when she was in her late twenties. Louisa had been only nine and still largely in her care and they had invented a new game. Emma would write a word and then ask Louisa to say it several times until she associated the movement of her mouth with that word. It was not a perfect art and there were slates and chalk in almost every room of Tremlow House in case of a misunderstanding or if the kindly lady simply became too tired. It required a great deal of concentration on her part and if a conversation went on too long or became too rapid, she would retreat into herself. Her own speech was not as clear as it had once been but was perfectly understandable once one became accustomed to its lack of expression.

As Emma was an excellent seamstress, it had been agreed that she would take Grace under her wing. She tutored her for an hour after breakfast whilst Louisa and Cassandra discussed their allotted tasks for the day. These were not onerous as Louisa employed, besides Mrs Larkin, her cook-housekeeper, a laundry maid, a kitchen maid, two housemaids, Mr Cooper – a strapping man who combined the duties of stable hand and gardener – and a footman. Louisa, who had been brought up to be thrifty, clearly felt a little guilty about the footman.

"William is an extravagance for such a small household, I must admit," Louisa told her, "but I can well afford him and one must have someone to answer the door and go and fetch the post, after all."

Cassandra did not think it an extravagance but a necessity and did not hesitate to say so. "Apart from anything else, he may accompany you when you wish to go shopping, for I think it must be some way to the nearest town of any size."

"It is," Louisa said. "Once every two months I make the trip to King's Lynn to acquire the few things I cannot purchase in the villages nearby, but it is two and a half hours each way in the carriage."

It was in King's Lynn that Mr Tremlow had conducted his business, a circumstance which led Cassandra to wonder why he had decided to live in such a remote spot. Over breakfast on her fourth morning at the house, she voiced the thought.

"I must admit," Louisa said, "that I am not completely sure why he built a house here. I am glad he did so, however, for although the servants he originally hired were not suited to the spot and left soon after his death, claiming that it was an uncanny place where strange lights and noises would float over the marsh, I have never experienced anything remotely strange." She laughed. "I expect someone from the village may have put such ideas into their heads, trying to make a May game of them. I must admit, however, that Clara had grown strangely twitchy and would jump merely at the hoot of an owl. Mr Tremlow seems to have made her sadly nervous.

"I did wonder if he had ambitions to set up as a gentleman for he purchased some land. But Willow Tree Farm is six miles distant and from all I could discover from Clara, he spent little time either here or there. He leased another house near his warehouse in King's Lynn and spent the better part of his week there."

"Poor Clara," Cassandra murmured.

"Harridan!"

Cassandra glanced over at Emma, surprised. "Was she really that bad?"

The little lady nodded and, her point being made, seemed to lose interest in the conversation, applying herself again to her breakfast.

Cassandra turned laughing eyes on Louisa, fully expecting her to share her amusement at this outburst, but although she smiled, her eyes held sympathy. "Clara was never kind to Emma, particularly after she lost her hearing, but I cannot help but feel sorry for her. She informed me during one of her many bitter rants that when it became clear she was not going to bear a child, Mr Tremlow was not kind to her. He was rather too fond of his brandy and when in his cups, would not hesitate to inform her of his latest mistress and enunciate all her charms whilst laying bare Clara's deficiencies."

The laughter in Cassandra's eyes fled, shock and then scorn taking its place. "How contemptible!"

"And cruel," Louisa added. "She married him because of his wealth, of course, and one cannot

82

blame her for that; we had always had to scrimp and save, but she made a very poor bargain, I think. After he died, she discovered his business was not as profitable as she had expected, and although when it was sold she was left very comfortable, she did not feel it enough to make up for the years of misery she had endured at his hands."

"No, I expect not," Cassandra said. "What happened to the farm?"

"She kept it on the advice of Mr Rythorne, the family lawyer who dealt with Mr Tremlow's affairs."

Cassandra put down her fork, her eyes sparkling with interest. "So, you, Louisa Thorpe, are a landowner?"

"Yes, I suppose I am," she said.

"How much rent does the farm bring you a year?"

Louisa mentioned a sum Cassandra thought paltry. She frowned. "How many acres has it?"

"I think in the region of four hundred acres."

"Then it should fetch a much higher rent," Cassandra informed her.

"Should it? I do not know about such things. Mr Rythorne has always seemed so solicitous and respectful on the few occasions I have met with him that I felt sure I could safely leave everything in his hands."

Cassandra became eager, finally seeing a way she could be of real use to her friend. "I may not be a dab hand at cutting and arranging flowers, but I do know about the management of land. I must see this farm."

Louisa smiled wryly. "I knew it would not be many days before helping me in the garden palled."

"It is not that, precisely. I have enjoyed a most

delightful holiday, I assure you, but you know how much I like to be busy."

"I know how much you were forced to be busy," her friend said gently.

"I was not forced," Cassandra said with conviction. "I have quite fallen in love with the country here, but there is so little to do that I imagine in time it might pall. Is it enough for you, Louisa?"

Her friend chuckled. "At the moment, certainly. I was quite worn out when Louisa died, you know, and have quite abandoned myself these past months to a life of leisure."

Cassandra felt a moment's remorse. She may not have chosen to live a life of leisure, but she could have if she had wished it. She smiled wryly at the thought that Mr Rushby, their bailiff, might have been happier if she had chosen such a life rather than overseeing him in her father's place. Louisa had not had the luxury of choosing but had resigned herself to a life of service, and however cheerfully she had done so, she had every right to relish her more favourable circumstances and the opportunity to live upon her own terms. "I understand, of course, and hope you have used the time to indulge your love of painting."

"I have," she admitted. "The vicar visited me frequently before and immediately after Clara's death, and during one of our rambling conversations, he confessed that he would like to have a miniature portrait of his wife done. As artists are thin on the ground in the immediate vicinity, I offered to do it." She assumed an air of consequence. "And that led to two more commissions: one from the doctor and one from a local farmer." She smiled. "I am not as skilled as you, my dear; the pupil most definitely outstripped the teacher in your case, but I do not think my efforts were contemptible."

"Of course they were not," Cassandra said. "But, Louisa, you do not need to paint for money, surely? That is not leading a life of leisure."

"Perhaps I crave fame and fortune," Louisa said with a twinkle.

Cassandra laughed. "Then you should aim a little higher. Ask the doctor or vicar to mention your excellence every time they visit one of the big houses around here, that might do the trick."

Louisa smiled. "I know my limitations. If any such commissions come my way, I shall pass them on to you."

"I would not accept them," Cassandra said loftily, before adding in dramatic tones, "to sell my soul for a few guineas would be a desecration of my art!"

"But a gift not shared is one that is squandered," Louisa shot back at her.

"Be serious for a moment, my dear," Cassandra said, chuckling. "Do you really mean to set up as a portraitist?"

"Of course not," Louisa said. "I did not charge the vicar; the portrait was my way of thanking him for his frequent attendance on Clara. He brought her some comfort, I think. I found it a little difficult to disappoint the others, besides, it was something to do whilst I was in strict mourning for my sister, but I have let it be known that I will not be accepting any more commissions." Her expression became more serious. "I sometimes help at the Sunday school in the village, but what I would really like to do is set up a proper school. There is a tumbledown barn on the other side of the village that would be the very place, but it would take a great deal of money to purchase and rebuild it."

"More than you can afford?"

"I think so," Louisa said. "Perhaps I will need to toad eat some of the local gentry, after all."

"Or perhaps you will not if you get a fair price for your acres. I think we should visit Willow Tree Farm; it is high time you met your tenant, Louisa."

Waiting only for Louisa to give her instructions to Mrs Larkin, they set off in the gig.

"I shall drive," Louisa said, taking the reins from Cassandra, who had automatically reached for them, "and then you may look about you."

Cassandra did look about her, for by the time she had hired the last chaise in King's Lynn on her journey into Norfolk, she had been too weary to do so. Once they ventured a little inland, a vista of gently rolling countryside that seemed to stretch for miles in all directions greeted them, and she discovered that the sky remained huge away from the coast, only broken by the occasional stretch of woodland, red-roofed farm building, or the odd windmill. She soon realised that this was due to the lack of hills or mountains in the region. Some might have thought this rendered the view dull and lacking in the picturesque, but she rather liked it. Perhaps it was the novelty of a landscape so very different to that of Derbyshire.

"This is excellent farmland," she finally said, indicating with a sweep of her arm the array of fields.

Some were still full of golden wheat rippling in the gentle breeze, but others were hives of activity, with groups of men, women and children engaged in the back-breaking work of gathering the harvest in. The men walked abreast of each other wielding the scythes, others raked the stalks into heaps, and the women and children tied the loose wheat into sheaves.

"I am even more confused by the ridiculously low rent your sister's husband demanded of his tenant."

"Perhaps, being a merchant rather than a farmer, he was ignorant of the true worth of his land," she suggested. "I had no idea of it, after all, and I must assume Mr Rythorne was also ignorant."

Cassandra gave a most unladylike snort. "Your ignorance is understandable, my love, but his cannot be so easily overlooked. It is his business to know of such things."

Willow Tree Farm lay between the villages of Sedgeford and Fring and was divided by the River Heacham, which abounded with the trees from which the farm derived its name. Cassandra frowned as they trotted along a sunken lane that was grassy in the middle, but full of dusty ruts to either side as if heavily laden carts frequently used it.

"My love? You look very stern," Louisa said. "Until this track took us below the level of the fields, I had been admiring the beautiful wild meadows." She smiled wryly. "I even knew the urge to run through the long grass and lie down amongst the remaining wild-flowers. I wish I had come to see them a month ago when they would have been at their best."

"Yes, they are very pretty," Cassandra murmured absently.

"But?" Louisa probed, sensing her friend's disquiet.

Cassandra turned troubled eyes on her. "There should not be so much land left as meadow or empty pasture; this is arable country. It might perhaps make sense near the river in case of flood, although I have observed enough drainage ditches to suggest that someone once knew what they were about, but it makes no sense to have acre upon acre left in such a way. Whoever farms this land is not utilising his acres to best advantage. And did you see the huge field that must have had at least ten horses grazing in it?"

"I did," Louisa admitted. "But a farm needs horses, does it not?"

"Of course," Cassandra admitted, "for ploughing, taking in the crops, and transporting them. They should be working now, not eating their heads off."

"Perhaps Mr Moore has already taken in the harvest."

As the road sloped gently upwards, there was indeed some evidence that a large field of perhaps eight acres had been recently harvested, and two others had mounds of hay drying in the sun, but there were many that lay fallow or in which the wheat yield was thin and still green as if it had been planted too late.

"It is as if," Cassandra said slowly, "whoever has taken on the farm has bitten off rather more than he can chew. Perhaps he moved from a smaller holding and has not the resources or skill to make so many acres pay. No wonder he cannot afford a proper rent. If Mr Rythorne was responsible for finding the tenant, he has again shown his incompetence. My grandfather always demanded references and proof that the applicant had enough experience as well as capital for seed, equipment and so on before he granted them tenancy of one of his farms."

The lane eventually led them to a substantial, three-storey farmhouse. It must have at one time presented a very respectable appearance but was now sadly neglected. A cursory glance showed that several tiles were missing from the roof, and one of the lower windows was boarded up. It was set in gardens, which had once had some sort of pattern to them, but now were only distinguished by overgrown shrubbery.

Louisa grimaced. "Oh dear, it appears I am as lax a landlord as my tenant is a farmer."

As they pulled up in front of the house, a black cat that sat upon a step in the porch, hissed and fled as the door opened. A lady with grizzled grey hair stepped out, her eyes narrowing as she observed her visitors; whether from suspicion or the sun that shone directly upon her was not immediately clear. The harsh light did not flatter her, highlighting her lined skin, which was marked with brown spots.

"Good day," Louisa said pleasantly. "I have come to see Mr Moore. Are you his wife?"

"I am," she said. "An' who do you be?"

"I am Miss Thorpe, your landlady, Mrs Moore," she said with an apologetic smile. "I am sorry that I have not visited you before, but I have been mourning my sister and am only just coming to grips with my new obligations."

"You've no need to worrit your head about us, ma'am," Mrs Moore said firmly. "Isaac deals with Mr Rythorne. Business is best left to the men."

Louisa's gaze roamed over the house. "I wonder if you are right? It seems to me that there are repairs crying out to be done here, Mrs Moore. Has your husband informed Mr Rythorne of it?"

"He don't need to," she said, a little defensively. "Them'll be done soon enough. Isaac will see to it."

"I see," Louisa said, "I should like to discuss them with him, however."

Mrs Moore folded her arms and her pointed chin jutted forward. "He en't here."

"No, apparently not. Where may I find him?"

The lady nodded in the general direction from which they had come. "He's helping Mr King with his harvest. He won't be back till dusk."

"One might have thought he would be better tending his own farm," Louisa said, her tone a little astringent. She was becoming tired of Mrs Moore's barely veiled hostility, which was as unmannerly as it was unwise considering her and her husband's future lay in the palm of her hand.

Cassandra approved of Mrs Moore's attitude no more than her friend, but an innate fairness made her say, "It is not unusual for farmers to help each other during the harvest, with either equipment or labour."

Mrs Moore smiled rather sourly, but her mouth tightened as Cassandra added, "Indeed, you have so many horses, ma'am, that I own myself surprised that they have not been sent to pull the carts."

"Isaac be fond of hosses."

"Clearly, as judging by the fields of hay and the amount of pasture they have to graze in, I would say they were the most cared for thing on the farm."

"'Tis no crime to cherish God's animals," she said belligerently.

Realising that this interview was going nowhere,

and that the woman had no intention of offering them any hospitality, Cassandra said, "No, indeed it is not. Good day to you, ma'am."

"I shall perhaps have the felicity of meeting your good husband another time," Louisa said with cool civility.

The woman took a step back saying, "Mind how you go."

As the gig moved off, Cassandra looked over her shoulder, frowning slightly, but the door of the farmhouse was already closing. She knew Mrs Moore's last words to be a traditional way of saying goodbye, but her rough way of speaking had made them sound almost like a threat.

CHAPTER 7

L aurence had spent a surprisingly pleasant few days. His siblings were all that was amiable and seemed determined to make him recall the best of his childhood memories. As the twins had been married at eighteen, these did not extend much beyond his thirteenth year.

He had been small for his age and extremely slender, a circumstance which had endeared him to his mother and sisters but had inspired in his father a disgust which he had done little to hide. He had observed the affection with which his wife and daughters treated Laurence with a jaundiced eye, but the secret fear that his puny son would not survive until adulthood had ensured that he had not interfered. By the time Cecelia and Anne had married, Laurence had survived several childhood illnesses and the viscount had realised that his son was hardier than he appeared. He had sent him to Eton with few qualms, insisting he returned to Westerby in the holidays, determined to overset years of female influence and put his own stamp on the boy.

And so Laurence had found himself bullied both at school and at home. At school, he had studied the weaknesses of his tormenters and found a way to utilise them to his best advantage, generally achieving a satisfying revenge without them ever being aware that he was the mastermind behind their downfall. It had been more difficult to overcome the challenges at Westerby.

He had made every effort to please the distant figure he hardly knew, applying himself to all the accomplishments his father admired, becoming, in time, an accomplished rider and whip, an excellent fencer, and a fine shot. If his progress in these activities had been overseen by a fond parent, he might have been said to have enjoyed an idyllic upbringing, but his father had been far from fond. Glowing reports of Laurence's academic accomplishments and his aptitude for painting had not impressed the fourth viscount but reinforced the image of his heir as a dreamy weakling who must be brought up to scratch. Although he had filled his house with both sculpture and paintings, his choices were driven by his wish to appear up to the knocker and impress his acquaintances, not by genuine interest.

Nothing his son achieved was ever good enough. He frequently taunted Laurence if he was thrown from a horse that such a lightweight should never have been given to ride in the first place or if came home with his game bag no more than half full.

The sensitive but sunny boy that his sisters had known disappeared behind a barrier of reserve as he learned to keep his thoughts and feelings to himself. Any show of emotion on his part would be judged as unmanly and result in a whipping. His mother had only once intervened and earned for herself a stinging slap across the face and a recommendation to visit her daughters. She had done so, frequently, partly because they produced five children between them within as many years, and partly because she could not bear to see her son so abused but was powerless to prevent it.

By the time Laurence turned sixteen, he matched his contemporaries in height if not in bulk, and by the time he left Oxford he was stronger than most of them and an excellent boxer. His father relaxed his attitude, but the damage had already been done. Laurence chose to live in the London house for all but a few weeks of the summer, knowing that his father was unlikely to leave Westerby unless a bill he was particularly interested in came under discussion, a circumstance that was increasingly rare. He preferred to reside in state at Westerby and invite his friends to come to him.

The viscount had not objected to his son's predilection for the metropolis; he knew him to be great friends with Lord Allerdale, son of the Marquess of Brigham, and could not help but be gratified by his son's connection to such a noble family. If Allerdale had already acquired a reputation for being a little wild, he contented himself with the knowledge that every man must acquire a little Town bronze as well as sow a few wild oats before he learned the business of his estates. But when he had been visited by an old crony a few months before his son's twenty-third birthday and had discovered that although Laurence was sometimes seen in his friend's company, he was more often to be found with a set of painters and sculptors in the most unfashionable of haunts, he had posted immediately to Town. He had arrived unheralded and unlooked for in Grosvenor Square and delivered his son a furious tirade on the ingratitude and downright disloyalty of sons, who ignoring their duty, indulged themselves in pursuits that could neither bring honour on their families nor help support the many dependents who relied on them to secure both their present and their future.

However much Laurence had resented his father, he could not deny the justice of his complaints and might have begged his pardon if his mother, who the viscount had thought to be with Anne at Malmsy Park, but had, in fact, been staying with Laurence for some weeks, had not just then come into the room. He had seen red and laid the blame for his son's weaknesses at her door. He would have struck her, but Laurence had stepped forwards and grasped his arm in a strong grip. It had not taken many moments for the viscount to realise that he could not resist his son's strength. Considering his many animadversions on Laurence's puny build when he was a child, some might have thought this would have at least provoked some amount of admiration in him, however small, but it did not.

Knowing full well that he could not physically hurt his son, he had torn through the house searching for his artistic endeavours. He had found them in the conservatory at the back of the house and ordered them all to be destroyed. He was rewarded with the pleasure of seeing horror briefly reflected in

Laurence's face and the more dubious satisfaction of reducing his wife to an extended fit of the vapours. This victory had been short-lived, however, for not long after he had supervised the removal of his son's work, he had suffered a seizure and the following day he was found to be dead in his bed. The doctor who had attended him had been in no doubt that the cause of his demise was heart failure.

The heavy burden of responsibility that was so unexpectedly thrust upon Laurence caught him ill-prepared, but a mixture of duty and guilt had ensured that he put away his brushes and chisel and set about understanding his obligations. Westerby continued to oppress his spirits, however, and it was rare that his visits lasted more than a few weeks.

His sisters knew it and regretted it. They hoped that if Laurence could be reminded of happier times, he might be able to see beyond the years of misery he had endured and begin to feel fonder of his home. And so the attics were ransacked and wooden sailing boats they had used to race on the lake were unearthed, an old kite found, and a set of quoits discovered.

These activities exactly suited his four nephews who ranged in age from eleven to fourteen, and Laurence could not help but see a reflection of his own boyish self in them. Miss Reynolds was content to sit under a tree with his sisters, watching them with a gentle smile on her lips, allowing ten-year-old Phoebe, Cecy's youngest child, to sit beside her.

This young damsel appeared to adore Miss Reynolds, a circumstance that did not surprise Laurence. Not only was she extraordinarily pretty, but she always seemed to be in a good temper, and once she had overcome her shyness, he had more than once discovered a mischievous twinkle in her eyes. But he had noticed that whenever he tried to discover her opinion on something, she would turn his question back, waiting to hear his thoughts before offering hers. When she did proffer her opinion, invariably it mirrored his own. This did not sit well with him; his father had expected as much from his mother, hating to be opposed on anything, but he was not such a man.

The only subject upon which Miss Reynolds did not hesitate to make her feelings known was Westerby. She wasted no opportunity to exclaim over the elegance of a room she had not before wandered into, commenting approvingly on the richness of the decoration, the magnificence of a mural, or the tasteful arrangement of the furniture. No fool, Laurence soon began to realise that she probably went to bed dreaming of becoming mistress of such an establishment. He did not blame her for that; as the daughter of Lord Malmsy's cousin, her birth was good but her fortune negligible, and what girl did not dream of making an excellent match?

But even as these eminently reasonable thoughts occurred to him, three ladies who had not been swayed by such considerations immediately came to mind. Although Miss Edgcott had eventually succumbed to the charms of his friend Allerdale, she certainly had not been on the catch for a husband, but then she had had a considerable fortune of her own, as had Lady Selena who had set her heart on Allerdale's cousin, the younger son of a baron. Miss

Reynolds was not in so fortunate a position, and neither was the third lady he had thought of.

He had been kept far too busy during the day to often think of Cassandra, but when he lay between waking and sleeping, her image would come to him, her eyes laughing and he would hear her say, *Of course I arrived safely. Did you doubt that I would?* Somehow, he did not, but he would be easier in his mind when he received a letter from Mr Blinksop assuring him of it.

His mind was to be relieved of any lingering worry sooner than he expected. He had promised his cousin that he would give him his undivided attention that day, and after a busy morning looking over applications for the upcoming vacancy of one of his farms, they rode out together to view the property in question. It marked the boundary of his estate to the west and as they drew in their horses to view the efficiency with which the fields were being harvested, he could not help but reflect that it was a shame he was to lose one of his most dependable and experienced tenants.

"Mr King feels he is ready to take on a larger enterprise," Alfred explained. "I must admit that I agree with him and had hoped that we might be able to acquire the neighbouring farm which is neglected and clearly beyond the capabilities of its tenant, Mr Moore. We could then have perhaps persuaded Mr King to stay, but when I approached Mr Rythorne, who is the owner's man of business, he assured me that she would never sell it."

"She?" Laurence enquired; his attention caught. "I had thought a Mr Tremlow owned the land."

"He did," Alfred confirmed, "but he died some

three years ago, and his widow inherited it. She succumbed to an illness a few months ago and it now belongs to Miss Louisa Thorpe, her sister."

They had been riding slowly onwards towards Mr Moore's farm, and now pulled up and surveyed the waist-high grass dotted with wildflowers.

"I see what you mean." Something was pulling at the edges of Laurence's mind. Why did the circumstances Westerby had explained to him resonate somehow?

"Have you met Miss Thorpe?" he asked.

Alfred's eyebrows shot up. "No, I have not. I could not approach her directly. For one thing, she is a woman, and for another, she is in mourning for her sister."

Laurence looked amused. "I admit your second objection is certainly a consideration, but that aside, is it your lack of an introduction which prevents you from making a direct approach, or your reluctance to do business with a female?"

"Well, both," Alfred admitted. "I would be at a disadvantage from the outset; I would not be able to drive so hard a bargain."

Laurence's eyes rested on his cousin's handsome countenance for a moment. "And yet, Westerby, I cannot help but feel that if you chose to exert your not inconsiderable charm, you might bring the thing about."

"It would feel as if I were taking advantage of her," he protested. "How ungentlemanly it would be to use such tactics against an ageing spinster who most likely has no head for business. I am amazed that you would suggest such a thing."

"I did not suggest you should try to fleece her," Laurence said gently. "Merely persuade her to part with the land. You would offer her agent a fair price, of course." His eyes returned to the view before him. "There is work begging to be done here, and much-needed employment for half a dozen men at least. I cannot imagine why our spinster is so determined to hold onto the farm unless there is some sentimental reason for it. If that is the case, you must not press her, and may even drop a word of advice in her ear. It seems to me that neither her tenant nor her man of business are serving her interests very well."

A swirl of dust in the distance caught Laurence's attention and his eyes narrowed as he saw a gig coming towards them. It was too far away for him to make out the features of the two ladies it carried, but the way one of them held herself and the dark green of her dress was familiar to him. Cassandra's words about her governess-companion suddenly came to him. *She reluctantly left me three years ago to live with her ailing, widowed sister.*

"I think," he said, his words much slower than the beat of his heart, "we are about to meet Miss Thorpe."

Alfred looked at him in some astonishment. "How can you possibly know that when you have never met her?"

Laurence smiled, for as the gig drew nearer the thought that he was guilty of wishful thinking was firmly banished. Cassandra's winging eyebrows, sculpted cheekbones, and luscious mouth were unmistakable.

"Call it a hunch," he said softly, urging his horse

towards the point where the sunken track met the road.

Miss Thorpe was driving, and as she was concentrating on the sharp turn from the track onto the road, she did not immediately perceive them. Cassandra did. Her eyes widened and a flash of surprise, followed swiftly by something that looked very much like pleasure came into them. She reached out a hand and placed it on her companion's arm, murmuring something indistinguishable.

The gig drew to a halt, and Miss Thorpe turned her head, her eyes alight with interest.

He swept the hat from his head and bowed. "Good day, Miss Fenton. I am very happy to see you again."

"And I you, Lord Carteret," Cassandra said easily. "I had not expected to have the pleasure, however. Are you staying in the area?"

"My land ends where this farm begins," he explained.

"I had not realised."

"How should you have done so? I do not believe the subject of my home came under discussion when last I saw you."

Cassandra turned a speaking look on her companion. "This is Miss Thorpe, my very good friend."

"Ah, Miss Thorpe," he said, tipping his hat to her. He noted that she wore a dark blue dress and so apparently was in strict mourning no longer. "My cousin and I were just speaking of you. May I introduce Mr Westerby, my steward?"

Alfred bowed, casting her a keen glance. It would have been quite understandable if the lady had been embarrassed by the revelation that two strange gentlemen had been discussing her, but she evinced no sign of awkwardness, however, her rather remarkable eyes showing only surprise and a hint of amusement.

"Good day to you, sir," she said calmly. "It seems very odd to me that my name should have been upon either of your lips. I do hope you mean to satisfy my curiosity." Her inquisitive glance again rested upon Laurence. "I cannot think why I should have come to your attention, sir, unless perhaps, Mr Rufford, the vicar at Thornham mentioned me to you?"

"He has not," Laurence said. "Should he have done so?"

"No, no. It is only that I painted a miniature portrait of his wife, and he was so pleased with it he mentioned it to a few others who sought me out. He overrates my skill, however, and so I am pleased he has not."

"I am sure, if Mr Rufford is pleased with it, you must be very talented, ma'am," he said smoothly.

A look of comical dismay crossed her face. "You must not think I was fishing for compliments, sir, for I most certainly was not."

Cassandra laughed. "Are you even acquainted with Mr Rufford, Lord Carteret?"

He smiled wryly. "Well, no," he admitted. "It was on another matter of business that Miss Thorpe's name came up, but we cannot discuss it in the road." He turned to that lady. "May we call on you tomorrow, ma'am?"

"By all means," she said. "You will find us at Tremlow House just outside Thornham."

He bowed again, his eyes lingering on Cassandra. "I shall bring your cloak to you, Miss Fenton."

"Thank you," she said, a smile in her eyes. "My luggage has yet to arrive, and I will be glad to have it."

Laurence watched them drive away until they disappeared around a bend in the road.

"How very providential," Alfred said, looking intently at Laurence.

"Yes, wasn't it?" Laurence agreed. "Tell me, Westerby, was Miss Thorpe quite what you expected?"

Alfred grinned. "Not at all."

"I thought you may have been surprised. She is not a beauty, but neither would I describe her as an ageing spinster."

"No, certainly not," Alfred agreed. "I believe her sister was considerably older and had assumed, wrongly, that they were of an age."

"You need not worry," Laurence assured him, eyeing him with amusement, "she will not hear of your slander from my lips."

"Thank you," Alfred said, his tone heavy with irony. "And here I was, quaking in my boots in case you did so." His eyes narrowed. "I don't suppose you care to tell me how it is you have Miss Fenton's cloak?"

Realising that to say nothing would only lead Alfred into unwanted speculation, he said blandly, "There is no mystery. I met the lady on my way here and took her up in my curricle for a few miles when she discovered there was no vehicle available to hire for the purpose. I did not realise she had left her cloak behind until much later."

Scepticism shone brightly in Alfred's blue eyes, but

he only said, "I see. The meeting was doubly providential, then."

"As you say," Laurence murmured, urging his horse into a trot. "But who am I to question the workings of fate?"

CHAPTER 8

"I think," Louisa said as they swept out of sight of the gentlemen, "that you did not fully do justice to Lord Carteret. You spoke of his dignity, his reserve, and of his manners, but you did not mention his noble brow, his firm chin—"

Cassandra sent a look half-amused, half-exasperated, at her friend. "Do not think to distract me, Louisa. You must have known that he lived somewhere in the vicinity and yet you neither told me of it nor warned me that there was every likelihood that I might come across him."

"It was more of a possibility than a probability. His family seat, Westerby, lies some nine or ten miles from Thornham, and as I do not move in the first circles, our meeting him was a very slim chance."

"Yes, that is very fine reasoning," Cassandra said dryly. "Did you not think that I might wish to be informed of it?"

"Well, yes, it did occur to me, but you did not speak of him again after that first evening, and so I have hardly had the opportunity to do so," Louisa said, unruffled by her friend's acerbic tone. "And as you seemed determined to keep your whereabouts secret until you had at least heard back from your lawyer, which you have not yet done, I did not see that it would serve any purpose to inform you of it imme-diately. I would have done so when you were settled, however, and intended to suggest that you wrote to Lord Carteret to inform him of your whereabouts so that he could return your cloak."

She did not doubt the last comment, at least. Having for so long regretted that Cassandra had had no opportunity to meet any eligible gentlemen, it was only natural that Louisa would have wished her to renew her acquaintance with a handsome viscount.

"You may be sure I would not have done so, however," she said firmly. "To have put him to so much trouble would have been ridiculous, besides being most improper, not to mention encroaching of me. I am quite shocked that you would suggest it."

"You are not at all shocked!"

Cassandra saw her friend's eyes brighten with laughter and grinned reluctantly. She was aware of how unusually prim she had sounded and could only be glad that Louisa was not fully aware of how free her manners had been with Laurence at their first meeting, for that would have made her little speech even more absurd. If she had known that she was to see him again, she would have been more circumspect.

"And if you *were* assailed by such qualms, I could have done it in your stead," Louisa added, "being a confirmed spinster, an ape leader, in fact."

"You are only a spinster through a lack of opportunity," Cassandra said severely.

"You forget Mr Brampton," Louisa murmured, looking crestfallen. "It is unkind in you to overlook the one marriage proposal I have received."

Cassandra chuckled, not for a moment taken in. "Through lack of a reasonable opportunity, then."

The smile faded from Louisa's eyes. "The same could be said of you, my dear, and it is quite shocking that one as beautiful, and lively, and energetic as you are, should dwindle into an old maid."

"Fustian!" Cassandra exclaimed. "I am not beautiful; it is only your partiality that makes you think it. I will allow the liveliness and energy, however, and it will ensure that I do not dwindle as you put it but roar into old maidhood with splendid eccentricity and complete unconcern for what anyone may say of me. You would make a far better wife than ever I would, Louisa. You are always so calm and efficient that you must bring order to any man's establishment, and yet you have such humour and wit that he would never grow bored of you. Perhaps *you* should throw your cap at Lord Carteret."

Louisa laughed and said, as if much struck, "Of course, I should. I have so much to offer him, after all."

"You have more than I. You own your own house, are comfortably circumstanced, and have some land that if I am not very much mistaken, would be a welcome addition to Lord Carteret's."

"Oh, so that is the business he and his steward wished to discuss with me. I was at a loss to understand what it might be." Louisa threw a rueful glance at her companion. "I will admit that the prospect of two such attractive gentlemen visiting us, momentarily overcame my curiosity as to what might bring them."

Cassandra chuckled. "I wondered if you had noticed how handsome Mr Westerby was. One might almost have thought that it was he who was the viscount; you cannot have missed the aristocratic cast of his countenance. That aquiline nose was most impressive, and his eyes almost hawkishly keen."

She had the satisfaction of seeing a faint blush creep into her friend's cheeks and chuckled. "It would appear that you are not so old-cattish after all, my dear."

"Being a spinster does not make me insensate," Louisa said reprovingly, but with a half-ashamed look in her eyes. It did not last for long, however. A hiccup of laughter escaped her. "I think Mr Westerby is even more correct than Lord Carteret. He looked most put out when the viscount mentioned that they had been speaking of me."

"Yes, I thought so too," Cassandra said. "But do not be deceived, Louisa. When he visits you tomorrow it will be with Lord Carteret's interests very much in mind. He will, of course, try to persuade you to part with Willow Tree Farm, but do not succumb to his arguments, at least not immediately."

"But why ever not?" Louisa asked, her brow wrinkling in thought. "We have already established that I know nothing of farming, and the capital it would produce might go a long way towards funding the school I would like to build."

"It would go *some* way towards it, certainly," Cassandra agreed. "But it would not be enough to maintain it or pay the teachers you must employ. Consider this, my love, the farm that is currently bringing you only fifty pounds a year, might easily, if the farmhouse were brought into good repair and a decent tenant installed, bring you somewhere in the region of four hundred a year. That would provide both you and Emma with a dependable income that added to your other resources, must ensure your future comfort."

"That much?" Louisa gasped.

"At least that much," Cassandra said. "The farmhouse is larger than Tremlow House and the land excellent. I suggest that you listen to any proposals Mr Westerby may have but turn his experience to your advantage. Ask him to explain why the farm is of such interest to Lord Carteret and what he perceives to be Mr Moore's faults; it will be as well if you have an opinion other than mine. Do not, however, commit yourself to anything. If you decide to keep the farm, you will at least know what to expect of your next tenant, and if you decide to sell it, your seeming reluctance to do so may bring you a higher price. I will draw off Lord Carteret so that you may speak undisturbed." A rich chuckle escaped her. "Otherwise, your usual calm good sense might be quite overset by the combined arguments of two such *attractive* gentlemen."

"Nonsense," Louisa said firmly. "I was taken a little by surprise today, but you may be sure that I am as unlikely to be swayed by a handsome face as you. It will be as well if you distract Lord Carteret, however, for Mr Westerby may well speak more freely if he is not present. I shall keep Emma by me, of course, so your newfound respect for the proprieties may be satisfied."

It was rather Lord Carteret who distracted Cassandra, however. She arose even earlier than usual having spent a restless night. Laurence had intruded upon her dreams, but he was not the only or even the principal cause of her perturbation. She had expected to hear from Mr Penwith by now, and his silence unsettled her. She needed her clothes, longed for her horse, and most of all wished for the comfort of knowing that someone she felt sure had her best interests at heart and would protect them, was fully aware of her situation.

Unable to gallop out her restlessness and having no business to attend to, she collected Louisa's paints and instructed the sleepy footman to accompany her with an easel and stool. He followed her through the gate that led to the creek, across the wooden bridge, and along a path that wound across the saltmarsh. A brisk breeze blew moody grey clouds across the sky and low-lying pockets of morning mist created an eerie atmosphere, the effect amplified when a high-pitched, piercing cry broke the silence and a marsh harrier ghosted out of the mist, gliding just above the height of the reedbeds.

They came to another waterway that cut a channel across the scrubby marshland before making its inexorable way to the sea. Once the footman had arranged things to her liking, she dismissed him. She retrieved her brushes, water, and paints from her satchel, emptied her mind, and sat for some time drinking in the view. Deciding it would be too ambitious to immediately attempt anything on a large scale, she quickly divided her paper into three sections. In the first she attempted to capture a section of the river immediately in front of her, edged with the long reeds, in the second, a glimmer of the sun just then peeping beneath the dark edge of a cloud, and in the last, the shifting colours of the sea. Only then did she put up a fresh sheet and attempt to capture the whole scene.

As always on the rare occasions she allowed herself to indulge herself in this way, she became completely absorbed in her task. It was a difficult one as the light kept changing, but gradually the wind abated, and the sky stilled. All but one burning gold edge of the sun was hidden but its rays found breaks in the dark mass that surrounded it, casting beams of soft, diffuse light down to the sea's surface. When Cassandra finally dropped her arm and surveyed her handiwork, she felt the familiar feeling of disappointment. Her painting was accurate, but she had somehow failed to capture the drama of the scene.

She sighed heavily and stood, murmuring, "Why does something always elude me?"

"May I?"

She turned her head quickly, her mouth opening on a gasp of surprise as she found Laurence beside her. He raised an eyebrow, and she nodded her head, moving a little aside so that he could take her place in front of the easel. As he picked up her brush, she realised for the first time how shapely his hand was. He went to work quickly, brightening the beams of light here, darkening the sky there, and adding subtle nuances of colour to the water. It took him no more than ten minutes to transform her painting from ordinary to sublime.

She looked at him admiringly, a rueful smile on her lips. "Did I not say you had hidden depths, Laurence? I do not know whether to be grateful or made wretched by your intervention."

A small frown puckered his brow and his eyes seemed to reflect the clouds above them. "Why wretched?"

"Because you have achieved in a matter of moments what I have been attempting for years. I will never be anything more than competent."

"You are hard on yourself," he said gently. "Your painting was very good and, as you saw, it only needed a few extra touches. Besides, you are not comparing like with like, Cassandra. This is my country and so I am bound to have an affinity to it, and I also benefited from the tuition of some fine masters."

She began to pack away her things. "It would not matter," she said confidently. "I am fairly certain that you have a gift that cannot be taught."

"I thought so once," he murmured, closing the easel, tucking it under one arm and picking up her stool. "But although I may have some skill when it comes to landscape painting, I have never attempted a portrait, and I am certain I could not match your skill."

She laughed off his compliment. "We are both now so set up in our own conceit that we can have no more to say on the matter."

They began to walk back at a dawdling pace natural to neither of them.

"You are earlier than I expected. Is Mr Westerby closeted with Louisa? I warn you that I have put her on her guard and told her not to agree to sell Willow Tree Farm."

"You guessed then," he said, a wry smile twisting his lips.

"I should think I did. What else could you want with Louisa?"

"Nothing, of course," he acknowledged. "What is it exactly that you have put her on guard against?"

"Capitulating too easily on a subject she knows little about for a start."

"You were right to do so," he acknowledged. "But I assure you that Mr Westerby would never bring any undue pressure to bear upon her. I hope you do not think it."

"I do not think it," she said, chuckling. "At least not in the sense you mean. But she would not be the first lady to succumb to a gentleman's charm."

She glanced across at him and saw him wince.

"Laurence!" she exclaimed, her brows snapping together. "Do not tell me you asked him to use such underhand tactics? I would not have thought it of you!"

"Westerby thought it as objectionable as you," he said wryly. "But you must not think I meant him to cheat Miss Thorpe in any way. That land is going to waste, and I have a very good tenant who wishes to expand his holding. It seemed to me that perhaps all of our interests might be served."

Cassandra could not fault his logic but could not approve his tactics.

"In that case," she said with some asperity, "he should have approached Mr Rythorne."

"He did," Laurence said coolly. "And was told that

she would not sell on any terms. That is why I encouraged Westerby to make a direct approach, but only to persuade Miss Thorpe that it would be to her advantage to sell an asset that appeared to be of little interest to her, not to talk terms. If she agreed, he would certainly have hammered out the details with her agent. I could not see why she should wish to keep the land unless she had an attachment to it, and I instructed him not to press her if that was the case and even to offer her some advice."

Cassandra felt a wave of relief wash over her. The thought that she had misjudged Laurence had caused her a pang of dismay. She came to a sudden halt, losing her balance a little as she attempted to avoid a fat slug that lay in her path. Laurence promptly dropped the stool and took her arm, steadying her. They had reached a point where the path was very narrow, bounded on both sides by pools of brackish water and so she found herself almost pressed against him, only her satchel separating them. Their eyes met and held, hers wide open and his slightly narrowed.

"Thank you," she said a little breathlessly. "You will think it extremely missish of me, but I cannot bear to injure any harmless creature, however unappealing it may be."

A gaggle of geese suddenly launched themselves into the air, honking loudly as if approving of her sentiment. Laurence released her and bent to pick up the stool.

"You are full of surprises, Cassandra," he said. "I can only be glad that you did not view Mr Chubb as a harmless creature."

It was not Mr Chubb who was uppermost in her

mind, and she murmured absently, "I only injured his pride."

Laurence would have walked on, but she detained him with a light touch on his arm. "Did you say that Mr Rythorne informed your steward that Louisa would not sell the farm on any terms?"

"I did," he replied, regarding her closely. "Was he misinformed?"

"He most certainly was," she said sharply. "She has received no communication from him on the subject. When Louisa informed me that Mr Moore paid barely more than a peppercorn rent, something she was unaware of, I suggested we went to look at the farm. I had already formed an unfavourable opinion of her agent for making such a poor bargain and when I saw for myself how ill-managed the land was, it sank even lower. But this beats all! The first black marks against him *might* be put down to incompetence and ignorance, I suppose, but to not even inform Louisa of Mr Westerby's enquiry speaks of high-handedness and a wanton disregard for her wishes at the very least, and dubious practice at worst, although I cannot immediately see how he could profit from his actions."

"Perhaps Westerby—"

"I assume that is your family name?" she interrupted.

"Yes, and the name of my house."

"Does it not seem a little odd to you to call your steward also by that name?"

"No, why should it?"

She saw that he was frowning and said quickly,

"Pay me no heed, it has always been a fault of mine to say what I am thinking."

"You may always do so to me," he said.

"It is fortunate that you take that view," she said wryly, "for I certainly seem to do so. It was just that I found it strange, at first, to call my cousin's mother, Mrs Fenton, although I did not do so for long as she begged me to call her aunt."

Laurence was becoming accustomed to Cassandra's quick brain jumping from one thing to another and did not lose the thread of their original conversation. "I see. What I had been about to say, was would you like me to ask my cousin to make some discreet enquiries about Mr Rythorne?"

"Yes, thank you," she said, smiling ruefully at him. "It seems we cannot meet without me being in your debt."

"The debt will not be yours, Cassandra, but Miss Thorpe's. However, if you wish to thank me for so small a service, there is something you might do for me."

She eyed him warily. "It is I who am now on my guard, sir, having seen a more ruthless side to your character."

His lips curled into the soft smile that had only last night intruded upon her dreams. "You must not feel yourself obliged to do anything for me, Cassandra; it is my pleasure to serve you. But I admit that I would like it very much if you would agree to do a miniature portrait of each of my sisters. They are staying at Westerby for another week or so. My father never commissioned a painting of either of them, and I would like to have their likeness in my private rooms."

They walked on more quickly as a few drops of rain began to fall. Cassandra could not help feeling flattered by his request, and her interest was piqued.

"They are twins and identical in appearance, although as soon as they speak one is left in no doubt of who is who. To be able to capture their unique selves in a portrait would be too much to ask; I would not expect it. You could, if you wished, take the likeness of one and copy it; I would not wish to take up too much of your time."

"But no," she said quickly, her interest now truly caught. "That would never do. Not only would it be to treat them as one person rather than separate entities, but it would not please me. My mettle is up, sir, and I accept the challenge of producing two portraits that you *will* be able to tell apart."

CHAPTER 9

As they reached the bridge, the rain came down in earnest making the trickle of sluggish water beneath them bubble into life. Laurence glanced upstream and saw the brick arch of the culvert that diverted the water under the garden of Tremlow House. He was pleased to see that it was of a generous size as although the creek appeared benign, he knew that it would become much fuller at high tide and a torrent on a spring one. Once they crossed the bridge, they ran the short distance to the house. Cassandra did not flinch from the downpour but momentarily raised her face and laughed, revelling in it rather than showing the dismay Laurence might have expected. He also welcomed the cool rain streaming down his face for it grounded him.

When Cassandra had stumbled and he had pulled her to him so that her large, startled eyes had been only inches from his, he had known the impulse to kiss her. He had not given in to it, of course. Years of practising self-control had stood him in good stead, and the raucous noise of the geese as they had taken flight had brought him if not completely, at least partially to his senses.

He had been interested in her revelations about Mr Rythorne and impressed by her summation of his performance, but all the while he had been aware that he must find a reasonable excuse to see her again. She intrigued him in a way no other woman had ever done. She did not wish to be protected and cosseted but to face any challenges life threw at her head-on, and yet she could not bear to tread upon a slug, not because she recoiled from the hideous prospect of feeling the invertebrate squelch beneath her foot, but because she did not wish to do it harm.

She was frank, her face an open book, and he felt sure she would never resort to sly feminine wiles to get her way or score a point. On the contrary, she was refreshingly direct. Nor was she so entrenched in her opinions that she could not listen to an explanation with an open mind, and then, when she realised she had been mistaken, smile in so rueful a way that one could not remain offended, or at least, he could not.

He was not at all sure, however, that he was wise to pursue her acquaintance. Her energy and quick intelligence enlivened him, her face mesmerised him, and her figure sent the blood coursing through his veins, but he had a suspicion that to live with her would prove exhausting. When he had imagined himself wed to Diana, he had envisaged her as a gentle and predictable presence in his house. Something told him that Cassandra would turn his world upside down. She had not been at Tremlow House for more than a few days and was already taking a hand in Miss Louisa Thorpe's affairs.

Cassandra's bonnet and the pelisse she had borrowed from Louisa had prevented her from becoming soaked, but Laurence had not been so lucky. He had left his beaver hat on the table in the hall and by the time they rushed into the flagstoned hallway, his hair was plastered to his head, his riding coat saturated, and water was dripping off the end of his nose.

"Oh dear," Cassandra gasped, swiftly removing her bonnet and pelisse and passing them to the footman. "You must get out of that coat immediately Lau… Lord Carteret." Her lips twitched. "I would not like you to catch a chill."

"No, indeed," said Louisa coming out of the drawing room. She took the pelisse from the footman. "I shall ask Mrs Larkin to hang this up in the kitchen, you take Lord Carteret up to Mr Tremlow's old room, William, and find him a towel and one of Mr Tremlow's coats to borrow." She glanced at Laurence. "You are in luck, sir. My sister left his room very much as it was, and I had not yet decided what to do with his things. I thought her suggestion that I burn them so very wasteful, you see."

"I shall hardly melt from a drop of rain, ma'am."

"No, I don't suppose you will," she said, calmly. "But as you can hardly leave until the rain eases off a little and you will not wish to sit in your shirt sleeves or continue dripping water all over the house, I think it is the most sensible course of action, don't you?"

Laurence looked a little ruefully at the puddle forming at his feet. "You are right, of course, Miss Thorpe."

Alfred stood in the doorway of the drawing room, a faint smile touching his lips at this masterful handling of his relative.

"I shall assist you," he said, "it might take two of us to lever you out of your coat."

They were shown to a very masculine room with dark heavy furniture that was practical rather than elegant. As Laurence's coat had been made to fit him to the inch and was now clinging to him like a second skin, Laurence did indeed need both the footman's and Alfred's assistance.

"I'll take this down to dry by the kitchen fire, sir," the footman said, passing him a towel. "Unless you wish me to help you dress?"

"Thank you, William, but that will not be necessary," Laurence said. "Mr Westerby will do all that I require."

He nodded to a door that presumably gave onto a dressing room. "Very well, sir. There's plenty of coats in there. Just help yourself."

Laurence wiped his face on the towel before vigorously rubbing his hair with it. As there did not appear to be a comb upon the dressing table, he ran his fingers through it instead. Alfred had disappeared into the dressing room but soon came back with a green coat in one hand and a shirt in the other.

"The coat will do," Laurence said, "but I draw the line at the shirt. Mine is only a trifle damp and will dry in no time."

"Squeamish?" Alfred said, grinning.

"Would you wear a dead man's shirt, Westerby?"

Alfred dropped the shirt over a chair. "No, perhaps not."

Laurence stood looking at the coat, a small frown between his eyes.

"Not elegant enough for you?" Alfred said.

Laurence's gentle smile dawned. "Let us just say that it is not what I would have chosen, but it was not the coat I was thinking of. It was you."

"Oh dear," Alfred said. "And what is it I have done to make you frown so?"

"Nothing it all, dear fellow. How long have we known each other now?"

"Eight years."

"Yes, I suppose it must be," Laurence murmured. "I do not know how it is, but it has never before occurred to me how odd it is to address you by my name. As you are my cousin——"

"Second cousin," Alfred corrected him.

"Let us not quibble. As you are my cousin, and the most intimate acquaintance of my family after my sisters, I think I shall call you Alfred from now on, and you may, of course, call me Laurence."

"Not Laurie?" Alfred said, a smile in his eyes.

Laurence looked pained. "Certainly not Laurie, just as I shall not call you Alfie. I abominate the shortening of names, unfortunately, it is a habit I cannot cure my sisters of. It is bad enough that I have been reduced to calling Cecelia Cecy, but she will have it so, and on reflection, it suits her better."

"Oh, I agree," Alfred said, helping him into the coat. "There is something rather serious about the name Cecelia. And Cecy has many admirable qualities, but a serious turn of mind is not one of them."

As Laurence turned, pulling at the cuff of one of the sleeves, Alfred said, "I will be honoured if you call me Alfred. You are certainly the best of my relations, and I am only sorry that the rift between our fathers prevented me from knowing you sooner."

"But if it had not been for the rift between our fathers, I might never have had the opportunity to know you at all, Alfred," Laurence said quietly. "I doubt he would have encouraged me to know my country cousins and I am sure he took you on only to annoy your father."

Alfred smiled. "I know it, and he succeeded to admiration. Papa was torn between a desire for me to know Westerby, and resentment at being so beholden to his cousin. But that generation has gone, and we will do better."

"I hope we already have done better."

"Indeed we have," Alfred agreed, "but if you would stay at Westerby for more than a handful of weeks at a time, I think we could do better still."

"Perhaps I will," Laurence said absently. "I wonder what did cause the rift between them."

Alfred's lips twisted. "I suppose I should not be surprised that you do not know. Your father had his share of pride."

"Most of it misplaced," Laurence said dryly. "But go on."

"Are you sure you wish to know?" Alfred said quietly.

"Do not concern yourself. You will not shock me, I assure you."

"Very well. They fell in love with the same woman, although not at the same time."

Laurence let out a dry laugh. "Surely you are

mistaken. My father did not know the meaning of the word."

"I hate to contradict you, Laurence, but apparently he did. He met my mother when she made her come out. She was a beautiful woman but painfully shy, and your father offered for her towards the end of the season. She turned him down and was taken home in disgrace. My mother was sent to her aunt the following season when her sister made her come out, and it so happened that her aunt lived within my father's parish. He fell in love with her and she with him."

"Good God!" Laurence exclaimed. "That must have been a blow indeed! Father would never have understood how she could have chosen a parsonage over Westerby, never mind a vicar over a viscount."

"Quite. Your father offered for your mother the following season."

"Poor Mama," Laurence said softly. "I knew he never loved her, of course, theirs was a marriage of convenience, a question of duty."

"As you say. He and my father had occasionally swapped letters but after the marriage, he cut the connection completely, and Mama's family also cast her off, apart from her aunt who approved of the match. But they were happy, Laurence. There was never a cross word between them. I wish it could have been the same for your parents."

"No more than I," Laurence said. "I am surprised you dared come to Westerby, for I cannot think he invited you out of any lingering sentiment for your mother."

"I did not think it. My father told me of their

history when it became clear that I was determined to
come. But I somehow felt it was my destiny to do so,
and I must admit that although your father kept me at
a distance, he treated me fairly." He smiled wryly. "I
think it helped that I was the spitting image of his
grandfather rather than my mother. But come, the
ladies will be wondering what delays us."

As they walked towards the door, Laurence said,
"Have you persuaded Miss Thorpe to sell the farm?"

Alfred smiled wryly. "I told you it would be difficult to deal with a woman. She bombarded me with
questions regarding my history, why you wished to
purchase it, and the deficiencies I had noticed on the
property. And all the while I was distracted by the
elder Miss Thorpe. She watched me so closely that I
thought her the strictest of chaperones for all she looks
so benevolent. But then Miss Louisa explained that
she was deaf and was watching my lips to ascertain
my words. A remarkable feat don't you think?"

"Indeed, it is," Laurence said. "You will not have
discovered, then, that Mr Rythorne never informed
Miss Louisa Thorpe of your enquiry."

Alfred had opened the door, but he paused at this.
"How very irregular."

"I begin to think the man is more than irregular,
cousin, and I am giving you the task of setting some
discreet enquiries afoot."

They went onto the landing.

"It will be my pleasure. Miss Louisa is both
charming and amusing, if a little garrulous, and
certainly does not deserve to be ill-used in any way."

Laurence smiled. "I think you may lay her talka-
tiveness at Miss Fenton's door. She had warned her

friend not to be persuaded, and I suspect, suggested she ask you all manner of questions."

"I am so glad you found something that fitted you," Louisa said as they entered the drawing room. "May I offer you some tea or would you prefer a glass of wine? We certainly seem to have an ample sufficiency of the latter."

"A glass of wine would be most welcome," Laurence said. "Thank you."

"I will take a cup of tea," Alfred said.

Louisa poured the tea and Cassandra the wine. She brought the glass over to Laurence, softly murmuring as she gave it to him, "Now I understand what took you so long. Is that the windswept or the frightened owl?"

His eyes gleamed with amusement, but his voice was perfectly serious as he replied just as quietly, "I think I have created a new style, Cassandra. I shall call it the bedraggled."

He looked up in surprise as the little white-haired lady, who had been quietly bent over her stitchery when he entered the room, laughed.

"I do not think you have been introduced to Miss Emma Thorpe," Cassandra said, leading him across the room. "Emma, this is Lord Carteret."

He offered her an elegant bow and she smiled and nodded, before returning her attention to the deep flounce she was attaching to a dress of pale grey satin.

"Emma is—"

"Deaf, I know," Laurence said. "A remarkable lady."

"Yes, and a kind one. She is adding a double

flounce to one of Louisa's dresses so that I might wear it."

"Ah, yes, your luggage still has not arrived. Have you heard nothing from your lawyer as yet?"

"No, and I admit that it is worrying me somewhat."

"It must be a great inconvenience to you," Laurence said, "but he cannot have received your letter until a few days ago, and if you fear being discovered I think I might set your mind at rest. I could find no trace of you upon the road, and Fadon, my groom, whilst discreet, was both subtle and thorough in his enquiries."

She smiled gratefully at him. "That is indeed reassuring. Thank you." As the import of his words sank in, she added saucily, "So you looked for me on the road? For all your gentle ways, I thought you would not like to have your wishes thwarted."

"Yes, you said as much in your letter," he replied blandly.

Her winging brows rose. "I see you do not mean to admit to it, sir, but I hope you will at least acknowledge that I am not quite so reckless as you first thought and am quite capable of handling my affairs."

"You certainly displayed a caution, that however unnecessary, was, at least, effective."

Judging by the sparkle of indignation in her eyes, Cassandra was not entirely satisfied with this response.

"Cassandra," Louisa suddenly said. "I know that you wished us to go to King's Lynn to see Mr Rythorne, but Mr Westerby does not think we should approach him before he has made some enquiries."

"Then we shall not," she said. "It will be as well if we know what and who we are dealing with."

"You are wise, Miss Fenton," Alfred said approvingly.

Laurence saw the mixture of amusement and challenge in the glance Cassandra sent his way but did not rise to the bait, merely smiling faintly and saying, "The rain appears to have stopped and so we must be on our way." He turned to Louisa. "Thank you for your hospitality, Miss Louisa. I would like the opportunity to return it. It would please me very much if you all came to a luncheon at Westerby tomorrow. I shall send the carriage for you, of course."

"We would be delighted to come," Louisa said. "Cassandra has told me that you would like her to paint your twin sisters, and the more time she spends in their company, the easier the task will be."

"I agree." He glanced at Cassandra. "Do not bring your paints tomorrow, Miss Fenton. Let it be merely an opportunity for you to make my sisters' acquaintance."

"I have my own carriage, Lord Carteret," Louisa informed him. "Mr Cooper or William are quite capable of driving it and so there is no need for you to send yours."

"I will do so, however," he said. "Mine is larger, very well sprung, and my coachman experienced. You will find it more comfortable."

CHAPTER 10

L aurence's carriage was not the first vehicle to arrive at Tremlow House the following day. The ladies were just rising from the breakfast table when the unmistakable crunch of wheels on gravel was heard.

"Did not Lord Carteret say to expect his coachman at twelve, my dear?" Louisa said, glancing towards the window.

Cassandra walked quickly over and peered outside. "It is a carrier's cart!" she exclaimed. "My baggage has finally arrived!"

She rushed from the room and then stood to one side as two men staggered through the front door beneath the weight of a large trunk.

"Shall I have it taken up to your room, Miss Fenton?" William enquired.

"Yes, thank you," she said eagerly, "and warn Grace that she is likely to be very busy, will you?"

"Of course, ma'am." He held out a letter. "I've

just come back from the village. This arrived yesterday but was somehow mislaid."

She smiled as she recognised Mr Penwith's neat hand.

One of the men put down his end of the trunk and reached into the pocket of his coat. "That reminds me, I was told to give this to you, Miss Fenton," he said, handing over a letter with no direction written on it.

"Well, what a multitude of riches are mine this morning," she said brightly, graciously accepting it.

She went swiftly to the small parlour at the back of the house, eager to read without interruption. As Mr Penwith was the only person who might have need to write to her and knew of her direction, she could only imagine that he had realised he had omitted something from his first missive and so sent another, although it did seem a little odd for him to send it with her baggage. If her surmise was correct, it would be sensible to read the one William had given her first. She quickly broke the wafer and unfolded it, her eyes devouring the neat rows of words.

My dear Miss Fenton,

You may conceive how disturbed I was to receive your letter; its contents seemed so fantastic that I had to read it twice through before I could credit them. Sir Francis had always seemed so very reasonable on the few occasions I had cause to meet with him that if it had been anyone else who had made such claims against his character, I must have doubted them.

You, however, have always had a quickness far above almost any other lady of my acquaintance, and a strength of character that precluded me from doubting. It was immediately apparent to me that for you to have left your home so precipitately, a great deal of pressure must have been brought to bear upon you. You may be sure that I visited Sir Francis at the first opportunity and asked him for an explanation.

The meeting was, as you may imagine, a rather awkward one. It was perhaps natural that he should resent my enquiries into his behaviour, and you may be sure that he did. I shall not repeat what passed between us but I assure you that my eyes were opened. However, I believe I was successful in bringing him to a realisation of how very wrong his actions have been. I do not believe they were motivated by any maliciousness towards you, however, but were rather the promptings of an autocratic nature.

As you know, your grandfather wished for the marriage, and Sir Francis clearly felt it his duty to marry you, although, if I am not much mistaken, it was not only that which drove him. There was such a strange light in his eyes when he spoke of you that I am sure his feelings, whatever they might be, were also engaged. It can make no difference, however, as he is certainly not the man your esteemed grandfather would have wished for you, and so I told him. This did not go down at all well, and I will be very surprised if he does not replace me forthwith.

I will say no more on the subject now, apart from that I am thankful that I persuaded Sir Thomas to at least consider the possibility that you and your cousin might not suit, but I would rather discuss this and some other matters of business with you in person. I must admit that I will be happier in my mind once I have seen for myself that you are comfortably circumstanced, although as I know what an estimable lady Miss Thorpe is, there can be no real doubt. You may expect me by the end of next week and not knowing the country, I would appreciate it if you would engage rooms for me at a suitable inn.

Your groom is bringing your horse to you by easy stages and should arrive within the next few days. I must tell you that he *hopes to remain with you, having been summarily dismissed by Sir Francis when he insisted that he should be the one to deliver the mare. I took the liberty of providing him with a mount as your cousin refused to permit him to take any of the horses from his stables and he will hardly be of use to you without one. I do not know how they treat servants in Jamaica, but his ways will not do here. That I also told him, and I leave it to your imagination to envisage how he responded to my impertinence.*

You may be sure I did not reveal your location to your cousin, and neither will the carriers I have employed. I do not think you need fear Sir Francis making any further attempt on your liberty. Now that I know how things stand, he cannot hope to gain anything by such a rash course of action.

Mrs Fenton joined us before I left Darley. She seemed very keen to know you were well and happy and requested that I send you her best wishes. I believe she was sincere. I think she would have said more but her son frowned her down.

I remain your dutiful servant,

Mr Lionel R Penwith

"Is everything all right?"

Cassandra glanced up quickly and smiled at Louisa who had poked her head around the door. "Yes, I think so. Here, read it for yourself. I will be very interested by what you might read between the lines, if anything."

"Certainly," Louisa said, coming into the room and taking it from her.

Cassandra opened her second missive and realised immediately that it was not from Mr Penwith. It was very short and difficult to read. The letters were erratic as if the words had been rushed or the scribe's hand had been shaking.

My dear child,

I am sorry, so very sorry that you have been driven from your home. You were quite right to go, and I can only regret that I did not have the opportunity to know you in happier circumstances, and also that I had not the courage to protect you as I should have.

Mrs Maria Fenton

"Well, this seems quite straightforward," Louisa said, handing back the letter from Mr Penwith. "He does not like Sir Francis any more than you do, I find the reference to his feelings interesting; *whatever they may be* is a peculiar turn of phrase. Perhaps he means to suggest that his affections are not quite natural in their intensity. The only other item of interest is the business he might wish to broach with you. It seems to me that as he desires to discuss it in person rather than through the medium of the post, it must be of some importance."

"I expect he wishes to discuss my future plans and whether or not it might be more convenient to have an agent closer to hand. Although if he can arrange for me the facility to draw on a King's Lynn bank, I would prefer to keep him." She frowned, passing her friend the other letter. "Read this, if you will. I shall be back in a moment."

She went into the hall and discovered the man she was searching for there.

"How came you to bring me that letter?" she said brusquely.

He looked startled and doffed his cap to her. "I hope I did right to bring it, ma'am. We were instructed not to mention our destination, but I couldn't see the harm in taking the sweet lady's letter.

She seemed all in a twitter but looked at me with such sad eyes I could not say her nay."

"I see," Cassandra said thoughtfully. "You were right to do so, of course. I just wondered how it came about."

"I felt sorry for her," he said abruptly. "No sooner had she thanked me than the tyrant who is apparently her son came out and told her in the most biting of ways to get herself back into the house. It ain't none of my business, o'course, but I'd say you're well shot of him, ma'am."

"Yes, I believe you are right," Cassandra murmured. "If you wait a moment, I will fetch my reticule."

He frowned at this. "If you are thinking to slip me a coin, I wish you won't, ma'am. We've already been amply recompensed for our services."

Cassandra looked surprised. "How very refreshing."

The man grinned. "Mr Penwith has a large stake in the company, ma'am, and he made it very clear that we was not to accept anything more than we have already been paid. Now, I'd best get on if it's all the same to you; we've still got some miles to cover this day."

"Then I bid you goodbye with no more than my thanks."

"And they're mighty appreciated, miss," he said, nodding and briefly touching his hat again.

"Now this," Louisa said as Cassandra came back into the room, "*is* intriguing. What are these happier circumstances she speaks of? Why had she not the courage to protect you? And what exactly should she have been protecting you from?"

"Is it not obvious?" Cassandra said, sighing.

"Perhaps," Louisa said.

Cassandra was not attending. "I begin to think I have not treated Mrs Fenton as I ought. She was a pleasant enough lady when she first arrived at Darley Manor, but it very soon became clear that she would support her son in any folly he wished to indulge in. And then she became increasingly erratic in her behaviour, at one moment sympathising with my lot and at another urging me not to provoke Francis but understand that he knew best. It seemed to me that she suffered with an irritation of the nerves, and I confess I began to find her most trying."

"Yes," Louisa said, with a sympathetic smile. "You would find such behaviour difficult. I completely understand, of course. Clara also suffered from the complaint."

"But you, my love, I am sure, displayed far more patience than I did. I begin to think that it was not mere irritation of the nerves, or at least, that Francis was the cause of them. Her words, written in such an unsteady hand, and so contrite, make me think that I never knew her at all." She began to pace up and down the small room with hasty strides. "Oh, Louisa, I think that she is frightened of him, and it is I who should have protected her!"

"She was clearly upset when she wrote the letter," Louisa said calmly. "From what you have told me, your cousin does not like to be thwarted and so I imagine that he may have been a little angry when he saw your things being carried from the house, but I fail to see how you could have done anything to protect Mrs Fenton. I regret to say that Sir Francis seems to me to be a bully, and that sort of gentleman, you know, can only be brought to book by someone with more power than he. I am very sorry for his mother, but if you had tried to come between them, I think it would only have brought more trouble upon her head. A bully will always take out his annoyance on whomever he perceives to be the weakest target, but now that you, who it seems were the largest cause of his dissatisfaction, through no fault of your own, I might add, have removed yourself from the scene, it may well be that he will regain his temper and Mrs Fenton, her nerves."

Cassandra stopped pacing. "You may be right. I did once or twice pull Francis up for the way he spoke to his mother, but she begged me not to do it."

"There you are then," Louisa said, rising to her feet. "Come, you must wish to avail yourself of the opportunity to change into a fresh dress now that your trunks have arrived, and if you do not hurry, Lord Carteret's carriage will be here before you are ready."

Cassandra closed the short distance between them and briefly embraced her friend. "You have always had the knack of making the darkest day seem brighter."

Louisa gave a low laugh. "It is you who are now suffering from an irritation of the nerves, my dear. This is hardly a dark day. Mrs Fenton's letter has unsettled you a little, that is all."

"No, of course it is not a dark day," Cassandra said, laughing a little self-consciously. "I only meant to say that you can always lighten my mood even when I am in a twitch."

"Well, when your groom arrives with your horse, you will be able to ride out any fidgets you may feel, and that will do you a great deal of good."

Her eyes brightened. "Very true, and I cannot tell you how much I am looking forward to it."

Cassandra had not been able to fully explain to Louisa feelings that were not entirely clear to herself, but a very real sense of uneasiness had come over her when she had read Mrs Fenton's letter. Although she had been incensed by Francis' increasingly despotic ways as the weeks had gone on at Darley, she had never been afraid of him, and it had not occurred to her that his mother might have been until she had perused those few lines. But on reflection, she thought she must have read far too much into them. Mrs Fenton had, at times, been as nervous with Cassandra as she had been with her son, and *she* had certainly never done anything to frighten her. If Louisa was right, and it had been the frequent clashes between herself and Francis that had caused the disharmony between them all, surely that lady would now be able to sink into the domestic duties she so enjoyed and resume the dull but peaceful existence she seemed to crave.

She entered her room to find Grace staring out of the window. She seemed to be strangely distracted and did not immediately notice that she was no longer alone.

"Grace? What is it that you find so interesting in the garden?"

The girl jumped and turned a flaming face to her

mistress. "I'm not sure what it was, ma'am, but I think it might have been a cat."

Cassandra gave her a steady look. "And does this cat happen to be well over six foot, have a mop of curly brown hair, and go by the name of Mr Cooper?"

Grace sighed. "Oh, miss. He is so very strong and handsome." She suddenly giggled. "He is more like a lion than a cat."

"Yes, well, I suggest you treat him very much like you would a lion in a menagerie. You may look to your heart's content, but never wander too close or you may get more than you bargain for."

"Yes, ma'am," Grace said obediently.

By the time Cassandra had changed into a white robe of jaconet muslin, donned an open pelisse of French grey sarsnet, and a satin straw bonnet with three rows of grey satin ribbon about the high crown, she was in a much more cheerful frame of mind.

"Oh, Miss Cassandra," Grace said, "you look beautiful."

Cassandra laughed. "Thank you, Grace. It is certainly pleasant to have something to wear other than my green cambric or the lavender silk. You, I am sure, must be as pleased as I that my things have finally arrived for you have had much to do keeping a wardrobe that consisted of only two dresses washed and pressed."

Grace flushed. "It was no bother, miss. But now your other dresses have arrived, I intend to put into practice some of the things that Miss Thorpe has taught me and furbish them up a trifle."

"Oh, do you?" Cassandra said, these tidings not inspiring her with any marked degree of delight.

Grace looked a little crestfallen at her doubtful tone. "Miss Thorpe says that my skill with the needle is much improved."

Cassandra could not bear to have her most faithful servant look so downcast and so said with more enthusiasm, "Very well, then. I shall look forward to seeing the result of your endeavours."

Grace immediately perked up, and Cassandra consoled herself with the thought that it did not matter if she made a few interesting additions to one or two of her gowns, for who, after all, would see them?

By the time she came down the stairs, the carriage had arrived and both Louisa and Emma were waiting for her in the hall. Cassandra had half-expected Emma to refuse to accompany them for she rarely went beyond the house or garden, but she was pleased that she had not refused. She could not think it good for her to be so cooped up and rarely see any faces but their own. She smiled as she saw the large basket she carried. It would be full of her sewing, no doubt, a safe haven for her to retreat to if she became overwhelmed by the occasion.

She had set what Cassandra suspected to be her best bonnet over her white locks and trimmed it with some ostrich feathers, dyed dark blue to match her pelisse. Miss Emma Thorpe might have been plain and over fifty, but it could not be denied that she had very good taste, which matched with her skill with a needle, ensured that not only did she always appear neat and trim, but elegant as well. Having had charge of Louisa in her formative years, it was not perhaps surprising that this lady also had a certain understated style when she chose.

In the days that Cassandra had been in residence at the house, she had not chosen to display it but had dressed very plainly, concerned as she had been with little more than gardening and housewifely duties. But Cassandra now perceived that whilst she had been smartening herself up for their forthcoming visit, Louisa had also been so engaged. She had never seen her so becomingly arrayed. Not being a hypocrite, Louisa had spent only three months mourning a sister for whom she had had little affection, and now wore a green pelisse, which exactly matched her eyes, over a dress of jonquil muslin. Her usually severe hairstyle had been softened to allow a few curling strands to fall over her ears. She looked younger than her years, and Cassandra thought, rather pretty.

"Well, and aren't we all smart," she said, smiling.

"Indeed," Louisa said, "I do not think we shall be at all out of place at Westerby, however grand it may be."

"And is it grand?" Cassandra asked, nodding her thanks to William as he opened the carriage door.

"So Mrs Larkin says," she said, once they were all comfortably settled. "But I dare say it will prove to be much like any other manor house."

Cassandra looked amused. "You talk as if you had been in a score of such houses. I see that now that you are a lady of substance, you intend to put on airs and graces."

Louisa assumed what she imagined to be the haughty pose of a lady of the first stare, lifting her chin a little and opening her eyes wide, but she did not quite have the way of it and merely looked startled.

Cassandra laughed. "No, my dear, you cannot carry it off."

Louisa accepted this with good grace, smiling at Emma who had given a deep boom of laughter. "Well, I have been in your house, my dear, and Darley Manor was not of an insignificant size."

"No, it was a rambling hotchpotch of rooms. Somehow I cannot imagine Lord Carteret in such a rabbit warren."

Louisa, who had not wasted her time in Mr Westerby's company, said knowingly, "Ah, but he is the fifth viscount, and however neat and understated he is, you cannot assume that his forebears were just in the same style."

They completed their journey in a little over an hour and amused themselves by creating for Laurence a host of eccentric relatives who had each added a new wing to the house, decorating it in their own style, ranging from the Gothic to the Chinese. Emma soon gave up trying to follow their fast-flowing conversation but smiled gently and pulled some knitting from her basket.

When the well-sprung carriage swung through two wrought iron gates, they lapsed into silence, glancing with lively curiosity out of the windows.

They drove for some time up a gentle incline with woodland spread out on either side of them, and when they eventually emerged from the trees, they saw a vast park spread out before them and a huge herd of fallow deer grazing. Beyond them, a neatly scythed lawn sloped gently up to a large fountain, with neat parterres set on either side, and beyond them stood the house. It was not quite as either of them had imagined. Although it had the neat, Palladian frontage that Cassandra had half-expected, it was on a scale that she had not. The middle section of the house, rising to three storeys and fronted by a long colonnade, would have been impressive on its own, but linked to it were two further wings built in the same style rising to two storeys.

Both ladies were too surprised to immediately voice their feelings, which was perhaps just as well for they differed widely. Louisa thought it very grand but would not have exchanged her current establishment for it if she had been offered the opportunity to do so. She doubted very much that there was a cosy room in the house. Cassandra, whilst never having had a desire to be mistress of such a large establishment, approved of what she saw; everything spoke of an order and symmetry that she admired. She had often wished that she could redesign Darley Manor, but although the estate was well managed, it would not have been able to afford such improvement and she could never have subjected her grandfather to such disruption. On top of this, however much she had been allowed to rule the roast, she had always known that the house would never be truly hers, and who was she to make sweeping changes which might not have been to the incoming owner's taste?

As the carriage pulled up on the wide gravel sweep in front of the house, Emma nodded approvingly and said, "Very nice."

Cassandra and Louisa's eyes met and they burst out laughing.

CHAPTER 11

On the south side of the house, a less imposing entrance circumvented the large entrance hall and some of the grander rooms on the ground floor. It had been Laurence's initial intention for his guests to be admitted there. It was the most direct way to the south drawing room where the family were to gather that day. It was situated at the back of the house and overlooked the gardens. The suite of rooms there lay in an original wing of the house that had not been extensively remodelled, although the small-paned windows had been replaced with sash ones. They had been his mother's domain and were the least imposing of the public rooms in the large edifice that was Westerby. However, when his sister Anne overheard him giving these instructions to Needham, she protested.

"You would not wish your guests to feel that you thought them unworthy of being shown in by the front door, Laurie." Her eyes glinted with mischievous humour. "Besides, I always think it so very revealing to see how strangers react to our gracious splendour!"

"I wonder then, what you make of Miss Reynold's reaction to it?" he said dryly, that lady not just then being present.

Anne sighed. "I must admit Kitty's excessive admiration is growing a little wearing, but she is young and so eager to please that it must have been so. I had hoped that her mixture of shyness and deference might have pleased you."

"And yet, dear sister," he said softly, "you assured me that you were not matchmaking when I arrived."

Anne pulled a face. "There is a vast difference between matchmaking and merely ensuring that a lady crosses your path. Have I made any extraordinary effort to throw her in your way?"

"No," he acknowledged, "but only, I suspect, because you know there would be no more certain a way of setting up my back."

She laughed, acknowledging a hit. "*Do* you like her, Laurie?"

"Not enough to marry her," he said firmly.

Anne accepted this with good grace. "Then there is no more to be said on the matter. But do allow your guests to see something of the house, I beg. However difficult the relationship you shared with papa, you cannot deny that he left you a handsome legacy. I have never thought you valued it as much as you should, which is most perplexing considering you used to very much enjoy painting and sculpture. You cannot deny that you have inherited an abundance of fine examples of both here at Westerby."

"An overabundance," he said dryly.

"Oh, how can you say so? Everyone who has been privileged enough to see our collection has admired it greatly."

"My dear Anne, if I were to show the apartments you refer to, to my guests, it would look as if I were puffing off my consequence."

"Nonsense," Anne protested. "You would be giving them a high treat, I am sure. If Miss Fenton is the daughter of a baronet, I daresay she will not be at all overwhelmed by it, and it will give the other two spinsters something to talk about for some time to come."

Laurence was fully aware that his consequence was of far more importance to his sister than it was to himself and that she very much hoped his guests would be, if not overwhelmed, at least brought to a realisation that although his manner was unassuming, he was a gentleman of the first importance.

He allowed himself to be persuaded and Anne accompanied him onto the colonnaded terrace when the butler informed them that the carriage was approaching. This was not done out of a wish to please his sister alone, however. Just as Anne thought it would be diverting to see the ladies' reaction to Westerby, so he thought it might afford him some amusement to see his sister's response when she discovered that Cassandra was not just in the common way.

He had told his guests the same story concerning Cassandra as he had told Alfred, and although Anne's eyes had brightened with interest when he revealed he had met Miss Fenton on the road, they had dimmed a little when he had described her in the most tepid of terms as a well-looking woman, and all speculation had fled from them when on asking her age, he had revealed her to be somewhere in the region of six and twenty.

He was to be proved correct, for when a liveried footman opened the carriage door and Cassandra and Louisa nimbly descended, still laughing at Emma's absurdly understated response to the edifice before them, they both appeared to great advantage. Only Emma, following them more carefully once she had handed the footman her basket, approached Anne's expectations.

"You sly thing," she murmured. "Is it Miss Fenton or Miss Thorpe that has engaged your interest?"

He looked down at her, a sardonic gleam in his eyes. "I find *all* of our guests interesting," he said, "as I am sure you will."

The very natural indignation she felt at this unsatisfactory response could not be expressed as Needham, having welcomed the visitors, was now leading them up the steps so that they must have heard anything she uttered. She discovered that she was even more piqued by the visitors than by her brother. Without ever really being conscious of it, she was rather proud of her family home, and whilst she had witnessed a variety of responses to it, never before had laughter been one of them.

Although Anne was perfectly polite, Louisa, who was almost preternaturally sensitive to those about her, immediately grasped this fact, and aware that Emma was still some distance behind her, offered an apologetic smile.

"I am quite delighted to make your acquaintance, Lady Malmsy," she said, "and must apologise for our unseemly merriment. You must not think that we meant any disrespect. I do not know if your brother has mentioned that my sister, Miss Emma Thorpe, is deaf?"

"Yes, he has, Miss Louisa," Anne said, feeling her indignation begin to abate, and it was completely banished when Louisa added with a rueful smile, "Well, the truth is, that she is a little removed from reality, and when she saw this splendid house, the comment that she made quite overcame us."

"Go on."

"You must not think that she meant to damn it with faint praise," Louisa said with a decided twinkle in her eyes, "but she thought it *very nice*."

Anne smiled and glanced at the neat matron who at that moment was involved in a tug of war over her basket with the footman, who did not seem to think that a petite lady of such advanced years could possibly carry such a burden up the steps.

"What on earth has she in there?" she asked.

"It is her work basket," Louisa confided. "If my sister becomes too fatigued trying to follow a conversation, she will occupy herself with her sewing or knitting."

Anne nodded. "I quite understand. It is amazing that she can follow the spoken word at all." She said in a more penetrating voice, "It is quite all right, Peter. Miss Thorpe does not require your aid with the basket."

"Thank you," Louisa murmured.

"Think nothing of it," Anne said, realising that she had quite lost the opportunity to study her brother as he greeted Miss Fenton.

On hearing his sister address the footman, Laurence took in the situation at a glance, ran lightly down the steps and offered the lady his arm.

"Welcome to my home, Miss Thorpe."

"Thank you," she said, and standing firm in her opinion, added, "it is a very nice house."

"I am glad you think so," he said gravely.

He was rewarded with a beaming smile before Emma returned her attention to the steps. Glancing up, his eyes met Cassandra's and a look of warm amusement passed between them. Miss Fenton was not at all the sort of lady Anne would have expected her brother to be attracted to. There was nothing at all delicate about her; she was built on queenly lines and carried herself with an unconscious pride. An aura of confidence surrounded her and if her character was as strong as her features, she suspected that she would be a force to be reckoned with. But that Laurence liked her could not be in doubt. They had looked at each other as if they were old friends sharing a private joke. She was not at all sure she approved and was even less so when they passed through the huge double doors that had been thrown open to receive them.

"Good Lord!" Cassandra exclaimed.

"You do not like what you see, Miss Fenton?" Anne said coolly, her tone nicely calculated to depress pretension.

Rather than being put out of countenance, however, Cassandra went on with disastrous frankness, "I'm not at all sure that I do."

But even as Anne raised her chin and eyebrows, effortlessly achieving the haughty look that Louisa had so abjectly failed to portray, Cassandra threw her a look half-amused, half-dismayed.

"Oh, pray don't be offended, Lady Malmsy," she said. "I have never learned to mind my wretched tongue. Not having gone into society a great deal, combined with the circumstance of my being brought up by my grandfather, who liked the word with no bark upon it, there was little need to do so. I own myself to be completely at fault and beg your pardon. I am sure this must be one of the grandest entrance halls England has to offer and that you are justly proud of it."

Anne was not proof against these words or the engaging smile which accompanied them. "There is nothing to apologise for, Miss Fenton," she said, her own smile a little rueful. "I have been justly served. My brother would have brought you in by a more modest way, but it was I who insisted that you should see Westerby in all its glory."

"My sister likes to observe what degree of awe it must inspire in our visitors," Laurence said, a strange smile flickering about his lips.

"The temptation must be irresistible," Louisa put in, "and it would have been a shame if we had not had the opportunity to see this splendid space."

"Well, that is what I thought," Anne said, turning a fascinated eye upon Cassandra. "Walk with me, Miss Fenton. I own myself agog to discover what you will think of the other rooms in this part of the house."

"I shall tell you now, ma'am," she said promptly, "before my unruly tongue can get me into any more trouble. They are all elegant to a fault, delightfully furnished, and can leave the individual fortunate enough to observe them in no doubt that the person behind their design must have possessed exquisite taste."

Anne was surprised into laughter. "Oh, I should dislike you excessively for you have made me seem like one of those stuffy creatures who only desire people to say what they wish to hear. No, no, do not try to deny it, for it is true, that is just how I sounded. How odious of me! I apologise. I insist you do not abate your frankness one jot."

They were led through a series of rooms in which the walls were covered in crimson cut velvet, the pattern and colour reflected in both the chair coverings and large carpets that covered the floors. Combined with the effusion of gilt which coated the picture frames, chair legs, side tables, and even the coffering of the lofty ceilings, they could not fail to dazzle the eye. For some reason, Cassandra was reminded of her youthful admirer's mother, who had once insisted on accompanying Mr Rutherford to Darley Manor to see for herself the young lady who had ensnared her son. She had been delightfully vulgar, bedecked in purple rather than crimson, and had worn a turban in which a huge ruby had been set. If that impressive jewel had been her only adornment, it must have drawn the eye, but its effect had been somewhat diluted by the massive array of other jewellery which hung about her neck, dangled from her ears, or weighed down her wrists.

Cassandra would not have called the rooms at Westerby vulgar precisely, but there was so much magnificence that one did not know where to look next. To add to the rest, busts were set upon mantlepieces or plinths, and other statuary into niches set into the walls, and her initial impression was one of confusion. Just as Mrs Rutherford had been under-whelmed by the unpretentious simplicity of Darley Manor, so the first-time visitor to Westerby, must be overwhelmed by a scheme of decoration that had no clear focal point and was so richly sumptuous.

Anne, not privy to these thoughts, had at last the satisfaction of seeing Cassandra struck dumb, and, when they reached the last of what she called the state apartments, aptly named the crimson saloon, said, "Well, Miss Fenton?"

Cassandra's first unwary words on entering the house had been uttered in a moment of unguarded surprise. She truly had no wish to upset Laurence's sister, so although Lady Malmsy had given her leave to speak freely, she chose her words more carefully. "I think the rooms very nicely proportioned, ma'am, and imagine that the Prince Regent himself must be impressed by such a lavish display."

"I believe he was," she said, with a complacent smile. "Although he was only the Prince of Wales when he came here. But are *you* impressed, Miss Fenton?"

"Certainly," Cassandra said, "although the rich-ness of the decoration is not perhaps quite to my taste."

Laurence had remained very much in the back-ground leaving Anne to lead the way and point out anything she thought worthy of especial notice but now said dryly, "Nor mine."

Cassandra looked at him in some surprise. "Then I wonder that you have done nothing about it."

"I would hardly have known where to begin. Perhaps you might advise me, Miss Fenton."

She looked at him closely but when she could see no sign of satire in his expression but only polite interest, she obliged him. "I would not have velvet crimson in every room for a start. Perhaps you might like to keep it in one of them, so that you may receive any particularly important visitors with due pomp, although you could hold any such reception in the great hall, which I am sure is grand enough to hold a ball in. I would certainly be tempted to strip it from the other rooms and perhaps paint one of them light blue, and another pale green. The more neutral colours would be more relaxing to the eye."

"Miss Fenton," Anne said, choking back an incredulous laugh, "have you any idea how much it costs to cover a room in cut velvet?"

"No, I have not," she said ruefully, "is it very dear?"

"You need give no thought to cost," Laurence interpolated. "Please, go on. Consider the cut velvet no more."

"Very well. I would remove a few of the paintings. There are so many that it is like being in an art gallery, or at least, what I imagine that would be like for I have never been to one."

"And what do you suggest we do with the ones we take down?" Anne said, bemused. "Sell them to the highest bidder and so start a rumour that my brother has lost his fortune?"

"Oh, no," Cassandra said quickly. "But perhaps you could store them in the attics, and then now and then rotate them, to give the room a fresh look."

"An excellent idea," Laurence said, encouragingly. "Are there any in particular that you feel should be the first to be so assigned?"

"But they are all done by the hand of a master," Anne protested in an uncharacteristically faint voice that hardly penetrated the concentration with which Cassandra was regarding the many masterpieces on offer.

"They are all so very good," she finally said, "that it would be a difficult task indeed, but I have noticed that there is no scheme to their hanging. Perhaps it would be better if those in each room shared a common theme; mythological subjects in one room, biblical in another, then landscapes and so on. Once so organised, it might be easier to decide."

"That idea does have some merit," Anne acknowledged, if a little begrudgingly.

"It has a great deal of merit," Laurence said, regarding Cassandra with an enigmatic smile. "Anything else?"

"Yes," Cassandra said thoughtfully, her eyes just then coming to rest on the bust of a serious-looking gentleman. There was a plaque attached to the plinth it rested upon, proclaiming him to be Thucydides, an ancient Greek historian. She had nothing at all against him but felt there were far too many such examples littering the rooms.

"Do not be afraid to consign Thucydides also to the attics, I beg," Laurence said gently, "this is only a Roman copy of a Greek original, after all."

Cassandra laughed. "Only? He is very well preserved considering he has such an ancient lineage and most certainly should not be put in the attics, but perhaps he might be more at home in the library. However, there are a great many statues, and it is a little disconcerting to have so many sightless eyes following one about. I would be tempted to assign a few to the garden, or if that is already overrun with them, design a gallery specifically for their display."

Anne's sense of humour overcame her indignation. "What very decided opinions you have, Miss Fenton," she said, a reluctant smile in her eyes.

Cassandra sent her a look of sympathetic understanding. "I know it. But it was only a hypothetical discussion, after all. I would not have been so comprehensive in my assessment if I had not been pressed, you know, and I expect my suggestions will be consigned to the devil without any more ado. It is very right that they should be, for what have I to say to the matter, after all?"

"I can't imagine," Anne said, casting her brother a quick glance. As usual, his expression gave nothing away. "Come, my sister will be wondering where we have got to."

"Just a moment, if you please," Louisa said. "We appear to have lost *my* sister."

By unspoken agreement, they all retraced their steps to the previous room. Emma was seated on one of the gilt-edged chairs, her work basket on the similarly finished table, and a needle in her hand. Her loss of hearing had heightened her other senses, and she was often observant of those little details that others might not notice. She had discovered a corner of fraying hem on the red, velvet curtains, and was engaged in correcting this oversight.

She glanced up, the faint vibration that went

through the floor alerting her to their presence. "I won't be above a moment. They are such nice curtains and only need a stitch."

It was too much for Laurence; he met his sister's astonished gaze, and his shoulders began to shake, and after a pregnant pause, the ladies joined in with his laughter.

CHAPTER 12

Only Cecy and Miss Reynolds awaited them in the south drawing room, otherwise known as the yellow saloon.

"What a charming room," Cassandra exclaimed, taking in the primrose walls and beamed ceilings, the floral chintz covering the comfortable chairs and sofas, and the complete lack of ostentation or display.

"Oh, I am so glad you think so," Cecy said, coming forwards to meet them. "Mama always had such good taste. This room used to have such a pretty view down to the lake, but papa thought it unremarkable and so added a more formal garden for interest."

Cassandra glanced through the windows glimpsing a wide terrace with steps leading down to an Italianate garden. She bit her lip as she saw an abundance of statues placed at regular intervals about it, the most splendid of which was the centrepiece of a fountain, depicting a man at repose on a couch of stone, his long flowing beard preserving his modesty, and water spouting from his mouth.

Laurence, who was standing at her shoulder, murmured, "The river god. There are many variations on the theme, but I have never seen another used in so original a manner."

Cassandra choked back a laugh as Laurence made the introductions. She at once perceived the difference between the two sisters. Their features might have been as alike as peas in a pod, but both their mannerisms and expressions were vastly different. Mrs Pellow fluttered like a startled dove, whilst she would rather have compared Lady Malmsy to an owl, her glance alert and watchful but her demeanour calm unless one ruffled her feathers.

"Why, Miss Fenton, how tall you are! I feel quite dwarfed," Cecy said, before briefly clapping a hand to her mouth. "Oh, dear. I hope you do not think me uncivil for I did not mean it so. I know some ladies appear terribly awkward when they are so unusually tall, but you are not one of them, I assure you, indeed you are not."

Cassandra laughed. "I shall take your word for it."

"But it is quite true," Cecy said, smiling gratefully at her. "You hold yourself so well and are not at all clumsy in your movements. I marked it particularly when you entered the room."

"You are very kind," Cassandra murmured, glancing over her head as the young lady who had been sitting with her rose and came forwards, offering Laurence a shy smile as she did so. *She* certainly held herself well, Cassandra thought, and moved with a grace she could never hope to acquire.

"Ah, there you are, Kitty," Anne said. "Miss

Fenton, Miss Louisa, and Miss Thorpe, this is my cousin, Miss Reynolds."

She curtsied very prettily, murmuring, "How do you do?"

"Dear Kitty was growing most impatient to meet you all," Cecy confided. "But she quite understood that you would not wish to hurry through the staterooms."

"No, indeed, how could anyone?" she said. "It does not matter how many times I visit them, I always see something I had not noticed before."

"That is because there is far too much to see," Laurence said, "but never fear, Miss Fenton has come up with an excellent scheme to make them more manageable to the eye."

Miss Reynolds gave a trill of laughter. "Oh, you are funning. They are quite perfect as they are."

"Yes, well," Anne said, perhaps realising how syco-phantic the girl sounded, "each to their own taste. Now, I suggest we partake of our luncheon before strolling down to the lake where my husband has taken the boys fishing."

"Oh," Cecy said, "I must go and find Mr Pellow. He will, of course, have his head buried in a book in the library, but he did ask me to remind him to join us."

"I suggest you accompany my sister, Miss Fenton," Laurence said, his voice deceptively bland, "and then you may judge for yourself if the library would be more fitting than the attic for our historian."

Cassandra met his amused glance and returned it, realising he was teasing her, but she did not refute his suggestion. She had spent many happy hours in the library at Darley with both her grandfather and Louisa and her natural curiosity was aroused. She smiled at Cecy, who was looking more than a little bemused. "I would very much like to see the library. Do take me with you, Mrs Pellow."

"Of course," she said, "please come this way."

No sooner had they left the room than she looked at Cassandra a little anxiously. "What could my brother mean, Miss Fenton? Who is this historian he speaks of, and why would he wish to put him in the attic?"

"I believe your brother was having a little joke at my expense," she said gently.

"Oh, no," Cecy assured her. "Laurence is not a great jokesmith, you know. On the contrary, his disposition is serious." A look of great sadness crossed her face. "Too serious. It was not always so, of course."

"Was it not?" Cassandra said, tucking Mrs Pellow's arm into hers. "Tell me what happened to make him so serious."

Cecy quite forgot her original query, and although some vague thought that she should not confide in a stranger crossed her mind, she found the sympathetic glance cast upon her too tempting to resist and launched into a catalogue of all her brother's trials. Cassandra was wise enough to realise that a lady of such sensibility as Mrs Pellow, was bound to exaggerate a little, but even so, she was a little shocked by her tale and saddened by the culmination of it.

"It was very wrong of papa to destroy all his work, well, almost all of it, for my sister and I have a painting each, and I also have a lovely sculpture carved in wood of a little boy standing on his head.

An odd subject you might think, but it is so well done and captures the innocence and exuberance of a young child so very well."

"It sounds charming," Cassandra said.

"Oh, yes. It is such a shame that Laurie gave up his artistic endeavours after papa died. He was convinced, you see, that the rage he put papa into when he discovered how he had been spending his time was the cause of his heart attack. He even told Mama that if Papa had not destroyed his work, he would have."

Cassandra was about to ask why a man who proudly displayed so many paintings and statues should have been so set against his son enjoying such a harmless pastime but glancing down at the soft gaze of the woman beside her, decided against it. She had already pried enough. Although she felt it was only fair that she should know something of Laurence's history having revealed so much of her own, she was a direct woman and was already regretting the impulse to discover it through a third party. She had certainly not expected so comprehensive an answer. Besides, she could hazard a very good guess herself; her recent dealings with a man of autocratic temper had shown her how unreasonable such a person could be if thwarted, and the way so many artefacts had been crammed together without any great thought to their arrangement spoke of a man more interested in displaying his wealth and consequence than of a person who was genuinely interested in his possessions.

"Here we are," Cecy said, opening a door and preceding Cassandra into the library. "I am sorry to disturb you, my dear, but I have brought Miss Fenton to see the library."

It was far larger than the library at Darley Manor, and the dark furniture proclaimed it a masculine domain, but Cassandra could immediately see that if the walls above the bookshelves and the ceiling were painted a cream colour, and some comfortable sofas placed here and there, it would be a very comfortable room. She perceived a studious looking gentleman bent over a large tome. He raised his eyes if not his head and peered over a pair of spectacles that were perched on his nose. He blinked and then an affectionate smile softened his countenance as he perceived his wife. He rose, saying ruefully, "My dear, have I lost all track of time again?"

"Yes, but it is all my fault. You requested me to alert you at the appointed hour, but I was trying to distract Kitty, who seemed unusually... oh, what do I mean? I had nearly said sulky but that would be unkind, so I shall rather say put out."

"Then she was most definitely sulky," Mr Pellow said, removing his glasses, closing his notebook and rising to his feet. "Good day, Miss Fenton."

"Well, perhaps," Cecy conceded, "but she does have an unaccountable liking for the staterooms and was most put out not to have another opportunity to explore them."

"Unaccountable?" Cassandra said, in amused tones. "Do not tell me that you do not also revere them, Mrs Pellow?"

Cecy looked a little self-conscious. "Well, I am sure they are to be admired, everybody says so, but I can never be comfortable in them. All those blank eyes following me about gives me the shivers."

"I quite understand. It is what I said myself."

"Oh, did you?" Cecy giggled. "Anne would not have liked that at all."

"No, I think I have given her a very odd opinion of me."

"No doubt," Mr Pellow said, "but you must admit, Miss Fenton, that there is much to be admired."

"Indeed," Cassandra said, her eyes scanning the room until she spied a niche housing a rather ugly vase. "And yet, sir, I cannot help but feel that Thucydides would be very much more at home here."

Mr Pellow looked impressed. "Miss Fenton, you have surprised me. It is rare that I discover a female with an interest in ancient Greek historians."

"I do not have such an interest, I am afraid," she said with an apologetic smile. "I read the plaque set beneath it."

"Oh," Cecy cried. "It was a statue that you wished to put in the library or the attics!"

"A bust, to be precise." Mr Pellow regarded Cassandra quizzically. "The attics, Miss Fenton?"

"It was Lord Carteret who suggested the attics. I thought he would be happier in the library, and I see that I was quite right."

Mr Pellow smiled in a bemused fashion. "I think he must have been teasing you, ma'am."

"Almost certainly," Cassandra allowed.

They enjoyed a very pleasant luncheon set out in the modest dining parlour next to the drawing room and discussed subjects no more controversial than the fair that was to be held in Burnham Westgate the following week.

"But the horse fair is always held at the beginning of August," Laurence said.

"It is not a horse fair," Anne informed him, "but a travelling fair with puppets, magicians, jugglers and so on. We shall have to take the children, of course. I hope you will accompany us, Laurie."

"I think I am engaged on that day," he said promptly.

Anne sent him a look of sparkling indignation. "How can you be when I have not yet mentioned the days it is to be held upon, dear brother?"

"I did not need you to inform me of it," he said. "Alfred has insisted that I devote myself to estate matters next week. I spend so little time here, you see, that there is always so much to bring to my attention when I am in residence."

"Poppycock!" Anne protested. "He is well able to take care of your affairs and there is no reason you cannot stay for as long as you wish. Besides, you so rarely see your nephews and niece that I think they have quite as much claim on your time. If it *were* the horse fair, I have no doubt that you would make time for it."

"But it is *not* the horse fair," Laurence said gently, snubbing her quite ruthlessly.

Cassandra exchanged a look with Louisa. It seemed that he was not a man to be coerced.

"There *will* be horses there," Miss Reynolds said, "for there will be a circus with acrobats riding them. Do you not think you might enjoy that, Lord Carteret?" She looked at him with large, hopeful eyes.

"Do come, Laurie," Cecy put in. "Not if you don't wish to, of course, but I can't help but remember when you were a boy, and we went to a similar fair in Fakenham. You enjoyed it so very much, although you put us all in a quake because you disappeared and after half an hour searching for you, we found you in the conjurer's tent. He was most put out for you had worked out how he had made a red silk handkerchief turn into a green one."

"Oh, do tell," Miss Reynolds begged in a breathless voice.

"It is out of my power to do so," Laurence said, smiling wryly. "He made me swear an oath that I would not betray his secret, and I never break my word."

"Quite right," Cecy said, looking at him with affection, "and if you are set against coming, then there is no more to be said."

Laurence capitulated. "Enough, I shall agree to come if only because you must all be boring our guests."

Cassandra amended her previous thought. He was not the man to be coerced by bludgeoning tactics. She was not sure if it had been Miss Reynolds' wide, pleading eyes or his sister's childhood reminisces which had made him change his mind, but one thing she felt certain of was that Miss Reynolds had a decided tendre for him. What Laurence felt was unclear. His manner to her was meticulously polite, his tone when he spoke to her kind, but there was nothing of the lover in it. He was not the man to show his hand, however, so she could not read too much into that.

Miss Reynolds was pretty, shy, and modest, and

just the sort of girl she had imagined would suit him very well. She did not warm to her, however, yet the only thing she could hold against her was her shrinking attitude towards Emma. Whenever that lady occasionally made a comment, in her flat, and sometimes overloud voice, she jumped and looked at her nervously.

Although Laurence had suggested that this be a social visit only, Cassandra wished to unobtrusively capture the sisters' likeness whilst they were enjoying their afternoon. When it became clear that everyone had eaten their fill, she smiled at Cecy who sat on her right. "I wish I had brought my sketchbook, for I really would like to take this opportunity to make some preliminary sketches, not in a formal way, you understand."

"Oh, I see. In that case, I shall fetch one for you, and a pencil, of course." She added confidingly, "I am afraid that neither I nor my sister showed any great proficiency in the art of drawing and so there are many unfilled sketchbooks in the schoolroom."

"There is no need for you to put yourself to so much trouble, Cecy," Laurence said. "You are looking a little tired. One of the footmen can quite as easily fulfil the task."

He glanced at Needham, who had come back into the room to enquire if anyone would like any further refreshment. "Send someone to fetch two sketchbooks down, will you? I think I might like to sketch the lake this afternoon."

The butler looked intently at his master and the merest hint of a smile tugged at his lips. After a slight pause, he said, "Certainly, sir."

Needham had not yet reached the door before Cecy burst into tears. "Oh, forgive me," she said, reaching for her napkin in a not entirely successful attempt to stem the flow. "It is just that I am s-so h-happy."

"Cecy!" Laurence said, on a half laugh. "What on earth have I said to make you dissolve into tears?"

"Oh, how can you ask?" she said between sobs. "When you have not sketched as much as a beetle for years."

He looked surprised and a little amused. "No, I have quite lost the habit of drawing, but I assure you, Cecy, I would not have chosen a beetle as my subject even if I had not."

A sharp kick under the table delivered to her shins by Anne reminded Cecy that the Westerby ladies had all agreed never to bring to Laurence's attention the fact that they had ever noticed this lapse. It had been their mother who had insisted upon it, explaining to them that it could only open old wounds.

"No, of course you would not," she said, "pay no heed to me. I am not quite myself."

Her husband was regarding her in some concern. "My dear? The only time I have known you to become a watering pot without the least provocation is when you are expecting a happy event. Is it possible that after all this time you are in the family way again?"

Cecy turned eyes half hopeful, half anxious upon Mr Pellow. "Oh, you have guessed. Do you mind very much?"

"Mind?" Mr Pellow said, pushing himself to his

feet. "Cecy, how can you think such a thing? I am delighted!"

Cecy once again burst into tears. "I am so glad. It is just that you have been so absorbed in your studies recently because you wish to write that book on the influence of ancient ideas on the modern world that I thought you would not like the disruption to our lives."

Mr Pellow looked stricken. "What a selfish fellow I am. Forgive me, my love."

This only made Cecy cry all the harder. "H-how can you t-talk such n-nonsense," she sobbed. "There n-never was a k-kinder husband."

"I shall take you up to your room to rest, my love," he said, swiftly coming around the table to take her arm and lead her from the room.

Louisa, noticing that her sister was looking worried, reached for the basket that sat at Emma's feet and rummaged in it for the slate and chalk she knew she would find there. She quickly wrote a message upon it and passed it to Emma.

"Wonderful!" she said, glancing at Laurence.

"Thank you. It is good news indeed. My sister always wished for another child."

"But is Mrs Pellow not too old?" Miss Reynolds said, her eyes wide with surprise and more than a hint of revulsion.

It was a naïve and untactful thing to say in the presence of Mrs Pellow's sister, who as her twin, must by implication, also be so struck by years that she should no longer enjoy those intimate relations with her husband that might lead to such an interesting condition.

"Clearly not," Anne said sharply. "Did you not promise to bring Phoebe down to join us when we were ready to take our stroll through the gardens, Kitty?"

A flush of colour rushed into the young lady's cheeks. "Yes, of course. I shall fetch her immediately."

"Then perhaps you will bring the sketchbooks to us when you have collected her from the nursery? I feel the need for some air."

The reduced party navigated the winding paths of the Italian garden.

"Will Mr Westerby be joining us this afternoon?" Louisa asked nonchalantly.

"I am afraid not," Laurence said. "The roof of one of my tenant's farmhouses is leaking, and he has gone to see what repairs need to be done."

"You are fortunate to have so assiduous a steward," Louisa said.

Laurence smiled "I know it. He is not only an excellent steward but the best of good fellows."

They passed through an arch in the high hedge that encircled the garden, and a picturesque vista opened up before them. Wide lawns interspersed with clumps of trees, artfully planted so that the eye was drawn to a long curving lake that disappeared into a wood were revealed, and in the far distance, a glimpse of the sea could be seen.

Cassandra much preferred it to the garden they had just left. "It is a pretty view."

"I am pleased you approve," Anne said. "As we have been speaking of making sweeping changes at Westerby, I would move the Italian garden and so open the prospect to the house again. Don't you agree, Miss Fenton?"

Laurence gave a dry laugh. "If I did not know that you two had not met before today, I might suspect that you were in cahoots to keep me here a twelvemonth supervising all these works."

Anne sent him a sideways glance. "Would that be so very bad, Laurie?"

He pondered this question for a moment before saying, "Perhaps not."

Anne offered him a swift smile but was wise enough to let the subject rest, and she dropped back to walk with the Misses Thorpe.

"I am glad to have this opportunity to speak with you," Cassandra said, "for I have at last heard from Mr Penwith. My trunks arrived too, and my horse will be arriving in the next few days."

"I had noticed how very smart you were looking," he murmured.

She chuckled. "I was not fishing for compliments."

"I did not give you one," he said softly. "If I had wished to do so, I must have said lovely rather than smart."

Her eyes flew to his and a faint colour touched her cheeks. She saw a quizzical gleam in them and laughed. "I begin to think you an accomplished flirt. You may save such nonsense for Miss Reynolds who deserves such an accolade far more than I."

"She would certainly value it more, Cassandra," he said with a wry smile.

"You must not call me so," she gently chided. "Your sister already has a very odd opinion of me, I am sure, and heaven knows what conclusion she will jump to if she overhears us."

"I doubt anything you might say could any longer surprise her. However, I would not like you to be made uncomfortable and so I shall accede to your request. How did your lawyer react to your news, Miss Fenton?"

"He was very much shocked and is posting down to see me at the end of next week. That reminds me, he asked me to book some rooms for him at an inn, perhaps you could advise me as to a suitable establishment. There are three inns in the village—"

"I would rather say alehouses," Laurence said. "And not much more than thirty years ago, they were all the meeting places for smugglers. Thornham was famous, or rather, infamous for the practice."

Cassandra's eyes widened. "No, was it? How exciting."

"I do not think you would have found it so," Laurence said gravely. "There were powerful smuggler barons who could command the majority of the populace to take part in the trade, and they were quite ruthless when confronted by customs officers or even dragoons."

"Good Lord! It seems like such a sleepy little backwater. You are quite right; I would not have liked it at all."

"I am afraid that there were and still are many poor labourers hereabouts and they could earn a week's wages in one night by assisting the smugglers by all accounts. It must have been a great temptation."

"Well, if they are no better off now, something must be done for them. Can you not use your influence to pass a bill that would ensure them better pay? Or perhaps incentives could be offered to farmers or other businesses to take them on year round."

He looked at her with a strange glint in his eyes that she could not easily interpret.

"What have I said to make you look so?"

"What most other ladies of my acquaintance would never think of," he said. "It would be impossible to regulate pay as different farms, as well as different areas of the country, produce vastly different yields, and the prices they can achieve for their crops or cattle vary widely. But the incentive scheme has some merit."

Cassandra's face lit up. "Thank you."

He laughed. "Now I must ask, what have I said to make you look so? I have only acknowledged that your idea was a good one."

"That is what I am thanking you for," she said. "You can have no idea how frustrating it is to not be taken seriously merely because one is a woman. I have always had a great many ideas—"

She broke off as something occurred to her. "Laurence!"

He raised a brow.

She smiled ruefully. "Oh dear, I should never have insisted we use our given names at our first meeting. It is a hard habit to break, and I cannot imagine now what made me do so."

"You wished to remain a lady of mystery," he helpfully reminded her.

"Did I say that? It was all nonsense of course. I must have been suffering from an irritation of the nerves."

"I do not believe you have any nerves," Laurence said.

"No, I believe you are right," Cassandra agreed. "What I was going to say was that Louisa mentioned that Mr Tremlow's servants left after he died, saying that it was an eerie place and that odd noises and lights floated across the saltmarsh. She thought that perhaps some people from the village had been teasing them, but now I wonder if it might have been smugglers, although Louisa has never seen or heard anything untoward."

"I imagine that she was in the right of it. There are many stories concerning Thornham in relation to the trade, and although the truth was bad enough, you may be sure they have become exaggerated over time. I would not be at all surprised if some smuggling still occurs, but you may be sure it is on a small scale and nothing for you to worry about. If you do happen to see lights on the marsh, I suggest that you ignore them. Now, as usual, we have wandered some way from the starting point of our conversation. The nearest decent coaching inn to Thornham is at Burnham Westgate, but as the fair is to be held there, I daresay there will not be a room to be had. Mr Penwith had better come to me."

"To you?" Cassandra said, frowning. "He would not wish to put you to so much trouble, I am sure. And why should you put yourself out in such a way?"

"I have discovered I enjoy puffing off my consequence," he said promptly.

When she did not laugh but looked at him, clearly a little troubled, he said, "Do not be such a goose. It will not put me out at all. I daresay he won't stay above a night or two, and I hardly think he would expect me to entertain him. My servants will look after him very well."

There seemed no more to say. They were nearing the lake and Cassandra's attention was caught by an old cottage situated on an island in the middle of it. It was partially obscured by creepers and the overlong grass which had clearly not been scythed for some considerable time.

"Who lives in that old cottage?"

"No one," Laurence said dryly. "Its sole purpose is to add a romantic aspect to the scene. My father felt there were already a plethora of grottos, hermitages and follies gracing other gardens the length and breadth of the country, and so was persuaded to build it."

"Did you used to play there as a child?"

"No. The building is not at all old but only made to look so. It was built when I was in my first year at Oxford and had outgrown such boyish whims. Besides, it is an empty shell inside. My father at least had enough sense not to build a series of rooms within it that no one would ever see."

Cassandra's eyes came to rest on a little group by the lake shore. Lord Malmsy was seated on a stool, and four boys ranged along the bank, fishing rods in hand. "But surely your nephews have explored it?"

"No, the island was never intended to be visited but left to nature, besides, my sisters are afraid that after eleven years of intentional neglect, the roof might fall in. That would, of course, only add to its romantic aspect."

She caught the irony in his words and laughed.

"Well, it seems a pity that they should not have the pleasure of exploring it. I know I would have wished to when I was a child, but at least it will add interest to the composition of your sketch."

A small, enigmatic smile curved his lips. "True. It is a pity that you will only have one subject for your drawings now that Cecy has retired."

She shrugged. "It does not signify. Perhaps Mrs Pellow will come and visit me when she feels well enough. I like to do sketches at first, and then paint various features and expressions on a larger canvas before I begin the more delicate task of a miniature."

"I am sure both my sisters will be delighted to visit you."

The rest of the afternoon sped by. Phoebe proved to be a charming girl and became very interested in Emma. When it was explained to her that she must look at Mrs Thorpe when she spoke to her so she could read her lips or write on her slate as she could not hear her words, she was intrigued. They struck up an instant rapport and before long the little girl was being instructed in the art of knitting. Louisa and Anne also got on very well, and Cassandra was able to make several sketches that captured her likeness in a natural manner rather than in a conscious pose.

Laurence, once he had spent some time talking to his nephews, retreated to a tree a short distance from the rest of the party. He sat beneath it, his back resting against the trunk and began to sketch. Both artists became completely absorbed in their tasks, although their eyes occasionally strayed to each other, usually at the same moment. The only person who seemed at all discontented was Miss Reynolds. Something approaching a pout disfigured the perfect bow of her lips when Anne refused to allow her to wander over to Laurence to have a look at his drawing.

"You must not disturb him. He has never liked anyone to see his work before it is finished."

The truth of this assertion was proven at the end of the afternoon when Cassandra asked to see his sketch.

"Like your work, Miss Fenton, it is only a first study. I shall show it to you when it is completed to my satisfaction."

CHAPTER 13

Lady Malmsy and Mrs Pellow visited Tremlow House a few days later, and a comfortable rapport was soon established between the ladies. Miss Reynolds and Phoebe accompanied them, the young girl naturally gravitating towards Emma who was equally pleased to see the child. Miss Reynolds sat on the periphery, rather quiet, her thoughts apparently elsewhere. Cassandra completed a series of sketches of Mrs Pellow whilst they drank tea and chatted, and it was agreed that the sisters should return the following afternoon for a final and more formal sitting in the summerhouse that was situated at the top of a gentle slope in the garden. It was fronted by a series of large windows that had the dual benefits of allowing great quantities of light into the building whilst offering its occupants a wide view of the marsh and the sea beyond.

After the visitors left, Cassandra retreated there and from her sketches of the twins completed two rudimentary watercolours, their images side by side on the canvas. By a subtle shift in expression, she had captured something of their different personalities she hoped. Tomorrow she would mix some gum into her paints to strengthen the colours and hope to accurately match the hue of their eyes, hair, and complexion. The painstakingly delicate work of the miniatures would take rather longer to complete.

The dinner hour passed unnoticed, as did Louisa when she quietly entered the room and left a glass of wine and a plate of cold meat and bread and butter for her refreshment. She was recalled to the lateness of the hour by a protesting rumble from her stomach and an appreciative smile curved her lips as she saw the repast laid out on a small table. It was set next to a cushioned cane chair, positioned to take advantage of the wide view beyond the window. The weather had cooled, and dusk was beginning to descend. A low-lying mist crept over the marsh, and the clouds above reflected the sunset, blushing a dull red.

Cassandra sank into the chair and rubbed gently at her tired eyes, before reaching for the wine and taking a small sip. She looked out of the window, her eyes feeling soothed by the gathering darkness and absently nibbled at a slice of bread and butter. Lights out at sea marked the progress of the dark hulk of a boat towards the entrance of the harbour. It was probably bringing coal in on the high tide to be offloaded in the morning into the barn built there to store it.

Her attention was caught by another light, closer in that was moving across the marsh. That probably belonged to a lone herdsman returning home after checking on his sheep. She had frequently seen such characters on her solitary walks. She sipped her wine, idly watching his progress. Every now and then the light disappeared, and she amended her first hypothesis. Many waterways criss-crossed the marsh that at high tide became navigable for small boats, and judging by the lamp's height and its intermittent visibility, it was probably a fisherman.

She smiled wryly. If she had possessed more sensibility, after her talk with Laurence she might have put quite another interpretation on the scene unfolding before her. She was not such a ninny-hammer as to automatically assume that any nefarious connotations pertained to the appearance of a single light on the marsh, however, and very soon had the satisfaction of discovering that her second conclusion had been correct. The boat came to a halt in the middle of the estuary that led to the harbour, and as the moon found a gap in the clouds and obligingly cast a cool pool of light onto the water, she observed the silhouette of a gentleman casting a line.

She rose to her feet, picked up her plate and made her way back to the house. She paused, startled, as she heard the rustle of a bush close by.

"Is anybody there?"

Someone muttered something in a low voice and then the curly head of Mr Cooper appeared. "Didn't mean to frighten you, ma'am."

"And you did not do so," Cassandra said. "I am not so easily frightened. You did startle me, however."

"I'm sorry, ma'am." He stooped and picked up a watering can. "I'm just doing a spot of watering."

Cassandra privately thought that there had been quite enough rain over the last few days to preclude the need for it, but merely said, "Very well, good night, Mr Cooper."

As she entered the house by the kitchen, a rather dour lady was just taking off her apron.

"Thank you, Mrs Larkin," she said, putting her plate and glass by the sink.

"You should take better care of yourself, Miss Fenton," that lady said with a sniff of disapproval. "Aside from the fact that you missed a fine dinner, if I do say so myself, a strapping girl like you needs a mite more than a bit o' bread and butter and a slice of ham to sustain her."

"Do not concern yourself, Mrs Larkin," she said, not taking the slightest umbrage at being so described, although for some reason the fairy-like delicacy of Miss Reynolds suddenly came to mind. "It will do me no harm to become a mite less strapping."

"I don't hold with ladies starving themselves," the blunt housekeeper said, "and what is more there is no need for you to do it. There's no spare flesh on you, ma'am, and your build perfectly matches your height, and *that* you can do nothing about."

"Very true," Cassandra acknowledged, amused at the implication implicit in the housekeeper's rough but sympathetic tones that being tall must be a great trial to her. "It is a lowering thought. I daresay there is not a gentleman alive who could carry me if I were to turn my ankle or fall from my horse. I shall take great care that neither of these unfortunate events befall me."

"You do that," Mrs Larkin said, much struck by these sensible observations. "I know one or two who could do it, but they are none of them gentlemen and they're not fit to touch so much as the hem of your dress."

The few early risers who had the privilege of seeing Cassandra enjoying a gallop on her bay mare over the common that lay south of Brancaster the following morning might have raised their brows if they had been privy to this conversation. Rather than riding with any noticeable degree of care, she flew across the ground as if she were in deadly peril. Her horse and her groom, Plackett, had arrived two days previously, but Blaze had needed to rest after such a long journey. The mare and her mistress, delighted to be reunited again, were each as eager as the other to indulge in a form of exercise so long denied them.

Cassandra had just reined in at the far end of the common when her groom said warningly, "We have company, ma'am."

She glanced in the direction indicated by the jerk of Plackett's head and perceived two gentlemen on horseback riding at a more restrained canter towards her. A wide smile crossed her face as she recognised Laurence and Mr Westerby.

She turned her horse and rode to meet them, her cheeks flushed and her eyes sparkling from the exercise. "I am acquainted with both gentlemen."

They both rode well but she thought Laurence had the better seat. She smiled as they came up to her.

"Good day, Lord Carteret, Mr Westerby."

"Miss Fenton," Laurence said, briefly removing his hat. "We shall ride back with you. We are on our way to Tremlow House. I apologise for the early hour but our business today will take us quite some distance and so it was now or not at all."

"Then you must break your fast with us," Cassandra said, resisting the impulse to immediately enquire what was so urgent that it could not wait until tomorrow. Instead, she said, "Well, Lord Carteret, do you not think Blaze a fine horse?"

"I think both horse and rider appeared to great advantage when in full flight," he said with a small twist of a smile.

"By God, Miss Fenton," Alfred said in admiring tones, "you are a slapping rider!"

"But not, perhaps, a very wise one," Laurence said softly. "The common is pocked with rabbit holes."

"Aye, and so I told her," Plackett said in a resigned voice.

Cassandra merely laughed. "Pooh! I have enough skill, I hope, to avoid them."

Laurence regarded her with a penetrating and rather stern stare. She returned his gaze but after a moment dropped her eyes. "Very well, I admit that my exhilaration at being again on horseback may have overcome my judgement."

She felt an undefinable tension stretch between them and after a moment looked up again. Laurence's eyes had gentled. "I applaud you for admitting a fault, Miss Fenton."

"I hope I must always do so when I am in the wrong," she said, very much upon her dignity.

His lips quirked into a smile. "It cost you something to admit it though, did it not?"

"Not at all," she said a trifle archly.

He merely raised an eyebrow and after a moment she chuckled. "Odious man!"

He was perfectly right, of course, and she was not

entirely sure how he had made her admit it, except that when he had looked at her so gravely, she had felt as if she had somehow disappointed him and discovered that she had not liked to do so. They had come to the road that led towards Thornham and Mr Westerby fell back beside the groom so that they would not entirely block the narrow thoroughfare.

Cassandra thought Laurence seemed a little pensive and said in a lively manner, "I shall restore your good opinion by displaying an example of my good sense. You will be pleased to know, sir, that I took your advice, and last evening when I noticed a light making its way across the marsh, I neither worried nor indulged in any wild imaginings. My first thought was that it must be a herdsman returning home but then I realised it was attached to a boat and so was most likely a fisherman, which proved to be quite true for when the moon peeped from between the clouds, I saw him cast his line."

"How happy it must have made you to be proven right," he murmured.

She laughed. "Indeed, it must always be a satisfying experience, must it not?"

"We shall see," he said a little grimly.

"Good Lord, Laurence. What has occurred to put you in so solemn a mood?"

The house came into view, and they turned onto a track that led directly to the stables.

"Forgive me," he said wryly. "I am refining upon something a little too much, I dare say."

A puzzled look came into her eyes, but she said no more as Mr Cooper just then came out of the stables. Cassandra thought he looked as if he had overslept for there was a slightly stunned expression on his face and his hair was rather dishevelled.

Laurence dismounted quickly and came to help her out of the saddle. She reached down to place her hands on his shoulders intending to jump down, but he surprised her by grasping her about the waist in a firm hold and lifting her down without, it seemed, any great amount of effort. It was a pleasant experience and made her feel ridiculously girlish. She stepped quickly away from him, her cheeks feeling a little hot.

"You will do yourself an injury, sir. I am no lightweight."

"And I am no weakling," he countered swiftly.

"You wretch," she said indignantly. "I was completely taken in when I thought you a true gentleman, such a one would have said I was as light as a feather."

Amusement flickered in Laurence's eyes. "Then he would have grossly exaggerated."

As Mr Westerby just then joined them, she did not dignify this with a response but turned and led the way to the house. She glanced over her shoulder as she heard Plackett berate Mr Cooper for not having yet swept out the stables and her eyes narrowed as she caught a glimpse of a slightly askew cap imperfectly concealing a head of blonde hair just visible above one of the stall doors.

Concealing her dismay, she showed the men into the hall and directed William to show the gentleman into the drawing room, saying that she would join them when she had changed her dress. She then lay in wait for Grace in the hall. The maid very soon rushed into the house, straightening her cap with one hand

and shaking a few stubborn wisps of straw from her skirt with the other. Her eyes widened as she saw her mistress and her mouth dropped open.

"Do not stand there gaping, Grace," Cassandra said sternly, "but come up to my room."

The maid scurried after her as she mounted the stairs swiftly not speaking again until she had closed the door behind them. Cassandra threw down her whip, followed swiftly by her hat, and began pulling off her gloves. She was seriously disturbed. She had a fondness for the maid and having been treated so well by her uncle and aunt, also felt an obligation to Mr and Mrs Blinksop. They would not thank her if she allowed their niece to get herself into trouble.

"Would you explain to me, if you please, Grace, what business you had in the stables?"

The girl wavered between shame and defiance, for although her colour was heightened, her jaw was set in a decidedly mulish manner. "It's not what you think, miss."

"No?" Cassandra said. "Then I am sure there must be a perfectly reasonable explanation for your cap being askew and the straw that is still stuck to your gown."

The girl, apparently overwrought, suddenly burst into tears. "How could you think such a thing of me? It was only a kiss, Miss Cassandra, and it was the first time things had gone so far."

"And the last time, I hope. If Miss Louisa knew that her servant was trying to seduce the maids, she would dismiss him, I am sure."

"It wasn't his fault," Grace said, wiping at her eyes. "It was me as kissed him."

Cassandra suddenly remembered the stunned look on Mr Cooper's face and despite herself, her lips twitched.

"And I wasn't being a hussy, whatever Plackett says," she continued defiantly. "We are in love, only Matthew, Mr Cooper I mean, kept saying as how I was better off being a lady's maid because he could hardly afford to keep me, and I wouldn't like to live over the stables. As if I cared for that. Anyway, I thought it was time to give him a little encouragement."

Cassandra knew her maid to be full of pluck, but she still felt a little stunned by her machinations. "I assume he has proposed?"

The girl nodded her head and Cassandra felt a measure of relief. "It is very sudden."

Grace sighed. "It was love at first sight."

"For him or you?" Cassandra said dryly.

"For both of us," Grace said with conviction.

Cassandra's impulse was to challenge the probability of this but for some reason, she checked her tongue. She had been struggling to undo the buttons of her riding dress, but now Grace rushed forwards.

"Let me, Miss Cassandra."

"Thank you," she said, already turning over in her mind what must next be done. She knew well the stubborn streak that lay at the root of her maid's character and if it was within her power, she would make sure Grace was happy. "You are still only twenty, Grace, and I believe the proper person to apply to for permission for this union would be your uncle."

"Mr Cooper is going to ask Miss Louisa for permission to visit him," Grace acknowledged.

"Very proper," Cassandra said. "As my groom is now in residence and the grass so recently scythed, I can see no obstacle to a short leave of absence."

She stepped out of her habit. "I shall miss you, Grace." The maid looked a little dismayed. "You must know that you must leave my service."

Grace nodded and began to sob again. "Come," Cassandra said gently. "Did we not agree that once I was settled, we would reconsider your future? You can hardly remain as my maid once you are wed. It may be that Mr Blinksop might appreciate the help of a strong, young man, however."

Grace looked more hopeful. "I would like it of all things if we could both set up home with my uncle and aunt."

"Then let us hope they are impressed with Mr Cooper. But in the meantime, I must insist that there are no more clandestine meetings between you. I shall discuss the matter with Miss Louisa and speak with Mr Cooper myself on the matter."

"Thank you, miss," Grace said earnestly. "You have always been the finest mistress any servant could wish to have."

"If I were such a fine mistress, I would have had an inkling that whilst I was out walking or riding, you were quite ruthlessly pursuing Mr Cooper," she said dryly. "And I suppose you were also behind that bush, last evening."

Grace giggled. "I know what I want is all."

"Apparently so, but it was very wrong of Mr Cooper to meet with you, not to mention lie to me. Now bustle about and bring me my pale pink muslin, will you? My visitors will wonder what has become of me."

"At once, miss," the maid said, disappearing into the dressing room.

She reappeared moments later with an air of anticipation and proudly held up the dress. "I furbished this up a little only yesterday."

Grace had attached a bright orange ribbon beneath the bust and two rows of the same ribbon to the hem of the dress, neither of which was straight, and, of course, the colours clashed horribly. Cassandra thought the effect quite hideous, but she knew the gentlemen were on limited time and could not quite bring herself to banish the proud glow from Grace's face.

"How very original," she said, allowing the maid to help her into it. "I begin to think Mr Cooper deserves you."

The subtlety of this statement went quite over the maid's head. The only dark cloud on her rosy horizon had been her mistress' disapproval. It was now banished, and Grace's happiness was complete.

CHAPTER 14

The occupants of the drawing room glanced up as the door opened, Louisa's eyes widening in astonishment. Emma put her hand to her mouth and was not entirely successful in stifling a laugh.

Laurence regarded Cassandra quizzically. "Do I detect the hand of your most original lady's maid at work, Miss Fenton?"

"Yes," she said, putting her chin up a little, "but it is of no importance."

"No," he agreed gently, "not if you mean to stay indoors today."

Alfred regarded his cousin in some surprise and opened his mouth to protest at this rudeness, but he just then encountered Louisa's eyes and could not mistake the twinkle in them or ignore the slight shake of her head. He closed his mouth again.

"I am sure Grace has done her best," she said, rising to her feet. "And Miss Fenton is quite capable of making any suitable alterations herself if she so wishes, Lord Carteret. It is only her kindness that has made her wear the dress, I am sure. Now, shall we go into the breakfast room?"

Once the footman had laid out the dishes and served coffee or ale, he withdrew and the commonplace chatter that had prevailed took a more serious turn.

Laurence laid down his fork. "You may recall, Miss Fenton, that we had some discussion earlier on the satisfaction of being proven right in our assumptions."

The grim tone was back, and Cassandra glanced questioningly at him.

"Before I continue, I should perhaps explain that I have seen fit to take my cousin into my confidence as to that nature of our first encounter. You need feel no alarm, however, Alfred is extremely discreet."

"I shall take your word for it, sir, but I would be interested to know what can have occurred for you to do so."

As he had expected, he heard both surprise and disapproval in her voice. "Of course. You may be sure I would not have presumed to discuss the matter without your consent if circumstances had not made it seem prudent to do so." He smiled wryly. "I felt I might benefit from a second opinion."

"I am surprised, sir," she said, still bristling. "It seems to me that it is you who always like to be proven right."

"I usually am," he said softly. He shook his head slightly as he saw the flash of exasperation that brightened her eyes. "That was not an assertion based on arrogance but on fact, ma'am. In this case, however, it is you who have been proven right. I asked Mr Blinksop to write to me when he had news from Grace that you had safely arrived at your destination. I, at last, received that now-defunct assurance this morning. I also received some news that was less welcome."

"Go on," she said, leaning towards him.

"Grace may not excel at either sewing or letter writing, but she has it appears, quite a talent for description. A man came to The Red Lion asking if a Miss Fenton had visited the inn only two days after your stay there. It appears Mr Chubb is developing a little more subtlety; he did not give his name but from the picture Grace drew for her uncle of him, Mr Blinksop was left in no doubt that it was Mr Chubb."

"Oh, is that all?" Cassandra said, relaxing back into her chair. "What is there to trouble me in that? The Blinksops would never betray me, I am certain."

"And they have not done so," Laurence said gently. "It is rather I who appear to have betrayed you, just as you prophesied in the letter you left for me."

"You mean someone did see me leave Stamford in your curricle?"

"I have no certain information on that head," Laurence admitted. "But I think it likely that someone saw us turn onto the Deeping road. Mr Chubb must have discovered it somehow to end up at the inn so soon. I am sorry, Cassandra."

He did not seem to realise he had spoken her name and nor did he perceive, as his eyes were fixed on hers, that Alfred and Louisa exchanged a look; his surprised, hers pleased. It seemed that Cassandra had also momentarily forgotten their presence.

"It was not your fault, Laurence," she said quickly. "You took every precaution, after all."

His lips quirked up at one corner. "I have given you the perfect opportunity to crow and you have not taken it. What an extraordinary creature you are."

She looked a little hurt. "I am no such thing. What a very odd opinion you have of me. I have not forgotten that I have every reason to be grateful to you, besides, you said yourself that you could discover no trace of me upon the road, so why should Mr Chubb be able to?"

Laurence frowned. "Taking you in an open curricle to West Deeping was only the first of my follies. The second was to drive there the following morning. Mr Blinksop said nothing of either of us, but the stable boy was not likely to forget either my equipage or myself, which perhaps helped him remember my title which he duly passed on to Mr Chubb for the princely sum of a shilling. He may not be able to immediately discover your whereabouts, but it would take no very great ingenuity to discover mine. I am very well known in Market Deeping, which is where he would have cast his net, next, I am sure."

"You think he may find me through you still," Cassandra said thoughtfully.

"I must admit it a possibility," Laurence said. "It is another reason I took Alfred into my confidence. He will keep an eye out for him and drop a word in a few of our tenants' ears to alert him if they see anyone hanging about in a suspicious manner. In the mean-time, I regret to say, that after my sisters' visit this afternoon, there should be no direct contact between us until I feel certain that it is safe. Alfred and I came today by a circuitous route cross country that I would defy anyone to follow."

"Is that really necessary?" Cassandra said. "Mr Penwith felt sure that now he was fully aware of my circumstances and had brought Francis to a realisation of the... the inappropriateness of his behaviour, I should have nothing more to fear from him."

"I am not *sure* if it is necessary," he allowed, "and I very much hope that it is not, but I believe it will be best if we are cautious. I must admit, I have no great faith in your cousin's understanding of what is appropriate. I would not have allowed my sisters to visit you today if I could have prevented them without sharing your tale, and I would not do so without your approval. My groom will accompany them, and he will keep a sharp eye out for anyone who might follow them and discover some excuse for them to turn back if he does suspect it. I would also suggest that you curtail your solitary rambles for the present." He looked at her, a measure of approval in his eyes. "I was very pleased that you had your groom with you this morning and would advise that you go nowhere unaccompanied."

Cassandra's eyes went to Mr Westerby. "Do you agree, sir?"

"I do," he said with an apologetic smile.

Cassandra looked dismayed. "But for how long must I exercise such caution?"

"At least until Mr Penwith arrives and I may discuss the matter further with him. I suggest you take your groom into your full confidence. If he is anything like mine, he will be fiercely protective of you."

"He is," she admitted with a wince. "He gave me a

rare trimming down for leaving without as much as a word to him. But I would not give Francis any excuse to get rid of him. He was not employed by me, you see. Whilst I was under my grandfather's roof it did not seem necessary for me to run independently. Only my horse was my own as it was a gift from him."

"Then he must be your watchdog, and you must not hesitate to send word to Westerby if there is any trouble."

"Very well," Cassandra said, seemingly resigned to his strictures.

Louisa looked at her, sympathy and understanding in her eyes. "It is less than a week now until Mr Penwith will be with us, and it will be no very great matter if we must be accompanied when we go out, after all. Although it must be Plackett who takes the groom's seat behind us if we go out in the gig; both Mr Cooper and William are too large. And perhaps you might still enjoy your rambles if you allowed William to walk behind you."

Cassandra gave a dry laugh. "That might pass if I went into the village and wished him to carry my basket, although even then I think it would raise a few brows and draw more attention than we might wish, but to have a footman trailing after me over the marsh or along the beach would be ridiculous as well as irksome."

"Very true," Louisa said, her eyes lighting with amusement at the picture this presented. "How bird-witted of me to suggest it."

"You will, at least, have your paintings of my sisters to keep you occupied," Laurence said gently.

Cassandra sighed and rose to her feet. "Yes, of

course. We have kept you from your business long enough, gentlemen."

"Before we go," Alfred said, "may I cast an eye over your account books and any copies of contracts or correspondence you have received from Mr Rythorne, Miss Louisa? I do not wish to pry unnecessarily into your affairs, but I intend to set some enquiries afoot in Lynn today and I would be interested to see if I can discern any anomalies in his dealings with you or your sister."

"Certainly," she said, briefly laying a hand on his arm, and saying with a grateful smile, "You are very kind, and I feel fortunate to have the assistance of a gentleman I feel sure I can rely on."

As she led him towards the door, Emma rose to her feet as if she would follow them.

"You stay with Cassandra, my dear," Louisa said, "she needs your chaperonage more than I."

The little lady's eyes turned towards Cassandra.

"Nonsense," she said. "Give Grace her usual lesson, Emma, if you will, heaven knows she needs it! I shall take a turn about the garden with Lord Carteret."

"I wonder how much of our conversation Miss Thorpe understood," he said as they crossed the lawn.

"You can never tell," Cassandra said, leading the way to the gate that gave onto the creek. "Sometimes I think she has not been attending at all and then she will say something that gives the lie to my assumption. Are you also going to King's Lynn? I assume that is what Mr Westerby meant when he said Lynn?"

"Yes, to both of your questions. Lynn is how we generally refer to it and I also have some business to attend to. Is there something I could do for you there?"

"That is a very gentlemanly offer, but the scales have quite fallen from my eyes," she said with some spirit. "You know very well that you are unlikely to be put to the inconvenience of carrying out any commissions when you will not be able to bring me my purchases."

His lips twitched. "You underrate my ingenuity, ma'am. I am sure I could find someone else to deliver them, or I might leave them somewhere within reach where you could collect them yourself."

She laughed. "Could you not let me get the better of you, just once?"

"I believe you did so at our very first encounter," he said softly.

"Did I?" she said. "It did not seem so to me. I may have provoked you out of your calm for a brief moment, but that was a paltry victory. I neither wished to tell you my story or accept your escort, and yet I did both."

He merely smiled enigmatically, and they walked down to the creek and onto the bridge where they stood leaning on the rail. The tide was out and a few boats, their paint peeling, could be seen stranded on the mud.

"The creek is not so pretty when the tide is out, but I think it has its own charm in this state. Close your eyes and tell me what you hear."

Cassandra did as she was bid, and a slow smile crossed her face. "How can I have been so unaware of the cacophony of bird calls? Can you tell them apart?"

He indicated a bird with brown flecked plumage and a long, slightly curved beak. "That is a curlew, and it has a long call that rises in pitch at the end. Close your eyes again and see if you can distinguish it."

He watched her lids flicker shut, her long black lashes appearing to become entangled as she did so. A small crease of concentration marked her brow, and he was aware of an urge to smooth it away.

She suddenly gave a delighted laugh. "Yes, I can. What about that one?"

She pointed to a distinctive bird with black plumage, a vibrant orange-red beak, and pink legs.

"That is an oystercatcher. It has a shorter, shriller call."

Without his prompting, she again closed her eyes. "Yes, I hear the difference."

He regarded her upturned face, the smile of pleasure such a simple achievement had brought to her lips and as her eyes sprang open, the warm light in her eyes. For a moment he basked in it and his hand reached out as if to touch her face but then veered upwards and brushed at a few locks of hair that had fallen over his forehead. He said rather abruptly, "Alfred will most likely be finished by now and we must be on our way. I am to dine with Mr Lapworth this evening; he is a neighbour and the magistrate of this district. I have warned him that I might be late and he has already put dinner back until seven, which I assure you is a great sacrifice on his part."

Alfred had indeed finished, and they took their leave. For some minutes Laurence did not speak, his mind preoccupied.

He had recently passed several weeks at the resi-

dence of Lord and Lady Bassington in Northumberland. Lady Bassington had been careless of
convention and outspoken, and he had found her altogether charming. Her words on taking a wife now
came to him. *Trust in serendipity. When the time is right, the
lady will appear.*

Cassandra had appeared out of nowhere and the
timing of their meeting had been most apt as he had
only moments before been considering his future and
wondering when he would meet a lady who could
pierce his reserve. She had certainly done that and
continued to do so. He had thought after the lesson he
had learned at the hands of Diana when still a green
youth that he was awake upon every suit, but he was
beginning to perceive that he was quite as blind as any
other man where love was concerned.

Cassandra's confidence, teasing manner, and frank
speech, not to mention her extraordinary actions on
leading a man, who had once been a Bow Street
Runner, on a wild goose chase without any great loss
of composure, had led him to believe that she was a
headstrong young woman who would constantly cut
up his peace.

She did cut up his peace, and he had no doubt
that she was headstrong. Yet he had discovered that a
look or a word from him could temper this character-
istic. He found that he enjoyed teasing her just as
much as she did him. She was a vital, expressive creature who embraced the world about her rather than
floating through it in a whisper of satin or silk. He
grinned as he recalled that ridiculous dress. No other
woman of his acquaintance could have borne to have
come into company in it, yet she had done so rather

than offend her maid. She had a sometimes too quick tongue, but a kind heart. She also had a ready sense of humour and a quick wit. Life with her would never perhaps be comfortable but neither would it be dull.

There had been a moment on the bridge when he had felt the urge to propose to her, but he knew it to be too soon and so had quickly brought their tête-à-tête to a close. That she felt some affinity to him, he did not doubt. He had seen the glow in her eyes when he had lifted her down from the saddle, the girlish blush, and even though she generally did not admire compliments, the pique when he had not denied that she was no lightweight. He had also seen surprise and confusion.

For all her confidence, Cassandra was an innocent where matters of the heart were concerned. She had all but convinced herself that she was not suited to marriage, and he would be a fool if he pressed her before she knew her own feelings. Besides, he would not declare himself whilst things were so uncertain; both her and Miss Thorpe's affairs must be quite settled before he did so. Having come to this not entirely satisfactory conclusion, he turned his mind to more pressing matters.

He glanced at his companion, fully expecting Alfred to make some comment on his abstraction, but his cousin also seemed lost in his own thoughts.

"Did you find something troubling in Miss Thorpe's accounts, Alfred?"

"Forgive me, I was wool-gathering," that gentleman said with a wry smile. "Apart from the anomaly of the rent on the farm, no. The money from the sale of Mr Tremlow's business has been sensibly invested in the funds along with the rest of his modest fortune. I find it interesting that the contract relating to the tenancy of the farm reveals it is let on a very short lease, renewable every year. It is not unusual for farmers on so short a lease to be reluctant to plough any great amount of money into the land; the lack of security poses the risk of them never having the opportunity to recoup their investment. Mr Moore's contract, however, has been renewed for the last eight years, which removes this excuse for his lax management."

"Will you see Mr Rythorne?" Laurence asked.

"Yes, after I have followed a few other lines of enquiry. Miss Louisa has given me a letter informing her agent that she wishes him to answer any questions I may have on the matter."

"I doubt he will like such interference. Would you?"

"No, but then I would never have made so poor a bargain. I have another letter that I am to give him if I am not satisfied with what I discover, terminating his employment and requesting that he give into my hands any documents he has in his keeping that relate to her affairs."

"Was that your idea or Miss Thorpe's?"

Alfred gave a rueful smile. "Mine. But you need not concern yourself; I shall not neglect your affairs."

"I am sure you will not, but do I understand that you intend to oversee Miss Thorpe's affairs yourself?"

He shook his head. "No, they are not so complex that she cannot quite easily oversee them herself if she is shown the way."

"And are you the man who is to show her the way?"

"Perhaps," Alfred said.

"You seem to be going to a great deal of trouble for a lady you have so recently met."

The sharp, blue eyes that Alfred turned upon Laurence were rather amused. "So, my dear fellow, are you."

"Touché," Laurence said, taking his reins in one hand and reaching into his pocket with the other. "Did you discover from Miss Thorpe the precise date of Mr Tremlow's murder?"

"Indeed. The fifteenth of August 1812."

Laurence glanced at the sheet in his hand and replaced it. "Interesting."

"Is it?" Alfred said. "Are you going to enlighten me as to the contents of that letter and why you are suddenly so interested in Mr Tremlow's death?"

"Presently, dear fellow," Laurence said, putting the paper away. "You must first allow me to complete my business in Lynn."

"Very well," Alfred said, his tone resigned. "You may be interested to know that I have in my possession clippings from the newspapers which mentioned his death and the circumstances surrounding it. Mrs Tremlow kept every one. It seems a rather macabre thing to do; they are quite graphic in their descriptions, but perhaps it is a sign of her devotion to her husband."

Laurence considered this, remembering something Miss Louisa Thorpe had said to him when he had needed to borrow one of Mr Tremlow's coats. *You are in luck, sir. My sister left his room very much as it was, and I have not yet decided what to do with his things. I thought her suggestion that I burn them so very wasteful, you see.*

This did not suggest to him any great devotion to her spouse but on the contrary that she had harboured great bitterness towards him. "Did you find any correspondence from Mr Rythorne to Mrs Tremlow that preceded her husband's death?"

Alfred frowned. "No, none. What is in your mind?"

"Nothing, a fleeting and not entirely welcome thought, but I feel sure I must be mistaken."

CHAPTER 15

W hen the door closed behind the departing visitors, Cassandra and Louisa sat for a few moments lost in their own thoughts. Cassandra's were apparently not entirely happy, for a faint frown marked her brow, but she soon pushed them away and said with rather forced cheer, "Well, Louisa? Did you discover anything interesting in the study?"

"Oh yes," Louisa said, with a rather misty smile. "I discovered the persuasiveness of a pair of clear, blue eyes."

Cassandra laughed. "You have fallen in love with a handsome face, after all."

"No," Louisa said consideringly, "there is much more to Mr Westerby than a pleasing countenance, and I am not in love, but I certainly like him."

Cassandra smiled indulgently. "And you have discovered this within half an hour?"

"It is the second half an hour I have spent in his

company. How long did it take you to know you liked Lord Carteret?"

Cassandra considered this but offered no other answer than a rueful smile. "And what, pray, did Mr Westerby persuade you to do? Should I have insisted Emma go with you, after all?"

"Of course not," Louisa said on a sigh. "Mr Westerby was all business, so efficient, and quite, quite ruthless."

Something in Louisa's tone indicated that she particularly admired this last quality.

"In what way was he ruthless?"

"He bade me write him two letters to Mr Rythorne; one stating that I wished him to answer all Mr Westerby's questions concerning my affairs, and the other terminating his employment if he was not satisfied with the answers."

"That is indeed ruthless and perhaps a little premature. It would be better if he gave you time to find a new agent first."

"Mr Westerby considers that my affairs are simple enough that should the need arise, I may manage them myself," Louisa said with studied insouciance.

"But you have admitted that you know nothing of business," Cassandra pointed out. "I would help you, of course—"

"You are very kind," Louisa said firmly, "but if Mr Rythorne does not answer Mr Westerby's queries in a satisfactory manner, which I think is the most likely outcome of his interview considering all the faults that you immediately perceived in his management, then he will show me himself what needs to be done."

"I see. Then I immediately withdraw my offer."

"Thank you," Louisa said, a twinkle in her eyes. "I believe that would be best."

"I begin to think it is you who are ruthless, my dear. Which reminds me, there is something I must discuss with you. Grace, not having your subtlety, has kissed Mr Cooper this very morning and persuaded him to propose to her. He is to go to Mr Blinksop to ask permission for her hand."

"She is very happy," Emma interpolated. "And is going to embroider handkerchiefs for you all to remember her by."

"At least I will feel no hesitation in using them," Cassandra said dryly.

That sent Emma into whoops of laughter which made both ladies smile.

"I should have noticed something, of course," Cassandra said ruefully.

"But then, you have been a little distracted of late," Louisa murmured.

"Louisa!" Cassandra said in accusing tones. "Do you tell me that you knew what was in the wind but neither told me nor dropped a word in Grace's ear?"

"I only noticed that she had discovered a hitherto unsuspected predilection for fresh air," that lady said innocently.

"What if he had taken advantage of her?" Cassandra protested.

"I would have been vastly surprised. Have you not noticed that Mr Cooper's disposition is shy? He is the gentlest of giants. Besides, he did not," Louisa said, unrepentant. "It appears to have been Grace who did that."

"Perhaps so, but I have told her that she is not to

arrange any more clandestine meetings until we know Mr Blinksop's feelings in the matter."

"Cassandra, my love," Louisa said, "I begin to think Lord Carteret has exercised a very good influence upon you. Never have I known you to be so concerned with convention."

"Someone in this house needs to be," she said acidly, rising to her feet. "Now, I must change my dress before our next visitors arrive."

"But what will you tell Grace?" Louisa murmured.

Cassandra picked up a cup from the table beside her and smeared a few dregs of cold tea carefully onto the orange ribbon. "There."

It appeared that no suspicious stranger trailed the Westerby barouche, for Lady Malmsy and Mrs Pellow duly arrived that afternoon, again bringing Phoebe with them. Miss Reynolds did not accompany them. Phoebe immediately went to Emma and sat beside her and began to write upon her slate.

Seeing her daughter happily diverted, Mrs Pellow said, "Poor Miss Reynolds is laid down upon her bed with the headache. I am not at all sure she should not see the doctor; they seem to be occurring more and more frequently."

Lady Malmsy gave a dry laugh. "It is quite remarkable how they generally coincide with my brother's absence but miraculously disappear when he returns home. The girl is becoming quite tiresome."

"I am sure it is not surprising that she has developed a tendre for Laurie," her sister said gently. "His manners must generally please. But I think she begins to understand that her feelings are not returned. She looked most disappointed when he did not join us in the drawing room after dinner last night but instead suggested the gentlemen play billiards."

Cassandra was relieved that Laurence had no particular fondness for Miss Reynolds; she felt sure they would not suit. She had very little to say for herself, and Cassandra could only imagine that a man of Laurence's intelligence would soon grow weary of her, especially if she took to her bed every time she was disappointed.

"I think petulant would be the more accurate epithet," Lady Malmsy said. "I did not blame Laurie for not joining us; Kitty's heart is worn upon her sleeve... no, she certainly hangs upon his sleeve, but I begin to think her heart has nothing to do with it. Either way, he is not the man to raise false hopes in her breast."

"Or any lady's breast," Mrs Pellow said on a sigh. "It is always so difficult to know what he is thinking."

Cassandra could not help but agree. He had looked at her in a most disturbing manner on the bridge and she had felt her pulses quicken in the oddest of ways, but then he had turned away from her abruptly and almost curtly informed her that he must go. Had she unwittingly done something to displease him? She could not think what it might be.

"Miss Fenton? Are you well? You seem quite distracted. We can always come back another day if you do not feel quite the thing."

Cassandra looked up quickly and stilled the hands that appeared to be busy pleating the muslin of her gown.

"I am quite well, I thank you, Lady Malmsy——"

"Oh, do call me Anne and my sister Cecy," she

said. "We are all friends now, and I always think that one is more at ease and natural when one is on first name terms."

"Very well, Anne. I was just thinking about how best to proceed. On reflection, I think it will be best if I take you up to the summerhouse first whilst Louisa entertains Cecy."

"Certainly," she said, rising to her feet. "May I hope to see the outcome of your afternoon's work or are you like Laurie and cannot bear to have anyone see the results of your travails until you are quite finished?"

"I am afraid I am," she said. "But I hope to have the miniatures completed before you leave Westerby."

"Very well," she said. "Lead on."

Cassandra discovered that Anne could be quite as subtle as her brother when she chose and found herself deflecting a host of seemingly innocuous questions interposed between general chit-chat that were designed to reveal her thoughts on Laurence. She answered in a bland fashion that more than once brought a gleam of irritation into Anne's eyes. But perhaps she was not as successful as she had hoped, for when Anne finally rose from her chair and Cassandra led her into the garden, she was more direct. "Laurence is often reserved, Cassandra, but his feelings, once engaged, run deep. You have a great deal of presence, my dear, far too much for such a modest establishment as this, pleasant as it is."

Cecy was not so subtle, but neither was she as probing. "I think it is you we have to thank for Laurie picking up his brush again, Cassandra. He has disappeared several times in the last few days although heaven knows where to, for when I sent one of the footmen to find him, he could not discover him in the house or the garden. When I asked him what he had been doing, he admitted that he had been working on his painting of the lake. We have much to thank you for; you have done him a great deal of good. He is more... I was about to say jolly but that would be wildly inappropriate – I should rather say humorous or relaxed – than I have known him since he was a boy. I really do feel we are very much in your debt."

"Nonsense," Cassandra replied, thinking he had not seemed very relaxed that morning. "If he seems more congenial, then I am sure it is because he is enjoying the company of his family."

"Oh yes, that too," Cecy agreed. "But there is a difference in him, only I cannot explain it very well."

After the visitors took their leave, Cassandra returned to the summerhouse determined to begin work at once on her first miniature. She drew a mahogany box with brass handles towards her. It had three slender drawers and a baize covered lid that could be locked at an angle creating an easel. She opened a drawer, removed a rectangular sliver of ivory and attached it with pins to the baize, but rather than pick up her brush, she sat staring rather blankly at the rudimentary portraits of the sisters she had completed.

Their words had affected her more than she had cared to show. It appeared that they would approve a match between herself and their brother, but they had said nothing about suspecting Laurence of having any great regard for her. Anne had said that his feelings once engaged ran deep, but she had not said that

Cassandra had engaged them. Perhaps she was suggesting that she should make a push to do so.

This thought unsettled her. Laurence was a man of contradictions and subtleties; he did not command, he suggested or gently persuaded but he got his way; he could be serious one moment and teasing the next or vice versa; he was generally gentlemanly but at other times provoking, and he certainly did *not* wear his heart upon his sleeve. In short, it was difficult to know quite where one stood with him.

There was a bond of friendship between them; she had felt it from their very first meeting, and there were times when she thought she saw a glow in his eyes that suggested warmer feelings towards her, but it was always so fleeting she could not be sure, and his subsequent words or actions spoke against it. And perhaps it was just as well, for she was uncertain of her own heart.

She no longer felt that his chivalrous instinct to protect would annoy her. He had thrown his mantle of protection over her from the start, and it had only been when she had carried on her journey without him that she had realised quite how comforting it had been. She may have been irked by the caution he had suggested she adopt for the next few days, but it was the curtailment of her freedom she resented rather than him. And that was the nub of the matter. She was used to making her own decisions, of doing what she pleased, but if she married, she would belong to her husband and no longer be a person in her own right.

She knew that she would not be able to ride roughshod over Laurence; she sensed the steel beneath his soft-spoken ways, and that was a point in his favour. She would never be able to respect a man she could so easily best. Neither would he try to dominate her in so obvious a way as her cousin had done. She did not believe he would try to dominate her at all, yet only this morning on the common, her eyes had fallen beneath the stern expression in his, the dismay at displeasing him forcing an admission of her impetuosity from her. It occurred to her that she might just as easily lose herself trying to please another as she might by giving in to the demands of a tyrant.

Or was such compromise natural when one fell in love? That thought startled Cassandra. She was intrigued by Laurence, she enjoyed his company, and when he had pulled her to him on the marsh to prevent her falling, she had felt breathless, and her heart had quickened its beat making her feel light-headed. It had happened again today when he had lifted her from her horse and on the bridge when he had looked at her with a strange light in his eyes. Was this love?

Cassandra suddenly envied Grace. *I know what I want is all.* Louisa also seemed to know it, or at least was prepared to explore the possibility that she might know it. Her friend had spurned the offer of a man she knew she could not like, preferring to earn her own living, but if she found the man she could love, Cassandra knew she would give up the independence her rise in fortunes had granted her without regret. But Louisa had a romantic streak that Cassandra lacked.

There were, however, more practical matters to consider. Anne had given her food for thought as she had meant to. She had said that Cassandra had too much presence for such a modest establishment as Tremlow House, thereby implying that Westerby would suit her better. Cassandra was not the woman to be tempted into marriage by a fine house, but she had to acknowledge that she was used to managing a much larger establishment than the one in which she presently resided. It had not been many days after her arrival that she had known that she still wished for her own establishment, but the sort of house she could afford to run would not be much different in size from Tremlow House and how would she spend her days?

Louisa did not need her and so she might feel no qualms in moving to a place that was a little livelier, Bath or Brighton perhaps. But she would have no acquaintance there and it was not the life that she was used to. It might be amusing for a while, but she would not like to live in any town all year round. Her resources would not support two establishments, however. Laurence could, if he wished to, offer her a life that would not only open vistas new but allow her a home in the country, and one that was near to her dearest friend.

Cassandra felt the knot in her stomach unwind a little. It was too soon to speak of love, but it was not perhaps too soon to explore the possibility of love and all that that might mean. Her eyes regained their focus and she picked up her brush and began to paint.

CHAPTER 16

L aurence and Alfred went their separate ways in Lynn, arranging to meet at the Duke's Head Inn before making their way home. Laurence arrived first and sat at a writing desk in the corner of the private parlour he had hired. The newspaper clippings lay with the letter he had glanced at earlier. He referred to them occasionally and made a list of points on the paper in front of him.

He glanced up and laid down his pen when the door opened, and his cousin entered the room.

"Why the frown, Alfred? Has your inclination to play the white knight backfired?"

The merest hint of a smile touched Mr Westerby's lips. He spoke three words, each one crisply enunciated, "Pot, kettle, black."

Laurence looked pained and said in a tone of gentle reproof, "I begin to think my father was right to keep you in your place, cousin. You show a shocking lack of respect. I am not just your employer remember, but also the head of the family."

"How pleased Anne would be to hear you reminding me," Alfred said, grinning.

"You relieve my mind," Laurence said, "to please Anne must of course be an object with me."

Alfred strolled over to a table that had been set with a cold luncheon and poured two glasses of wine from the decanter that was set there. "Whether it is or not, I have a feeling that you are going to please her, if not quite in the way she originally intended."

Laurence picked up the papers in front of him and came unhurriedly across the room, laying them on the table and pulling out a chair. "We have wandered some way from the point. How did you find Mr Rythorne?"

"I did not find him at all," Alfred said, accepting that his cousin would not be drawn. He reached for a slice of chicken and placed it upon a thick wedge of bread. "He has gone out of town to some race meeting or other and will not be back until tomorrow. I did discover a few interesting tidbits of information, however."

He bit into the bread and chewed hastily, but when he opened his mouth to speak again, Laurence said, "Finish your repast before you tell me any more, I beg. I do not wish your no doubt fascinating insights into the character of Mr Rythorne to be constantly interrupted by your need to masticate."

Alfred reached for a baked egg. "A man must eat, old fellow. I have walked this town from end to end and am extremely hungry."

Laurence did not appear to have any great appetite but toyed absently with a slice of ham and veal pie, his mind wandering to another inn some distance away at which he had shared a meal with a very different companion who had also treated him without any marked degree of respect.

"Care to share what has put that smile upon your face?" Alfred said, at last pushing away his plate.

"Oh, just a memory," Laurence said.

"It looked to be a very agreeable one."

"It was," Laurence confirmed. "But we must, unfortunately, return to less agreeable matters. What have you discovered of Mr Rythorne?"

"The man who bought Mr Tremlow's business is not overly enamoured with him. He does not accuse him of any injudicious business practices but the client list he inherited with the business proved to be not so lucrative as the books suggested. Several of them did not continue to buy in such bulk as they had before. He furnished me with the names of two gentlemen who had once used Mr Rythorne's services whom I duly visited. They both described him as a quiet and respectful gentleman who was diligent in his work. About six years ago, however, he became known for gambling. He was never accused of using his client's money to do so, there is no suggestion of that, and he always paid his debts, but when he began to play for high stakes, he began to lose business. No sensible man would wish to put his interests in the hands of someone who could not manage his own, after all. As far as I can discover, Miss Thorpe is now his only client." He took a sip of his drink. "Which begs the question; how does he afford to maintain the neat little house he resides in or meet his obligations?"

"Did he lease land for any of these gentlemen?" Laurence asked.

"Yes, a farm near Great Massingham for which he secured a good rent. I cannot see, therefore, why he should have done such a poor deal on Willow Tree Farm."

"You must apply a little imagination, dear fellow," Laurence said, "tempered with a dose of logic."

"I suppose," Alfred said thoughtfully, "that Mr Moore might have some hold over him."

"I think it far more likely that it is the other way around," Laurence said softly. "I begin to think Mr Rythorne a very dangerous man."

Alfred had a great deal of respect for his cousin's intelligence and regarded him intently. "Go on."

Laurence pushed back his chair, crossed his legs, and drummed his fingers gently against the table. "Let us consider first the bare facts as we know them. Mr Rythorne, a once very respectable gentleman, has become addicted to the vice of gambling and appears to have an unknown source of income that funds his lifestyle. He has purposefully kept the rent on Willow Tree Farm at a ridiculously low level but has, however, in all other ways acted in a responsible manner in his management of Miss Thorpe's affairs."

"You think the farm is the key," Alfred said.

"I do," Laurence agreed. "Let us now add another fact. The man who bought Mr Tremlow's wine and spirits business found that several of the clients on his list were buying less than they had before. Why do you think that might be the case?"

Alfred sat forwards and laid his arms on the table, his eyes alight with interest. "Because they could purchase some of their wine and brandy elsewhere for a lesser price."

"Very good," murmured Laurence. "Especially if the seller of these goods had not paid duty at any port."

"Smuggling," Alfred said softly. "You think that Mr Rythorne is bringing in goods illegally and selling them on to some of Mr Tremlow's clients to fund his habit, using the farm as a place to store the goods before moving them on to the London markets."

"I think it is a possibility, certainly. Do not forget a river runs through the farm and down to the sea at Heacham, which makes it an extremely conveniently placed property for such activity."

Alfred said slowly, "Mr Tremlow first leased the farm at the current rent, so it would follow that he too was smuggling goods, using his legitimate business to cover his activities." He frowned. "Yet I could find no evidence in Miss Thorpe's accounts of any large sum of money that was unaccounted for."

"That does not mean that it does not exist, however. Mr Tremlow, I imagine, had an agreement with some of his clients that they would purchase a certain amount of his goods at the standard price and then he would provide them with a certain amount of the smuggled goods at a reduced price. It is only sensible that these customers should still purchase from his successor; they must maintain a respectable front, after all, but no such agreement would exist between them and the new owner and so they might purchase less at the standard price, and more from Mr Rythorne at the lesser."

Alfred ran a hand through his hair and gave a low whistle. "It is all conjecture, and yet it makes a deal of sense. If it is true that he has taken over the smuggling operation, he will not be pleased by the prospect of losing Miss Thorpe's business and so control of the farm. Is that why you say he is dangerous? Will such an action put her in peril?"

"I do not know that; he can have nothing to gain by harming her. However, if we are correct in our assumptions, Mr Tremlow's death was certainly to his advantage for he could take over the venture."

He reached out a hand and tossed the letter to Alfred. "You may finally satisfy your curiosity. I found this interesting missive in the pocket of the coat I borrowed from Mr Tremlow's wardrobe."

August 15th, 1812

My dear sir,

I regret disturbing you when I know that it is your intention to spend another few days at Tremlow House with your good wife, but a most pressing matter of business has come to my attention which is why I have sent these tidings express. As it is of a most delicate nature, I shall not commit the details of this matter to paper but request that you make all haste back to town.

You may be sure that as always, I am acting in your best interests when I urge you not to delay. As I doubt you will receive my letter much before four o'clock, I shall not expect you before eight and will have a late supper prepared for you at my house.

Respectfully

Mr James Rythorne

Alfred looked up from the letter. "This was sent the same day that Mr Tremlow was murdered."

A glimmer of appreciation brightened Laurence's eyes. "I knew there was a reason I put up with you."

Alfred leant forwards and grasped the pile of newspaper cuttings. He spent a few minutes scanning them.

217

"None of these mention that Mr Tremlow was either on his way to or from his agent's house when the murder occurred."

"Which circumstance persuaded me to visit Mr Hadley who is mentioned as the coroner involved in the case," Laurence said, taking a sip of wine. "Fortunately, he keeps meticulous records. Mr Rythorne was asked if he knew of anyone who might harbour a grudge against Mr Tremlow, to which he replied that he did not, and he was asked when he had last seen him, to which he replied some days before, but he never mentioned that he had summoned him back to town."

"Did you show Mr Hadley the letter?" Alfred asked.

"I did," Laurence confirmed. "He agreed that the omission was peculiar but was of the opinion that neither it nor the contents of the letter would be enough to justify casting suspicion on a gentleman who had nothing to gain from his death."

"You did not mention your suspicions of the smuggling operation to him then?"

"No, for as you have pointed out, it is all conjecture." Laurence began to turn his wine glass by the stem, a thoughtful expression on his face. "Has it occurred to you, Alfred, that if my suspicions prove correct and Mr Tremlow's and Mr Rythorne's activities come to light, they will cause a public sensation? Miss Thorpe will be left in the uncomfortable position of having her brother-in-law exposed as a smuggler, her agent also, as well as perhaps a murderer, and she may herself be scrutinised for allowing the farm to be used for such purposes by her agent."

"Good God!" Alfred exclaimed, frowning. "They could not prove such a thing of course, and her wish for us to investigate why Mr Rythorne was hiring the farm at so low a rate must clear her of suspicion, but it would be perfectly awful for her."

"It would," said Laurence. "Rumours have never needed truth to sustain them and they would abound, if not in the immediate vicinity certainly further afield, fuelled by the circumstance of her living at a place that was once a hotbed of smugglers."

"Yes," Alfred said, "and every time she came into Lynn to do some shopping, people would stare and whisper. Cousin, what must we do?"

Before Laurence could answer, a waiter came in. He made no move to clear the table but rather hovered by it, his gaze fixed on Laurence.

"Is it true, sir, that you are offering five guineas for any information regarding a man going by the name of Chubb?"

Alfred glanced quickly at his cousin. "You have been busy."

Laurence did not respond but regarded the waiter, an arrested expression in his cool eyes. "To be precise, I have offered five guineas for accurate information that can be proven."

"Oh, it can be proven all right," the waiter said. "He's enjoying a tankard of ale downstairs as we speak. Several tankards, in fact."

"Describe him to me."

"He's a fat cove with a greasy brown beaver and a yella waistkit."

Laurence produced a money pouch and poured five golden coins into his palm. "If you will inform Mr

Chubb that a gentleman wishes to speak with him and bring him to this parlour, these will most certainly be yours."

"Right away, sir," the waiter said, "but I warn you, he looks to be out of sorts."

"Do not concern yourself," Laurence said.

The waiter rushed from the room with no more ado.

"Be so good, Alfred, as to stand by the door, will you?" He passed the coins over. "Give these to the waiter and then close the door behind our guest."

Laurence stretched his fingers as he spoke, curled them into a fist and stretched them again.

Alfred raised an eyebrow. "Do you intend to mill him down?"

"I fear that will not be necessary," Laurence said regretfully.

Alfred leant his shoulder against the wall by the door, crossed his arms, and grinned. "Am I to block his retreat if he tries to bolt?"

"I doubt he will," Laurence said. "But we will leave nothing to chance."

The door duly opened, and Mr Chubb stepped into the room. He may have imbibed several tankards of ale, but he was a large man, and his eyes had a sharp, calculating look that did not suggest inebriation. He took a few steps into the room, his eyes narrowing as he saw who had summoned him. The click of the door shutting made him glance over his shoulder. Observing Alfred's wide-legged stance and hard stare he said quickly, "There's no need for any trouble."

He turned back to Laurence and removed his hat.

"In fact, I'm delighted to see you, sir. You might say your being here today is providential, for I had been thinking I might pay you a visit."

"Ah," Laurence said softly. "Do I take it that a certain gentleman has dispensed with your services?"

Mr Chubb snorted. "I wouldn't rightly call him a gentleman."

"I assume then, he did not appreciate you bungling your attempted abduction of Miss Fenton?"

"He did not," Mr Chubb muttered darkly. "I never thought to hear such language from a gentleman's lips; anyone might have thought he was born in a back slum. But I can't say as I'm sorry Miss Fenton escaped me, for it went against the grain with me to do it, and I wouldn't have taken such a job if Sir Francis had not assured me that she was a danger both to herself and the public at large, and when she ran away in that crazy fashion, knowing as how I had a gun, I could well believe it. But after Sir Francis sent me away with a flea in my ear, and what's more, not even giving me the money to cover my expenses but saying as I would see nothing until I could at least furnish him with her whereabouts, I discovered I might have been mistaken in the lady."

Laurence raised his wine glass to his lips. "And how, my good man, did you do that?"

"I stopped for some sustenance at an inn nearby Darley Manor and heard a deal of talk. It had somehow got round that Miss Fenton had upped and left her home in a hasty manner, and the consensus seemed to be that Sir Francis had driven her off as he had a host of servants from the house. They said as how it was an outrage and that she was as fine a lady as you would find anywhere, that her disposition was as handsome as her looks, and that for all she would not suffer fools, she was more than fair with honest folk." He shook his head and said ruefully, "I don't like to be made a gull of, sir, and it occurred to me that you had more of the gentleman in your little finger than Sir Francis will ever possess. I had already discovered that you had been seen turning onto the Deeping road with a lady in your curricle—"

"How did you discover it?" Laurence asked with an air of polite interest.

"Your crest is on your curricle, sir, and is well known in Stamford. A stablehand from The George happened to be returning from an assignation with a young lady and he spotted you just before you turned off."

"I did not see him," Laurence said frowning.

"Perhaps you was distracted, my lord," Mr Chubb suggested. "I am sure it is not to be wondered at. However it was, you were seen and the stablehand happened to come in my way and so I found you out."

"And then you discovered I had been to The Red Lion and left without Miss Fenton, and I imagine, that someone other than yourself had been enquiring for her in Market Deeping."

Mr Chubb looked pleased that someone, at last, appreciated his dogged but often successful methods. "I knew you was as bright a spark as has been my pleasure to encounter," he said, his manner becoming more jovial by the moment. "You needn't think I bear a grudge for you slumguzzling me at our first encounter, for haven't I already said you were a gentleman? As such, it is only natural that you would offer your assistance to a lady."

"I must applaud your forbearance," Laurence said with a gentle irony that was quite lost on his guest.

"And so you might," Mr Chubb said. "There are many others who would not see the matter in the same light, but I venture to suggest that I have a larger vision than the average man."

"And does this vision include you offering me your services?"

Mr Chubb smiled. "You're a knowing one, sir, and it is a pleasure to do business with a man of your intelligence."

"Are we doing business?"

"Come now, sir," Mr Chubb said in a benevolent tone, "let us not beat around the bush. I will admit that my initial thought was that as you was the last person to have seen Miss Fenton, you might be the one to lead me to her. But then I realised that you would hardly have been trying to discover her in Market Deeping if you knew where she had gone. I am sure it is only natural that you should wish to know, and it will be my pleasure to furnish you with that information."

"You have it then?" Laurence said, his voice deceptively soft.

"You may be sure I do."

Laurence was out of his chair in a flash and before Mr Chubb quite knew what was happening, he found his throat taken in a firm grasp by a surprisingly strong hand, its fingers exerting just enough pressure to leave him in no doubt that the gentleman before him could strangle him if he so wished.

"Have you furnished Sir Francis with this information?"

Mr Chubb's eyes bulged and his voice came out as no more than a squeak. "No, I swear it, and I can prove it too."

Laurence's fingers relaxed their grip a fraction. "How?"

"A letter," Mr Chubb gasped. "In the pocket of my coat."

Laurence raised his eyes. "Alfred."

His cousin came forwards and removed both a pistol and a letter from Mr Chubb's pocket. Laurence released his victim. "Give me the letter, Alfred, and use that pistol if our guest makes any attempt to move from his chair."

Mr Chubb coughed a little and rubbed at his throat. "There was no need for you to go adoing that, sir," he said reproachfully.

"We shall see."

Laurence unfolded the letter and perused its contents.

September 5th, 1815

Mr Chubb,

I must ask you to cease your investigation forthwith. I have no longer any interest in Miss Fenton's whereabouts and have enclosed twenty pounds in recognition of the time and expense you have been put to.

Sir Francis Fenton

Laurence looked up. "How did he know to find you here?"

"I wrote to inform him that I had discovered the lady's whereabouts and said that I would remain in Lynn until I had his instructions. I wasn't foolish enough to give him the information before I'd seen any payment."

The tight line of Laurence's lips softened. It appeared that Mr Penwith's knowledge of Cassandra's situation had indeed influenced her cousin. "Alfred, you may return Mr Chubb's pistol to him, and I beg you will step downstairs and request that some brandy is sent up to alleviate any discomfort I may have caused our friend."

Alfred was not put to the trouble as, after a timid knock on the door, a serving girl entered. She came forwards, a large tray in her hands, and loaded it with plates, promising to bring the brandy immediately.

Laurence passed the letter to his cousin. "It seems Sir Francis has had a change of heart."

Alfred quickly read the lines. "This is good news indeed."

"You think so, do you?" Mr Chubb said bitterly. "I was promised two hundred pounds and twenty will hardly cover the cost of my travel, board and lodging."

Laurence's lips twisted into a smile. "I am sure it must have been a blow coming, as it did, just when you had apparently discovered Miss Fenton's whereabouts."

The wily look was back in Mr Chubb's eyes. "There's no apparently about it, milord, and that knowledge will be yours once we have discussed terms."

"Before we do discuss terms," Laurence said, seemingly resigned to this eventuality, "perhaps you will enlighten me as to how you came to unearth your quarry."

The maid came again into the room, placed the brandy along with three glasses on the table and withdrew. Mr Chubb took advantage of the interlude to consider this request, his brow creased in concentration as if weighing up the chances that his information might be used against him, but seemingly concluded that it was not a likely chance as a rather self-satisfied smile crossed his round face.

"I am nothing if not thorough," he said. "It came to me that Miss Fenton, who on reflection I must admit to be a most resourceful lady, an attribute I must admire, I assure you, well, that she might have had the wit not to use her true name in Market Deeping."

"Very astute of you," Laurence approved.

Mr Chubb reached for the decanter, filled his glass, and took a sip of his brandy. "Thank you, milord, I was thought to be so, I admit, before an unfortunate misunderstanding ended my career at Bow Street."

Laurence's lips twitched; now that he knew that Cassandra stood in no danger from her cousin, he was developing a reluctant admiration for the rogue who sat opposite him. "I am sure it was their loss."

"You speak like a sensible man again, sir, and I am relieved, very much relieved. I returned to Market Deeping and instead described her appearance, for I must say, that never have I seen another female with such striking features. Those eyebrows are particularly extraordinary, and I felt sure anyone who had once seen her would not easily forget her." He looked complacent. "And so it proved. I discovered that a lady of her description going by the name of Miss Tatler, had indeed hired a chaise, and once I had a name, the rest was not so difficult to discover." He put down his glass and rubbed his hands together. "Now, sir, shall we talk terms?"

"You, sir, are a rogue and an opportunist," Laurence said, but without heat. "If you had not received that letter from Sir Francis Fenton, I feel sure you would have milked us both for the benefit of receiving the same information."

"And so I might," Mr Chubb admitted without a blush. "Times have been hard recently, and I could do with the money. I assure you it pains me to be placed in such a position, but any qualms I might have felt would have been ameliorated by the knowledge that once under your eye, Miss Fenton must have been safe. This is your county, after all, and your influence cannot, I am sure, be negligible."

"In that, at least, you are correct," Laurence said, his voice steely. "And I would ask you to remember it. I am about to enter into a bargain with you, Mr Chubb, but not the one you thought to make."

A look of confusion came into Mr Chubb's eyes. "Have I mistaken your interest in the lady?"

"Oh no," Laurence said gently, "but I already know of Miss Fenton's direction and so in that matter, you cannot be of use to me."

Mr Chubb looked crestfallen as well he might. He had spent a great deal of time and effort in discovering the lady's whereabouts, but he had not grudged it when he had thought he might be paid handsomely for his troubles by two gentlemen. Sir Francis' rough dealings with him had left him with no qualms about this course of action, but now it seemed his efforts had all been for nought. Added to this, the gentleman presently in front of him would be, he felt, a dangerous man to cross. Sir Francis may have raged at him and called him all manner of things that had been hard to bear, but he had never wrapped his fingers around his throat and threatened to strangle him.

"Go on," he said cautiously.

"Before I do," Laurence said, "you should understand that you will work for me and only me. In return you will receive your two hundred pounds and two hundred more, but only if I am completely satisfied that you have been both diligent and honest."

Alfred looked askance at his relative. "You cannot mean to trust this rogue?"

Laurence gave an understanding smile. "I appreciate your qualms, my dear chap, but I feel sure we can rely on Mr Chubb in this instance."

Mr Chubb's eyes had brightened at the prospect of such largesse, but he could not imagine what service he could do the viscount that would deserve such payment. Although he had always bent the law to suit his purpose, he had never put himself at risk of the hangman's noose, and four hundred pounds would be of no use to him if he were to find himself dangling at the end of a rope.

"I am sure I am happy to be of service to your lordship," he said, "but I won't do murder."

Laurence laughed. "I am happy to know it. You will not be called upon to do so, and you will be pleased to know that in this instance you *will* be acting in the public interest."

"Then I'm yours to command," Mr Chubb said, grinning. "Would it be possible to have a little on account?"

Laurence threw him his purse. "Use some of that to purchase a change of raiment. I wish you to present a respectable but unremarkable appearance; the yellow waistcoat and hat must go. Visit the shop in High Street which sells used clothes and deck yourself out as a respectable farmer."

CHAPTER 17

Cassandra sat forwards, magnifying glass in one hand, brush in the other and with delicate strokes added a touch of colour to the skin tones of Cecy's cheeks. She had been working on the portrait for several hours and was aware of a growing ache at the base of her neck. When the ache turned to a burning sensation, she laid down the glass and brush and straightened her shoulders, absently rubbing at the offending spot. Cecy's interesting condition had given her skin a luminosity that had been challenging to capture, but as she sat back from her work, Cassandra realised she had finally done so.

After cleaning her brushes and palette, she slipped them into one of the drawers of her box and went back to the house to change for dinner. Emma passed her in the hall. She did not speak but patted her arm and smiled up at her in a conspiratorial fashion. Cassandra watched her disappear through the door to the kitchen and wondered what precisely she was supposed to be conspiring in.

The door to the parlour was slightly ajar and she paused, one foot on the bottom stair as she heard a man's voice coming from the room followed swiftly by Louisa's laugh. Intrigued, she turned and went to the door, gently pushing it open just as Louisa said in tones of mock severity, "I will have you know, sir, that I am a vicar's daughter and have been brought up by the strictest precepts, and there is nothing improper in inviting a weary traveller to dine with three spinsters. It is, after all, the Christian thing to do."

As they were not seated, it seemed that the visitor must only just have arrived. Mr Westerby looked down at Louisa, an amused smile playing about his lips. "And I, ma'am, am a vicar's son, and take leave to tell you that if I had a shilling for every time I have heard someone twist the Lord's teachings to suit themselves, I would be a rich man."

"Mr Westerby!" Louisa said as if shocked. "I had not thought you so conceited. Of what possible advantage could it be to me to ask you to dine?"

"I am not at all conceited," he said, unabashed. "I know, alas, that it is the information I possess that you desire rather than the pleasure of my company."

"You are mistaken, sir," she said, a dimple peeping in her cheek, "I desire both things."

A soft but audible gasp escaped Cassandra. She knew her friend to be amusing, witty, and intelligent. She had cause to know that she could be subtly persuasive. But never had she seen her flirt so boldly. She had never seen her flirt at all. Her position, together with their restricted society at Darley would have made it impossible, of course.

Louisa showed no embarrassment at being thus

discovered. "You are in good time, my love. Join your voice with mine and persuade Mr Westerby to stay for dinner."

"Yes, of course," she said. "But, sir, what can have happened? I thought there was to be no contact between us for some days."

"You need no longer worry about Mr Chubb, my dear," Louisa said. "Mr Westerby came to tell us so but as yet I know no more."

"Then you must certainly stay to dine," Cassandra said with firmness. "I sense that you have had an interesting day and insist that your tale should not be rushed."

"My sentiments exactly," Louisa concurred.

"But I am in all my dirt," Alfred protested.

"That does not signify," Louisa assured him. "We shall not change for dinner either and so you may be comfortable."

Cassandra thought he looked far from comfortable and so, it appeared did Louisa, for she said, "I begin to suspect, Mr Westerby, that you are reluctant to share your news."

"I am," he admitted. "I fear you will be shocked."

Cassandra chuckled. "Louisa is never shocked by anything, sir, and I am rarely, so you need fear nothing."

Emma just then came into the room. "I have told Mrs Larkin there will be one more for dinner, and William is laying another place."

That seemed to settle matters and Alfred capitulated. "It is true that what I have to say may take some time, so I will stay rather than force you to sit down to a burnt offering."

The ladies at Tremlow House did not require their footman to wait upon them, and so once William had brought the various dishes to the table, he retired to the kitchen for his own dinner. As soon as the door closed behind him, Cassandra said, "Now, Mr Westerby, explain to me, if you please, why I must no longer fear Mr Chubb."

Alfred's brow creased thoughtfully as if he were considering how much to tell them. "We discovered him in Lynn and——"

"That will not do," Louisa protested. "You must not be so sparing of the facts. How did you discover him?"

Alfred eyed her in tolerant amusement. "I knew that if I stayed to dine you would have everything out of me, ma'am."

Louisa reached out a hand and laid it on his arm, laughter tinged with a hint of ruefulness in her eyes. "Please, do not withhold anything from us, Mr Westerby. It is so rare that anything remotely exciting happens here and I promise not to interrupt again if you will but tell us everything from the beginning."

He was not proof against such an appeal and did so. Emma frowned and watched him carefully, and seeing this, he slowed his speech a little. Cassandra and Louisa frequently exchanged glances. A touch of colour tinged the former's cheeks as he mentioned the five-guinea bribe, how Laurence had taken Mr Chubb by the throat, and again when he mentioned the huge sum he meant to pay him for his services. Louisa blanched a little when this last point was mentioned.

Alfred had been carefully watching all the ladies' reactions to his tale, but particularly Louisa's, fully prepared to edit it if they looked distressed in any way. He laughed softly. "What a remarkable woman you are, Miss Louisa. My cousin offering so large a sum for Mr Chubb's services has shocked you, I see, a sentiment I fully understand; I was shocked myself. But when I mentioned our suspicions that Mr Rythorne might have murdered your brother-in-law and was using your farm to hide and distribute smuggled goods, you looked surprised, intrigued, and even excited—"

"I was, but only because something occurred to me which I will explain when you have finished your tale, and you cannot know it, but Mr Tremlow was quite beastly to my sister and if he treated any others of his acquaintance in such a way, I am sure I cannot be shocked that someone murdered him."

Alfred shook his head. "And you a vicar's daughter."

"I did not say that I wished for someone to murder him," she pointed out. "And if I looked shocked just now, it was because it is a great deal of money that I had hoped to use for quite another purpose. Not that I begrudge it, I assure you."

"But you will not be asked to pay it," Alfred said frowning.

"But I must," Louisa said. "Lord Carteret is acting on my behalf."

"Yes, but not yours alone. As an important landowner and peer, he would be expected to take an interest in this affair. It is to the benefit of no one that we return to the days of lawlessness which used to be found in these parts. The violent gangs that led the smuggling trade then were not afraid of anyone. I do not say that this operation is of that ilk; for it to have gone so long unnoticed or unreported suggests that it is not, but it must be stamped out, nevertheless."

"Oh, I see," Louisa said, much relieved.

"But what is Mr Chubb to do for such a sum?" Cassandra asked.

"Little more than to keep his ears and eyes open," Alfred said. "Surveillance work you might call it." He glanced at Louisa. "Now, what was it that occurred to you, ma'am?"

She leant forwards eagerly. "Mr Rythorne came here not long after Mr Tremlow's death to offer his condolences and assure my sister that he would continue to look after her affairs. He spent some time in the study going through my brother-in-law's papers, putting them in order and it occurred to me when you mentioned the letter, that he might have been searching for it and perhaps removing any evidence of Mr Tremlow's more secret affairs."

"Very likely. We must be grateful that he did not also look through the pockets of his coats."

"I expect he could not think of a reasonable excuse to do so," Louisa said thoughtfully. "But I think that tomorrow I shall begin to pack away his things. I have decided to take them to that shop in Lynn High Street that sells good quality used clothes, but you may be sure I shall check the pockets of every one of his coats very carefully. Perhaps I shall find something else that may be of use."

"An excellent idea," Alfred said absently, his eyes looking inward as if turning over a memory. "Tell me, did your sister seem on good terms with Mr Rythorne?"

Louisa considered this for a moment. "I was with her, of course, when he came; she would not be left alone for a moment at first and I am sure it was not surprising after receiving such a shock. She had no reason to love her husband, but the nature of his murder upset her greatly. She said very little to Mr Rythorne and from that time on they only communicated by letter. But it was I who answered for her as she went into a deep decline within weeks. What is in your mind, Mr Westerby?"

"I am merely trying to discover as much about the man as is possible," he said lightly.

Louisa looked at him intently. "I am not sure why, but I think that is not quite true, though I shan't press you to tell me anything you do not wish to."

"Thank you," he said. "My cousin considers it would be best if we do not just yet inform your agent that he is under suspicion in any way, and so if he communicates with you over any matter, please reply as usual."

The ladies retired to the drawing room when their guest departed.

"Well, my dear," Cassandra said. "It seems you are embroiled in an adventure that quite eclipses my own."

Louisa did not immediately reply, her gaze far away. When she looked up, her usually clear green eyes were clouded. "He is worried about my sister," she said. "Or, to be more precise, what my sister might have done."

Emma suddenly said, "No! She would not have done it!"

Cassandra looked confused. "Done what?"

Louisa exchanged a look with her sister and when Emma nodded said, "Clara, no matter how difficult her marriage had been, would not collude with Mr Rythorne in the murder of her husband. However unpleasant Clara could be, she would not have committed so unforgivable a sin."

Cassandra sucked in a breath. "Good gracious! Why would he think so?"

"Because Mr Rythorne was not the only one who might benefit by Mr Tremlow's death. Clara was made miserable by him, but I can assure you that she would rather have lived a martyr than to have been a part of such a deed."

"I am sure you are right," Cassandra said, "but now you have explained it, I can see why the thought might have crossed Mr Westerby's mind."

"Oh, yes," Louisa said, "and I do not blame him for it in the least." She still looked concerned, however.

"Put the thought out of your mind," Cassandra advised. "You can disabuse Mr Westerby of his notion when you next see him."

"Yes, of course," Louisa said. "But you know how once a notion is put into your head, however ridiculous, you suddenly begin to see things that might support it."

"Such as?"

Louisa reached for her teacup and sat swirling the dregs for some moments. "Well, she insisted on acquiring both the local and London newspapers to discover any mention of the murder, and she cut out all the clippings and kept them. She did not do so because she rejoiced in his death, however, they almost seemed to make her afraid. And when night fell, she would jump at the slightest noise even if it was only the whistling of the wind."

"You think her conscience might have been troubling her?" Cassandra said.

"I don't know; that or perhaps she suspected Mr Rythorne might have had a hand in it." She suddenly sat bolt upright. "Oh! I have just remembered something she said to me. I paid little heed to it at the time for towards the end she became quite delirious. But on reflection, I do not think she was delirious at that moment; her eyes cleared, and she grasped my hand and said, 'If they come, pretend not to notice. Go to your room and stay there.' Of course, I asked her who she meant, but she merely shook her head and slipped away into a troubled sleep."

Cassandra's eyes widened as a thought occurred to her. "Louisa! Mr Westerby said that the river made the farm a convenient place to unload smuggled goods, but this house would also be an extremely convenient place so near to the sea as it is and standing alone some way from the village. Perhaps at one time, smuggled goods were brought here too and stored in the cellar until it was convenient to move them on. Or they might have simply been unloaded here. The track that leads from the stables to the road would make it easy to get them away without having to go through the village at all. Perhaps Clara had been told to see and hear nothing. And after Mr Tremlow's death, she may have feared that the smugglers would still come."

"Poor Clara!," Louisa said. "She would not have liked anything of that nature going on under her nose, but I think that you are right, and that might explain why the servants left after his death. They must have been involved somehow, either directly or they were paid handsomely to be deaf and blind to it. They spoke the truth about the noises and lights on the marsh, but it was not that which drove them from here, it was the lack of opportunity to be any longer paid extra for their silence."

Emma rose to her feet and picked up a candle.

"Are you going to bed, dear?" Louisa asked.

Emma shook her head. "I'm going to look in the cellar."

Louisa laughed. "There is no rush. Wait until tomorrow, at least. It is time I did an inventory of what is there, I admit. I wished to do so when I first took over the household accounts soon after I came, but Clara was adamant that I should not. I thought it another of her distempered freaks and it did not seem important enough to go against her wishes." She smiled ruefully. "Besides, she mentioned rats and I must admit I have an irrational fear of the creatures. It is why I have put the task off these last three months. I cannot imagine that we will find anything very interesting because William has never mentioned anything out of the way."

"Could he not have done it for you?" Cassandra asked.

"Unfortunately not," Louisa said, smiling wryly. "I did not hire him for his brains, but because he was strong, fit and trustworthy. Mrs Larkin suggested him; he is her nephew, you see. She told me at the outset that he was a moonling, but that he was perfectly capable of carrying messages, running errands, and, as a clincher, that he could drive the carriage if need be; also that he was very handy with his fives, which, I believe, means he can box. He cannot, however, read and can write little more than his name." She sighed. "And he is hopeless with numbers. I tried to teach him at first, but he would get the letters jumbled up and wrote his numbers backwards and I soon realised that I was embarrassing him rather than helping him."

"Then we will do the inventory together tomorrow," Cassandra said smiling. "I am not frightened of rats and will endeavour to protect you."

"No, you must work on your paintings if you are to have any chance of finishing them before Cecy and Anne leave Westerby. They will be very disappointed if they do not have the chance to see them. Besides, I have become shockingly lazy, and it will do me good." She turned to her sister. "Emma, will you help me pack away Mr Tremlow's things in the morning and then assist me to begin an inventory of the cellar in the afternoon?"

The next day's activities agreed, the ladies retired to bed.

CHAPTER 18

Mr Lapworth's estate lay some few miles outside Sedgeford. He had been one of the few acquaintances of Laurence's father that he had liked. He had not been a close intimate of the late viscount but his position as a landowner and magistrate had secured him an invitation to dine at Westerby on several occasions. Unlike his father, Laurence was not in the habit of giving large, formal dinner parties to impress the local gentry when he was in residence, although he generally paid at least a morning visit to some of them when he was at home.

He was glad that he had accepted Mr Lapworth's invitation; not only would it alleviate the necessity of having to parry Miss Reynold's increasingly obvious and he had to admit, ill-bred ploys to obtain and keep his attention, but he would need his assistance in the coming days if the plan that had been gradually forming in his mind was to be carried out successfully.

Mr Lapworth was a congenial host, more interested in his comfort these days than dealing with the assaults and petty larcenies that made up much of his work and had pronounced when last Laurence had visited him, that he had a mind to retire and allow a younger and more energetic man to take on the role. Laurence could only be grateful that he had not yet done so, for he did not wish the matter in hand to be taken on by a young man so set on proving his worth that he might overlook the delicacies of the case. Such a one would use a sledgehammer to crack a nut rather than chiselling away at the most important aspects of the matter. Mr Lapworth might not appreciate being forced out of his lethargy, but Laurence felt sure he could be brought to understand it was in his interests to do things his way.

A rather rotund man, with thinning grey hair and apple red cheeks, Mr Lapworth heartily welcomed his visitor.

"My dear Carteret, how happy I am to see you. Come in and sit by the fire, for I have no doubt you are feeling a little chilled. Or are you devilish sharp set? Dinner can be produced in a trice if you are, but as I have had a little something to keep me going, I am quite happy to partake of a glass or two of wine with you first."

"How do you do, sir?" Laurence said, shaking his hand and taking a chair set a little back from the blazing fire that raged in the hearth. "A glass would be most welcome."

"Quite right, quite right," Mr Lapworth said. "I never think one should eat immediately after exercise, you know, and if you have been to Lynn and back today and then ridden over from Westerby, you have had a great deal of it."

Once the butler had given Laurence a glass and refilled his master's, he discreetly withdrew. Laurence had not intended to broach the topic of smuggling until after dinner, but Mr Lapworth unexpectedly provided him with an opening.

"It's as fine a Burgundy as ever I tasted," he said with some satisfaction. "It's been hard to come by in recent times, but would you believe I found it on the riverbank when I went down for a spot of fishing?" He chuckled. "It took me back, I can tell you. There was a time when most of us landowners would find an offering somewhere on our land every now and then, but that was before the business got out of hand. Of course, when it came to excise men and dragoons getting murdered and little or no effort to be at all discreet on the part of the smugglers, we could not look the other way anymore."

Any remaining doubts that Laurence might have had fled. The river that meandered through Mr Lapworth's land was the same one that divided Willow Tree Farm.

"But you feel you may look the other way again now, sir?" he said.

"Well, there's been no trouble that I've heard of, after all. As long as it's only done on a small scale and all is kept peaceable, I say live and let live."

Laurence frowned and Mr Lapworth began to look uneasy.

"Come now, my boy, you must know as well as I that there are dozens of places where goods could be brought in along this coast. It would take an army of customs officers to keep them all under their eye, and thankfully they don't need to anymore in the general way. It would be a waste of money and resources for a few ships that have been lucky enough to escape the customs cutters. Not many do, you know. Only a few days ago a ship was caught just off Hunstanton. The days of the lawless smuggling gangs are long gone, but, unfortunately, the lot of the common labourer has improved hardly at all. Indeed, it is worse, for so much land has been enclosed that they are lucky if they have anywhere but the saltmarsh or a scrap of common to graze their animals. Would you have them hanged merely because they wish to feed their families?"

"No, sir, I would not. It is why I have brought my problem to you. I knew I might rely on your good sense."

Mr Lapworth relaxed back into his chair and took a sip of the fine wine. "And so you may, so you may. You have had an offering left for you too, eh? If you take my advice, you'll enjoy it and look the other way."

"I might do so," Laurence said gently, "if it were a case of a few local men banding together to pay for the odd anker of Geneva and a few casks of wine to sell on for a profit. But I do not believe it. If any of our people are involved, I believe it to be in a minor role to collect the goods and bring them inland a little way before the hardier land smugglers take over and deliver the contraband to its destination. I doubt very much it is quite as small an operation as you believe, nor do I think you were left an offering to look the other way. I think it far more likely that the wine you found had dropped into the water and been washed

up by the river. A careless error that confirms all my
suspicions. On top of this, a possible murder is
involved."

Mr Lapworth choked on his wine, his already rosy
complexion turning quite purple. "Carteret!" he spluttered. "I am due to retire from my office in precisely
three weeks and you come to disturb all my peace."

"Do not worry, sir. I have it all in hand. All you
need do is be ready to summon the militia when I give
you the nod and capture the culprits red-handed. You
may retire with honours, and I see no need for you to
mention that they have been audaciously running the
goods along the river which flows through your land."

The magistrate groaned. "You had better tell me
all of it. It is enough to put a man off his dinner."

～

Cassandra lay awake for some time, her mind
wandering vaguely over all they had discovered that
evening. Laurence's worries about her safety had been
unfounded, after all. But he had worried. He had also
wrapped his hands around Mr Chubb's throat in
order to discover if he had told her cousin of her
whereabouts. She caught her bottom lip in her teeth
and felt an undeniable rush of pleasure at this. Not
because he had offered the man violence, but because
it spoke of the strength of his feelings. He might not
be the man to spout flowery nonsense as had Mr
Rutherford, her only other admirer, but his actions
spoke for him.

They also spoke of the strength of his character.
Although Mr Westerby had said that as a peer and a

landowner it was only natural that his cousin take an interest in any unlawful acts being committed in the locality, they had not happened on Laurence's lands. He might just as easily have informed the customs men of his suspicions, or the magistrate he was dining with this evening, but his hiring Mr Chubb suggested he was not content to do that. She was glad of it, for although she had not mentioned anything to Louisa, it had occurred to her that any official investigation might prove rather awkward for her.

When she, at last, fell asleep, her dreams were a hotchpotch of vivid images, blending reality and fantasy in an indiscriminate manner. Her cousin had apparently given up any hope of binding her to his will, and yet he grappled with a shadowy figure she somehow knew to be Mr Rythorne on the bridge below the house, whilst smugglers' lights moved stealthily across the marsh. A sheen of sweat covered her body as, still locked in her dream, she awoke to the acrid smell of smoke, the curtains about her bed aflame. Before she could react to these alarming circumstances Laurence was there, scooping her up in his arms and rushing from the room. The landing was filled with smoke. Her eyes stung with it, but she blinked away the tears from her watering eyes and saw Mr Westerby carrying Louisa from another room. William came down from the attic and Louisa begged him to get her sister, but Emma was nowhere to be found. They rushed down the stairs and saw Emma holding open the door that led to the cellar. Their escape was blocked by hundreds of rats pouring down the hallway and out of the front door.

Cassandra awoke with a start and found herself

drenched. She sat up, wiping at the water that streamed down her face and dripped off her chin. Grace stood by the bed, a jug in her hand.

"You seemed to be having a nightmare, Miss Cassandra," she said apologetically. "I couldn't wake you and I heard once of a lady who died of shock in her sleep when she was having an unpleasant dream."

"Grace," she spluttered, "I could just as easily have died from the shock of such a rude awakening!"

"I'm sorry, miss," she said. "I did it for the best."

Cassandra threw back her covers and left the sodden bed. She suddenly laughed. "Never mind. I wished to be up early today anyway; I have a great deal to do." She glanced at the window and saw the sky lightening to a dull grey. It was not yet light enough to paint. "My riding habit, if you please, you absurd child."

"I'm not a child," Grace said, suddenly very much upon her dignity. "I am about to be married, remember?"

"I am counting on it," Cassandra said. "Let us hope Mr Cooper has made a favourable impression upon your uncle."

Cassandra led Plackett along the track from the stables and turned onto the Brancaster road intending to head for the common again, but she paused by a smaller byway that was signposted as leading to the village of Summerfield some four miles distant. She knew that Willow Tree Farm was only a mile or two further on and on impulse, turned down the lane. Plackett obediently followed but when they passed through the village without stopping, he brought his horse alongside hers.

"Care to tell me where we're headed, Miss Cassandra?"

She said casually, "Miss Louisa owns a farm near here. There is a river that runs through it where we can allow the horses to drink before we turn back."

"If we'd stopped in the village back yonder, we might all have enjoyed a drink," he said dryly. "Lord Carteret asked me to keep a close eye on you, miss, and I'd be a mite more comfortable if we were a bit closer to home. I don't know this country and I wouldn't know which way to take you if there were to be trouble."

"Plackett, don't be such an old woman!" Cassandra said, her words softened with a smile. "Mr Chubb is working for Lord Carteret now and not my cousin. We have nothing to fear."

"We'll see," he said, unconvinced, adding as he cast a jaundiced eye up at the heavens, "if nothing else, we're likely to get a soaking."

That was true, the sky was low and leaden, casting a dim half-light over the countryside.

"We had our fair share of rain in Derbyshire, I believe," she said lightly.

A scowl was her only answer. In other circumstances, she might have tried to cajole the groom out of his bad humour but it suited her purpose for him to remain as sullen and silent as the sky above. If Plackett knew that they were visiting a possible smugglers' haunt he would be more unhappy still.

She had not meant to come but the impulse had been irresistible. She wished to cast her eyes over the farm again with its new purpose in mind. She would stay on this side of the river so that the willows would shield her from view of the house. Where could be the harm, after all? The smugglers would hardly carry out their work in daylight, what little there was of it. It seemed rather tame somehow to be painting in the summerhouse with such skulduggery afoot. She would just satisfy her curiosity and then return home.

Knowing she could not easily access the meadow by the sunken lane, she followed the road towards Docking hoping to find a gate. She did not find one and was just contemplating leaping the hedge when she saw a hat moving in the long grass. Its wearer was crouching low and moving towards them.

Feeling a little alarmed, she was about to suggest they move on when the hat stopped, and the head it was perched upon popped up. Her eyes met Mr Chubb's. The head disappeared again and came on faster. Plackett had not noticed, his eyes scanning the farm, a frown set between his eyes.

"This is the strangest set up I've—"

He broke off as the hedge began to rustle and shake. Both horses sidled and the groom reached under his leg and pulled a pistol from a holster he had hidden there.

"Either that's the largest fox I've ever seen or we're about to have company, ma'am. And if you can tell me what honest man needs to go pushing through hedges, I'd be interested to hear your explanation."

"You won't need that," she said quickly. "It is Mr Chubb."

Her eyes dropped to the hedge and a section at the bottom popped out onto the road revealing a hole. Mr Chubb squeezed through it, pushed the twigs and leaves back into place and got to his feet, brushing at the detritus that liberally coated his trousers and coat. Straightening, he lifted his hat to her, for all the world as if he usually crawled through hedges to greet his acquaintances.

"Good day to you, Miss Fenton. I hope there are no hard feelings over our little misunderstanding."

"None at all," she said promptly. "If my cousin had not sent you after me, I might never have realised just quite how despicable he could be."

"Just so, ma'am, just so," he said. "The more I think of it, the more I realise just what a service I have done you, Miss Fenton. Not only have you learned what a cad your relative is, but without my pursuit, you may never have met a certain titled gentleman of our acquaintance."

Cassandra laughed, amused at his audacity, but Plackett growled low in his throat. Mr Chubb glanced at the groom, his eyes widening as he saw the pistol trained on him. "Now, sir, don't you be doing anything hasty."

"Oh, put it away," Cassandra said. "Did I not tell you he is working for Lord Carteret?"

The groom reluctantly complied, his eyes still fixed on Mr Chubb. "I can't see what you might be doing for him that you needs be crawling through hedges."

Mr Chubb tapped his nose. "That's between me and his lordship."

"I am glad you have learned such discretion," Cassandra said. "I might have wished you had learned it earlier so that you might not have left my name and no doubt a lot of speculation at various posting houses between Derbyshire and Norfolk."

"I regret it," Mr Chubb said, shaking his head. "I

never was so taken in by anyone as I was by Sir Francis. Now, I must be on my way. I have some information his lordship will wish to know of."

The threatened rain suddenly burst from the sky above them, a rumble of thunder swiftly following it. Mr Chubb looked gloomy.

"I'll be drowned before I get halfway."

Cassandra pulled the hood of her woollen cloak over her shallow bonnet. "Mr Chubb, I feel for you. I already know of Lord Carteret's investigation and assume you have discovered something pertaining to the practice of smuggling. Might I suggest you allow me to pass on your information? I will reach Westerby much sooner than you, after all. You may then retire to the nearest inn and wait the storm out."

Mr Chubb's eyes brightened. "Well, if you already know it all, I can't see the harm. Besides, I've an inkling where I can find out something more important still. Tell his lordship that hidden in all that overgrown grass, there must be upwards of forty barrels. I've an idea they'll not be there long as I overheard some talk last night about some ship being seized not far from here and mutterings that the customs men would be haunting the place before long. I hope to be able to send more information on that head later. If you go through Docking and onto the Stanhoe road, you'll see a pair of gates that give onto a track through some woods, and you'll be on Westerby land. Follow the track until you come to a carriageway; it will take you to the stables. That's how his lordship described it to me at any rate."

With that, he rushed off down the lane as fast as a man of his size was able. Cassandra urged her horse into a trot and then a canter. She was aware of the same thrill of exhilaration she had felt when escaping Mr Chubb's clutches. How narrow her horizons had been before she left Derbyshire.

Mr Chubb may not have been an accomplished rider or particularly stealthy, but he was observant, had excellent hearing, and could hold his drink better than most. He returned to the inn at Heacham where the night before he had not only overheard, whilst ostensibly drunk and snoring in a corner, mutterings about customs men but also one gentleman comment on how it was lucky that they had already done their part in the business. It was that information that had taken him to the farm that morning.

He felt certain there would be more talk today, and that the bad weather would ensure that several villagers would be enjoying a tankard of ale rather than working in the fields. When he entered the inn, apparently much out of temper, a mien not hard to assume after having tramped some six miles in lashing rain, not to mention the thunder and lightning which had accompanied some of it, he was reassured rather than dismayed when the room fell silent.

"I take it your business did not prosper," the landlord said, not unsympathetically.

"It did not," Mr Chubb said, shaking his head. "No doubt it's my own fault; I only stopped here to wet my whistle, not dreaming you'd have some of the finest brandy as has ever been my pleasure to sample. Well, I admit I got carried away, the result being, that

Mr Westerby informed me with no roundaboutation that a man who was late for such an important meeting would no doubt be late in paying his rent. He said Mr King had been as fine a tenant as he could hope to find, and he would be replaced by no less a man, no matter how much he had to invest."

"Here," said the landlord, pushing a glass of brandy towards him. "This one's on the house as I am, in some way, responsible for your predicament."

Mr Chubb raised the glass. "You're a gentleman, sir."

He downed the fiery liquid, reached into his pocket, and carelessly threw some coins onto the bar. "But you'd best give me the bottle, for I'd my heart set on that farm."

He went to the same dark corner as the evening before, which the landlord's wife had tried to brighten with a flower arrangement, and proceeded to enjoy his brandy, although more than half of it went to nourish the flowers. No one was surprised when his head slumped on his chest, although they shook their heads at a respectable gentleman drinking such a quantity of hard liquor at so early an hour.

The hubbub of conversation resumed, and Mr Chubb learned that the cargo would be taken by way of an old drover's road that ran by Willow Tree Farm and for some twenty miles beyond. He also discovered that although the local gentlemen had always resented that they would only be paid to deliver the run goods to the farm and not reap the greater rewards for taking it on in stages to Lunnon, they were happy they did not have that task tonight. Many of them also voiced the thought that it might be time to call time on this source of additional income, only they did not know how to be out of it.

The entrance of two riding officers, demanding to see the landlord's cellars, not unnaturally emptied the taproom allowing Mr Chubb to depart in all the confusion.

Lord Carteret's instructions had been to pass on his information to Mr Lapworth, a magistrate whose residence was close to Sedgeford, and that that gentleman would send him on to Lynn with a message to deliver. He should then wait for him at the Duke's Head Inn where he should receive full payment for his services in due course.

Having received many a knock in his career, Mr Chubb could not quite believe that something would not happen to upset this plan, and it was not until he was bowling along in Mr Lapworth's private coach, that he allowed himself to smile at his good fortune. The coves at Heacham had given him something to mull over, and he began to think that it might be time to have a change of career himself. There was no doubt that the type of person who usually wished for his expertise, was not always as respectable as he could wish, and although a sense of self-preservation had prevented him doing anything that would take him to the gallows, he felt sure it was only a matter of time before he found himself either murdered or in Newgate. A neat little inn somewhere quiet would suit him nicely.

"If you're thinking Lord Carteret will thank you for this morning's work, you've got a surprise coming, I reckon," Plackett said, as they passed through the gate and entered the wood.

"Nonsense," Cassandra said blithely. "Why should he not thank me?"

"Because he won't be any happier than I am that you went to that farm knowing what it was likely used for."

"No," Cassandra admitted, "he probably will not be. I must hope the news I bring him makes up for it."

"I wouldn't wager any great sum on the chance," Plackett muttered darkly. "I've known you since you were a child, Miss Cassandra. You've always been fearless, and I must admit that when you took over after Sir Thomas became ill, you did a grand job. None of the servants or tenants could pull the wool over your eyes, and they soon learned not to try. I understand why you had to leave Darley; it's my belief Sir Francis is dicked in the nob, but you had no need to go to Miss Louisa's farm today. You knew what was likely going on and you put yourself in danger for nothing. It seems to me Lord Carteret knows what he is about, and what you thought you could do has me in a puzzle."

"Enough!" Cassandra suddenly snapped. "I didn't think I could do anything but merely wished to take a look. I cannot sit on my hands sewing, gardening, or painting forever. I am used to doing, Plackett, not sitting idle and allowing events to pass me by. It was I who first noticed that something was amiss at the farm and for all Lord Carteret has taken matters into his own hands, Louisa is my friend, and I will do anything that is in my power to help her out of this mess. I should not perhaps have gone to the farm, but at least I can carry Mr Chubb's message and so be of some use."

A rather grim smile twisted Plackett's lips. "You've always had more energy than is good for you, miss, and you've always put yourself out for others at your own expense. You're a good girl and I only hope you haven't shot yourself in the foot this time."

They left the shelter of the trees as he spoke, and cold rods of rain slashed down at them as they turned onto the carriageway. Cassandra kicked her heels against her horse's flanks and flew up it, sudden tears of frustration stinging her eyes. She knew her groom was probably right. Laurence would in all likelihood be furious with her. If he disapproved of her galloping across the common in case her mount stepped into a rabbit hole, she could not imagine what he would say to this morning's ride. She gritted her teeth and pushed the horse harder. So be it. She had acted according to her nature, and if Laurence did not want her for who she was then she was better off without him.

CHAPTER 19

L aurence had had a late night. Mr Lapworth had been so much upset by the revelations he had been presented with, that he had only managed to consume as much of his dinner as the average man. He had washed it down with several glasses of wine, although he had sent away the Burgundy as if offended by it and requested some Madeira be brought instead. Out of politeness, Laurence had been forced to drink far more than he usually did. He rarely drank overmuch, hating to feel that he might lose the control he had so carefully culti-vated over the years and make a fool of himself. He had not drunk enough for that, but by the time he had persuaded the magistrate to fall in with his plans, he had not been completely sober.

He was an early riser, but the wine combined with a late night had their effect. His slumber was only disturbed when his valet pulled back the curtains, although it was his discreet cough rather than the dim light that disturbed him. He opened bleary eyes and observed the lowering sky outside.

"It is a dull day," he murmured.

"Yes and no," replied the valet in an expressionless voice.

It was not like Salop to make ambiguous statements, and if he had been feeling more the thing, he would have enquired what he meant. But as he sat up, his head began to thud in a most unpleasant way, and any desire to speak at all deserted him. He briefly closed his eyes as a clap of thunder sounded overhead.

Salop thrust a tankard into his hand. "Drink this, my lord. It's only ale with a few spoonfuls of honey, but it will make you feel much better, I assure you."

Laurence put the tankard to his lips and discovering that it tasted quite pleasant, soon drank it. As the thud in his head receded, he smiled gently at his servant. "Thank you."

Salop removed the tankard from his hands and crossed the room to a low table. He returned with a tray which he set on Laurence's lap. He whisked a domed cover from it, very much in the style of a magician about to produce some marvel, revealing a plate of eggs and some toast.

"I know you do not eat breakfast in bed, as a rule, sir, but there is nothing like eggs to set a man to rights after he has overindulged."

Laurence meekly ate his breakfast and discovered that his valet was quite right. He smiled wryly. "Either you have a percipience I had not before noticed, Salop, or I fear I must have been in a worse state than I supposed last night."

The valet removed the tray, saying as he carried it

away, "You were no more than half sprung, my lord, and no one who didn't know you intimately would have been aware of it. But as it is a rare occurrence for you to be so affected, I thought it likely that you would suffer for it this morning."

He went to the washstand, picked up a ewer of water, and poured it into the basin. "The water's cold, my lord. Bathe your head in this and you'll find you have all your wits about you again."

This also proved to be true, and neither a bright streak of lightning nor the next boom of thunder had the power to disturb him. Laurence wandered over to the window, still towelling dry his hair. "It is an impressive storm."

He discarded the towel, pulled the shirt Salop passed to him over his head and reached for his breeches, suddenly remembering the valet's first words. "What did you mean when in response to my saying it was a dull day, you said yes and no?"

The valet cast an eye at the window. "When I said yes, I was referring to the weather, sir. It has livened up considerably since I made that statement, however, although I think the storm will pass soon enough."

Laurence finished buttoning his breeches and took the neckcloth offered him. "And the no?"

"Well, sir," the valet said, his voice at its blandest, "It is not every day that a lady comes calling at eight o'clock in the morning."

Laurence had turned to the mirror to arrange the neckcloth, but his fingers stilled, and his suddenly intent eyes sort out Salop's. "What lady?"

"Miss Fenton, sir. She arrived some half an hour ago. She was enjoying a morning ride when the rain began to fall, and as she happened to be close by thought to seek shelter at Westerby. No doubt it was the inclement weather that caused her to come flying up the east ride at what Peter footman called a spanking pace." Seeing that the sudden twitch of his master's fingers had produced an unfortunate crease in his neckcloth, the valet held out another. "It is why I woke you, sir," he said, his face expressionless. "I thought you would wish to know."

Laurence tore off his ruined neckcloth and threw it aside.

"There's no need to hurry, sir. Lady Malmsy has taken Miss Fenton to her bedchamber to dry off a little. I believe her cloak kept most of the rain off, but she was a trifle damp."

Laurence muttered an oath under his breath, but he took the neckcloth and arranged it calmly enough.

As the valet assisted him into his coat, he said softly, "Thank you for helping me to clear my head, Salop."

The valet tugged a little at the tails of his coat, picked up the unused neckcloths and began to stow them in a drawer. "There's no need for thanks, sir. It is my job to make you as comfortable as I'm able."

Although Laurence was feeling far from amused, a crooked smile twisted his lips as he left the room. He had thought the valet he had hired a little over a year ago quite disinterested in anything but the appearance he presented and that had suited him very well. But it appeared he was mistaken, and Salop noticed far more than he had given him credit for. He had certainly discerned his interest in Cassandra. At the thought of her, his lips thinned.

He could think of only one reason she might have come by way of the east ride; her morning's exercise must have taken her near, if not directly to, Willow Tree Farm. Laurence was known for having a cool head, but he was aware of a rare blaze of sudden anger.

As he approached the head of the stairs, he saw Cassandra and his sister coming in the opposite direction. He bowed with rigid formality. "Good morning, Anne, Miss Fenton." His eyes skimmed over her bluish-grey riding habit. The body appeared dry, but he could discern damp patches about the voluminous skirts. "It was most imprudent of you to come so far on such a day."

Cassandra raised her chin a little. "It was not raining when I set out, sir."

Anne looked from one to the other uncertainly, sensing the strange tension that stretched between them. "You must not scold, Laurence. I have already told Cassandra as much. I would have given her one of my dresses to wear had she not been so tall. She would have cut a ridiculous figure wearing a dress that barely reached beneath her knees, besides, it would have been most improper of her to do any such thing."

Laurence's eyes did not leave Cassandra's as he said in a cutting tone, "That Miss Fenton might be deterred by the first of your assertions I can well believe, but that she would be overly concerned with the second, I cannot allow."

Cassandra's eyes flashed and Anne gasped. "Laurence, it is not like you to be so rude. I must ask you to apologise to our guest."

He raised an eyebrow. "Do you think I owe you an apology, Miss Fenton?"

"I would not accept it if you offered me one," she snapped.

"Come now," Anne said, "I do not know what has caused this falling out, but I recommend we all go down to breakfast. Everything always seems better on a full stomach."

"I have already eaten," Laurence said, his gaze still riveted upon Cassandra.

Her eyes did not fall before his. "And I am not hungry."

"Then might I suggest you come with me to my study, ma'am? There is something I wish to say to you."

"Certainly, sir," she replied with cold dignity, "for I have a message to convey to you from a mutual acquaintance."

His eyes narrowed and took on the sheen of polished steel, but he merely turned and strode swiftly back down the landing towards his rooms, leaving Cassandra to follow and Anne to stare after them in astonishment.

They did not get as far as the study. As soon as the door of the parlour which led to it shut behind them, Laurence said curtly, "I assume the mutual acquaintance you spoke of was Mr Chubb?"

"You assume correctly, sir," Cassandra said.

"And that you met him somewhere in the vicinity of the farm?"

There was a challenge in her eyes as she said, "Again you are correct. I thought I might as well ride in that direction as any other. My meeting with Mr

Chubb was a coincidence, of course, but a fortuitous one as I was able to save him tramping all this way in the pouring rain to bring his news."

Her description of their meeting and delivery of Mr Chubb's information only fanned the flames of Laurence's wrath. "Do you expect me to thank you for saving a man, who is being very well paid, a few miles walk in the rain? I said you were reckless when we first met, Miss Fenton, but on that occasion, you had, at least, some excuse for your rash behaviour. What possessed you to go there when you knew of my suspicions?"

"Curiosity," she said. "I wished to look at the farm afresh with your suspicions in mind. I hardly think, sir, that I stood in any danger in broad daylight with my groom beside me."

"Not in any danger?" he bit out. "A recently run cargo of contraband is hidden in those meadows, most likely with someone watching over it until it can be moved. If you had discovered it and been seen, I do not think your groom would have been protection enough. Have you forgotten that we suspect Mr Rythorne of already having committed murder? He may well do so again to protect his interests."

She paled a little at that and although she protested, it was with less vehemence. "I did not know it was there. It was all conjecture; nothing had been proven. And I never would have considered that the barrels would have been left in the open. I would have thought they would be stowed in a barn or the house."

"As might any enthusiastic excise officer, ma'am. Your ignorance does not excuse a piece of the fool-hardiest meddling I have ever encountered. Not only did you put yourself in unnecessary danger, but you might have upset my plans also."

His scathing tones brought her chin up again. "No harm was done, and I kept out of view of the house, you may be certain."

He was not mollified in the least. "I am certain of nothing, Miss Fenton. I had thought that you had too much sense to follow such a course, but I was wrong. You are wilful, stubborn, and unpredictable. I have tried to protect you since the moment I met you and had begun to hope that I might earn the right to continue to do so as your husband, but it is an impossible task if you will not take any steps to protect yourself!"

Cassandra turned to the door, yanked it open and said in a low, trembling voice, "And I, sir, had begun to think that you would make a tolerable husband, but I see that I was mistaken. We can have no more to say to each other and I will bid you good morning."

Laurence stood for some minutes, rooted to the spot, feeling as if she had taken all the air from the room with her. Eventually, he walked as if in a trance to the window, pushed it up and sat on the window seat, taking long calming breaths. It had been many years since he had felt such an ungovernable rage, and it left him dazed. The storm outside had passed, and as the one inside him dissipated, he groaned. What had he done? His words had been true but never had he spoken to a woman in such a way. *Never have you cared for a woman in such a way.* As these words whispered in his mind, he heard the sound of hooves scattering gravel and, raising his head, saw Cassandra tearing down the drive, her cloak flying behind her, and her groom following in her wake.

The rain may have ceased, but hot, scalding tears raced down Cassandra's face. Damn her pride! Just when she knew she should have capitulated, not because Laurence's will was any stronger than her own, but because he had spoken the truth, she had uttered words that could not be unsaid, words that had ended any possibility of a union between herself and the man she had come to love. She could no longer be in any doubt, for with every yard her horse put between herself and Laurence, she felt her desolation grow.

If only he had spoken to her more gently, the result might have been different. But the scathing way he had raked her down had left little opportunity for apologies or admissions of her foolishness but goaded her into wild speech. And perhaps it was for the best; she was all the things he accused her of, and if these characteristics so disgusted him, there could be no more happiness in a marriage between them than if she had married her cousin.

The fault, she knew, lay with her. Her suspicions that she was not made to be a wife were confirmed. This thought only made her tears fall faster so that they almost choked her. Hardly able to see where she was going, and with her nose streaming in a most unladylike way, she was forced to pull up in the woods. She was grateful that Plackett remained some distance behind her as she wiped her face and blew her nose.

This prosaic action calmed her somewhat and she continued her journey at a more respectable pace, carefully picking her way between the water-filled ruts.

The rain began to fall again as they reached Tremlow House. Cassandra handed the reins of her horse to Plackett, who looked at her with some compassion and said roughly, "No doubt you've had a rare trimming down, miss, but don't take it too much to heart. What's said in anger is often regretted soon after. It'll all blow over, you mark my words."

Cassandra could not agree in this instance and only smiled rather wanly. Unable yet to face Louisa, she made her way to the summerhouse. Her friendship with Laurence might be at an end, but she would finish the commission he had given her to the best of her ability regardless. Perhaps when he looked at the miniatures of his sisters, he would think of her more kindly.

She put the finishing touches to her painting of Cecy and soon became absorbed in her portrait of Anne. In this way, she escaped the leaden feeling inside her for a few hours. Louisa came to her in the early afternoon, bringing with her a thin, leather-bound notebook and an air of excitement. It became somewhat muted when she looked closely at her friend. She put the notebook on a conveniently placed table and glanced at the sodden cloak that was thrown over one of the cane chairs by the window, a puddle of water beneath it.

"My dear," she said, "you have not changed out of your riding habit, and you look quite pale."

Cassandra laid down her brush and rose, putting

her hands to the base of her back and arching her spine to relieve her stiffness.

"I went a little further afield than I had intended when I took my ride and thought I had better not waste any more time. I only have a few days left if I am to complete the miniatures before Anne and Cecy leave Westerby."

Her voice cracked a little on the last word.

Louisa said soothingly, "You must have got caught in the rain and are probably a little chilled. Come in at once and change; the skirts of your riding habit are still damp. I will help you dress, and you can tell me what is troubling you."

By the time Louisa had helped her out of her riding habit and into a long-sleeved dress of jonquil muslin, Cassandra's tale had been told in a flat, expressionless voice that in no way hid her distress from her friend.

Louisa sat down on the edge of the bed, pulling Cassandra down beside her. She slipped an arm around her waist. "I am sure I am not surprised that you flew out at him, my dear. It was perhaps not very wise of you, but it was quite Lord Carteret's fault. He has known how to deal with you to a nicety until now. I do not think you should despair, however. His maladroit handling of the situation is most promising."

Despite herself, Cassandra laughed. "Oh, Louisa. You have allowed your romantic nature to get the better of you. He perceives almost as many faults in my character as Sir Francis did and he is right."

"But he is not Sir Francis," Louisa pointed out. "He does not, I am sure, wish to change your essential nature. He has fallen in love with you despite what you call your faults, and perhaps even because of them. It is easy to put negative connotations onto what in other circumstances might be considered positive attributes. For reckless, stubborn, and unpredictable, substitute brave, determined, and interesting."

"But he was so angry, Louisa, so disgusted—"

"Angry, most certainly," Louisa interrupted. "But if he is disgusted, I suspect it will only be with himself. He is a man who does not easily show his emotions, my love, and that he let his anger get the better of him is very revealing. It was driven by the knowledge that you may have put yourself in danger, not by his disgust of your character, and it reveals the depth of his feelings for you. Let things settle for a few days. I will be very much surprised if you do not receive some sort of apology."

"Perhaps I should send one to him," Cassandra said tentatively.

Louisa smiled knowingly. "It is much to your credit that the thought has crossed your mind, but if you will be guided by me, don't. Let him come to you, and when you have graciously accepted his apology, then you may freely give your own."

She stood and picked up the leather-bound note-book that she had brought with her.

"What is that?" Cassandra asked.

Louisa's eyes lit up, and she held it out. "Have a look and tell me what you think."

Cassandra opened the slim volume and saw that each page had the date at the top and was divided into five columns. The first listed the names of various wines and spirits, next to each item was the quantity, the price it was purchased at, the price it was sold at with some initials inscribed next to it, and finally, the profit.

A puzzled frown wrinkled Cassandra's brow. "It is one of Mr Tremlow's account books, but I cannot immediately see what has caught your interest, Louisa."

"Ah, but perhaps it might become more interesting when I tell you that I discovered it in a locked box at the back of Mr Tremlow's wardrobe. I could not find the key and so William had to break it open for me. What does that suggest to you?"

"That he did not wish for anyone but himself to know of it?"

"That is just what I thought, and possibly not even Mr Rythorne. I begin to think it is the account book as well as the incriminating letter he was looking for when he came here. Now, look at the dates, my love."

Cassandra glanced again at the book and turned several pages. "The entries are made every two months only."

"Precisely," Louisa said. "If that book had been in relation to his usual business, the entries would have been far more frequent and list who had bought what, I imagine, rather than just initials, and there would be no need to hide it away."

Cassandra looked again at the first page and then the last. "The first entry was made some eleven years ago, and the last a month before Mr Tremlow's death."

"They start," Louisa said momentously, "soon after this house was built."

Cassandra looked again at the book. "Louisa, when did Mr Tremlow purchase Willow Tree Farm?"

"In April 1806, two years later."

Cassandra thumbed forward a few pages. "The quantities being sold doubled soon afterwards. This house *was* being used to smuggle goods and once Mr Tremlow had established himself, he expanded his business."

"So it would appear," Louisa concurred. "I have not calculated in any precise fashion you understand, only done a quick estimation in my head, but over the eight years he must have made somewhere in the region of twenty thousand pounds, and yet I can find no evidence of such a sum. What, Cassandra, did he do with that money?"

Cassandra smiled. "I have no idea, but I suspect you are about to overcome your fear of rats."

Louisa laughed. "It would be very nice if it was stored in the cellar, but I think it a slim chance."

"Come, let us partake of a light luncheon before we explore," Cassandra said. "I have eaten nothing today and am famished."

"We?"

"I shall just satisfy myself that there are no chests of gold in the cellar, and then I shall continue with my painting."

Grace knocked tentatively on the door and then poked her head around it. "May I come in now, Miss Cassandra?"

"Yes, Grace. My riding habit is a trifle damp, find somewhere to hang it to dry, will you?"

"Certainly, miss. Is that why you were not feeling

quite well when you came in? Have you caught a chill?"

"No, I am perfectly well, but the gloomy weather put me quite out of temper."

Grace looked a little sheepish. "I'm not surprised, that's two soakings you've had in one day."

"The least said about that, the better," Cassandra said firmly.

"Two soakings?" Louisa said.

"Grace thought I was having a nightmare and threw a jug of water over me," she explained dryly.

"Oh dear," Louisa said, her voice not quite steady.

Grace suddenly grinned. "Well, you won't have to put up with me much longer, Miss Cassandra. William was late today fetching the post because of the rain, but he's just given me a letter from my uncle. He's only gone and fallen down the stairs and broken his leg. Luckily, Matthew, Mr Cooper that is, was still there, and he managed to carry him back up the stairs and put him to bed before sending the stable lad to fetch the doctor. The thing is, my uncle wants to keep Matthew with him until he can get about again." She held out a letter to Louisa. "He enclosed this with his letter. It's from Matthew."

Louisa quickly scanned the few lines. "Of course he may stay with your uncle."

Grace turned back to Cassandra. "I don't like to desert you on such short notice, but he suggests I take the stage from King's Lynn to Market Deeping as soon as is convenient. He says Matthew will make me a fine husband and the sooner the banns are read, the better. He is happy for us to live with him. May I go, ma'am?"

Cassandra smiled. "Of course, you may. I am sure Mrs Blinksop will be very happy to have your support. I shall put you on the stage myself."

"We shall all go," Louisa said. "I had intended to go into Lynn tomorrow to take all Mr Tremlow's things anyway."

CHAPTER 20

They had barely sat down to their luncheon when William brought Cassandra a letter. She opened it quickly, her hands not quite steady and her throat suddenly dry. A sharp pang of disappointment smote her when she recognised the hand as that of Mr Penwith. She laid it down for a moment unable to concentrate on the words which seemed to jump about on the page making her feel dizzy. She glanced up to see Louisa's questioning gaze upon her and shook her head.

"It is from Mr Penwith," she said, reaching for a bread roll.

She crumbled it between her fingers for a few moments and then again picked up the letter. This time the words obligingly stayed in their place, and she read it slowly, paraphrasing it for the benefit of Louisa and Emma.

"Mr Penwith is in Lynn at the Duke's Head Inn and hopes that I will visit him there at noon tomorrow. He says that as he is not alone, he feels that he cannot impose either on our hospitality or that of Lord Carteret. A part of the inn is given over to a bank called Massey & Co, which is run by Benjamin Massey and his wife Mary Massey. He thinks the bank trustworthy and recommends I bank with them if I decide to remain in this area. He will introduce me to Mrs Massey if I do so decide, however, he hopes very much that I might reconsider my future after I have been put in possession of the information he brings with him and have met his fellow travellers."

"How intriguing," Louisa said, "but I must admit I wish he had not been quite so sparing of the facts."

"As do I," Cassandra agreed. "He mentioned in his last letter something about having persuaded my grandfather to at least consider that I might not like Sir Francis, so perhaps some further provision was made for me in that event." She shrugged and put down the letter. "We will know soon enough."

William came into the room and announced that Mr Westerby had called.

"Oh," Louisa said, dabbing at her lips with her napkin, "I shall come directly."

She stood and picked up the notebook which she had brought with her into the dining room. "No, no," she said to her sister who had also risen. "Keep Cassandra company and finish your meal, my dear."

She found Mr Westerby standing by the fireplace, one booted foot on the fender and his arm resting on the mantelpiece. He was staring at the unlit logs and frowning slightly, but his brow cleared, and he straightened as he perceived her standing just inside the door. He bowed and smiled.

"Good afternoon, Miss Louisa. Judging by the

brightness of your eyes, I suspect you have news. Do I take it that you have found something interesting in Mr Tremlow's pockets?"

Louisa laughed and came forwards, brandishing the notebook. "Not in his pockets but in a locked box at the back of his wardrobe."

He took it from her and leafed through it. "It seems smuggling is a profitable business."

"Indeed," she agreed. "It is very distressing, of course, but if you look at the dates, it becomes clear that both Tremlow House and Willow Tree Farm have been used for the purpose. When I discovered it, I was thrilled to think that I had proven your suspicions, but then Cassandra informed me that Mr Chubb had beaten me to it, which quite cast me down."

He did not smile at her light-hearted words, rather his frown descended again. "Miss Louisa, you are not at all distressed, but perhaps you should be. If it were to become public knowledge that this house and the farm had been put to such use, it would not reflect well on you, your late sister, or her husband. And if it can be proved that Mr Tremlow was indeed murdered, further awkward questions might be asked."

"Please, sit down, Alfred," she said.

He looked surprised, but not unpleasantly so.

"Do you mind?"

"No," he said with a crooked smile.

"Good. It seems to me ridiculous to be so formal when we share so many secrets." She sobered for a moment. "I do not think that my sister colluding with Mr Rythorne to murder her husband is one of those secrets, however. I can assure you she was not capable of it. I do think she knew of the smuggling and was rather frightened by it. I also think she was ashamed as she never mentioned a word of it to me, apart from on one occasion when she was in a fever, and she told me to pretend not to hear if they came. As for it becoming public knowledge that this house was used for the purpose, I suspect we are not the only ones who know of it; in such a community as this, something must have been at least suspected."

"Perhaps," he acknowledged. "The country people are known for being close-lipped, and they have no love of the customs men. They have long memories and more than one of their own was likely hung or transported for such activity in times gone by, which brings me to the reason for my visit." He gave her a steady look and a charming smile. "Well, one of the reasons for my visit."

Louisa's eyes dropped for a moment and a slight blush crept into her cheeks. "I am not sure I perfectly understand you."

He sat forwards and reached out as if to take her hand, but the door opened before he could do so, and he let it drop. William came in, handing her a card. "There's a Mr Gill as wishes to see you, Miss Thorpe."

Louisa glanced at it and a tiny gasp escaped her. "A riding officer. How unexpected. Put Mr Gill in the back parlour please, William, and tell him I will be with him in a moment."

"That is what I came to warn you about," Alfred said. "A smuggler's vessel that was taken off Hunstanton is suspected of already having disposed of some of its cargo, and several riding officers have been sent out to search the places on record as having been involved in the trade in the past. As you know, Thornham was one of them. I did not want you to be in any way alarmed or think that you were under any suspicion if you received a caller."

He saw she was looking a little pale. "You have nothing to fear, Louisa. Let him search. I suspect he will wish to look in the cellar and then he will be on his way."

"I am sure you are right, but I do not know what, precisely, is in the cellar. My sister did not wish me to do an inventory when she was alive; perhaps she feared what I might find. Emma and I were to start it this afternoon."

"But surely your footman would know if there was anything unusual down there?"

"Yes, I am sure you are right," she agreed, rising to her feet. "Although as the wood is kept in a shed next to the stables, he rarely has need to go down there, and he is not overly inquisitive. Having no gentlemen in the house, we do not go through wine at any great rate." She smiled ruefully. "I don't know how it is, but although I have done nothing wrong, the presence of a riding officer in my house makes me feel quite guilty."

"You have no need, I assure you. Laurence has everything in hand. As soon as the barrels are moved, which I suspect will be this evening before the riding officers turn their attention to less obvious places, the word will be sent, and the land carriers intercepted once they are well away from your farm."

She stretched out a hand. "Would you come down with us? My sister said something about rats."

He took the hand and raised it to his lips. "It is my honour to serve you in any way I may."

They found Mr Gill looking out over the marsh at the back parlour window. He had a pleasant countenance and the bearing of a soldier. When Louisa mentioned this, he smiled.

"Yes, ma'am. I did serve but now the war is over, I've had to find a new profession and as the government is determined to strengthen the preventive forces to discourage smuggling taking hold again, I thought I'd try my hand at being a riding officer."

"I am pleased you have found employment."

Louisa thought it a shame that she could not put such a nice man in possession of information that must stand him in good stead in his new profession. Perhaps sensing this, Alfred strode forwards, shook his hand, and introduced himself as the cousin and steward of Lord Carteret, adding that the viscount was a good friend of both Miss Thorpe and Miss Fenton, who was presently residing with her.

The man looked impressed and a trifle embarrassed. It could not, after all, further his new career if he were to upset one of the largest landowners in the area by importuning his friends in this way. Louisa surmised that it must have been Alfred's intention to convey this idea to the riding officer and that he must have thought better of allowing him to search the cellar.

"What is it I can do for you, Mr Gill?" she asked.

"I'm sorry to incommode you, ma'am, I am sure, but I have my orders, and they are to search anywhere in this vicinity likely to make a convenient place to store smuggled goods."

She looked at him with polite interest. "I see. And you thought that perhaps a household consisting of three spinsters would be the very place."

He began to shuffle uneasily, and she smiled kindly at him. "Do not, I beg, feel any embarrassment. You are only doing your duty, after all."

Emma just then came into the room, carrying a plate of biscuits and a glass of wine.

"How thoughtful of you, my dear," Louisa said. "Please, sit down, Mr Gill."

He did so and Emma placed her offerings on the table beside him. He thanked her and when she did not respond but sat in the chair next to him and pulled out her knitting from the basket at her feet, Louisa said, "My sister is not being uncivil, Mr Gill, she is deaf and did not hear you. She generally sits in here in the afternoon with her knitting. She is making socks for the poor children of the parish."

Mr Gill looked at Emma, who was the picture of harmless domesticity, and his colour deepened.

"I, alas," Louisa continued, "am no great hand at knitting, but I do my poor best by helping now and then at the Sunday school in the village. Where would you like to look first? The cellar would be the most obvious spot or perhaps the summerhouse. I am sure my friend, Miss Fenton, will not mind us disturbing her. She is painting miniatures of Lord Carteret's sisters, Lady Malmsy and Mrs Pellow, who have been kind enough to visit us several times."

Mr Gill had heard enough and rose to his feet. "I am sorry to have disturbed you, Miss Thorpe. I was asked to look in likely places, and I am no longer of the opinion that this is one of them."

"I see you are a sensible man, Mr Gill," Alfred said. "I shall come with you to the stables and ask you a few questions, if I may?"

"By all means, sir," he said, crossing the room. "Although I haven't much time. I've to return to Lynn this afternoon. Another officer has been sent to replace me. Apparently, some trouble is brewing, and they want someone with my experience to bolster the ranks of the militia."

"Wait!" Emma suddenly said.

He turned and she came to him with the biscuits wrapped in a handkerchief and a kindly smile on her face. "You must keep up your strength."

Mr Gill bowed and went hastily from the room. Cassandra entered it a few moments later. "William told us of the visitor. You got rid of him, I see. I must admit I think it was wise. Did Emma do the trick? I thought you might do better without my presence."

"We all got rid of him," Louisa said. "Between the name dropping and our charitable works we put the poor man quite out of countenance, although it was Alfred who sowed the first seed of doubt."

"Alfred?" Cassandra said, with a knowing smile. "You have been busy. Now, shall we go and discover whether it was at all necessary to be rid of him?"

"My thoughts exactly," Alfred said, coming back into the room. "There's a veritable army of recruits that have been taken on. They're concentrating their search around Thornham, Heacham and Snettisham today, and will move their search inland tomorrow. We may have dissuaded Mr Gill, but there's no saying another, more zealous officer won't come after him."

Candles were gathered and they all made their

way down to the cellar, or more accurately cellars, as there were four different rooms. They were accessed from a door at the back of the hall. The first held row upon row of bottled wine and brandy, many covered in a fine layer of dust. The second, casks of wine, brandy and beer, a few shelves of empty bottles, and a long table.

"This might have raised some interest," Alfred said, "although it could all be easily explained as the former owner was a wine and spirit merchant. The quantity is not excessive."

"You do not think so?" Louisa said. "It would take me a lifetime to drink it all."

The third room had two doors set high in the wall and a chute. It was empty apart from a few wooden boxes set against the walls.

"Now this would have been a handy place to receive illicit goods," Alfred said. He suddenly laughed. The ladies were peering into the boxes. "What is it you hope to find?"

"Mr Tremlow's profits," Louisa said. "It would be fantastic if they *were* here for anyone to find, of course."

"Ah, we are treasure hunting," he said, smiling. "What would you do with the ill-gotten gains?"

Louisa got up from her knees and brushed the dust from her dress. "Build a school and provide a decent education so that the next generation need not be tempted into crime by poverty but enter into a decent trade."

"It seems fitting," Alfred said softly, a glow of admiration coming into his eyes.

"This door is locked," Cassandra said on a note of

rising excitement. "Do you have a key for it, Louisa?"

"I don't know. I shall go and fetch all that I have."

She returned presently with a large bunch of keys, but none of them fitted the lock.

"How very frustrating," she exclaimed.

"There is damp in this part of the cellar and the door has begun to rot," Alfred said, indicating a hole at the bottom corner of the door and worrying it with his boot. "Stand back, ladies, I would not like you to be injured by a stray splinter."

They dutifully withdrew to the other side of the room and Alfred raised his knee and gave the door a strong kick. The wood shuddered but did not give way. He stepped a few paces back and then ran at the door, barging it with his shoulder. It flew open and he stumbled through it.

Louisa rushed forwards. "Are you hurt?"

He smiled down at her, rubbing his maltreated joint. "Not at all."

In contrast to the order that prevailed in the other cellars, this one was full of a bewildering array of odds and ends, ranging from chests ranged one on top of the other, to chairs, bandboxes, portmanteaux, and even a huge, heavy wardrobe.

"You would think Mr Tremlow had moved here fifty years ago rather than merely eleven," Cassandra said dryly.

"And why on earth would he lock the door on such a jumble of valueless items?" Alfred said, perplexed.

"Treasure!" Emma said, laughing.

"Of course, there must be something of value here," Louisa said. "I shall go and fetch William to help us search or we will be here all day."

Between them, Alfred and William unstacked the chests, but nothing of note was found in any of them.

"What is that I can hear?" Alfred said as he opened the last one, only to find a pile of bed linen in the bottom. "It is faint, but it sounds like running water."

"It will be the culvert," Cassandra said. "It must run under the house at this point. Perhaps that is why this room is damper than all the others."

"Most likely," Alfred said, closing the box. "The tide is in and after the storm, the water is running high."

"I am sorry to have wasted your time," Louisa said, with a rueful smile.

"Not at all. It reminded me of when I was a boy and used to search the attics at home for treasure. I must go now, however."

"Of course."

Louisa began to pick her way around the various obstacles in her path. Alfred held out a hand to help her, but she screamed and jumped up onto one of the chests. A rat jumped up beside her and she launched herself at Alfred. He caught her to him, staggering slightly, and carried her swiftly from the room, the fine lines about his eyes deepening as he grinned.

"So, you really are frightened of rats," he murmured into her ear. "What a fortunate circumstance."

"It is not at all a fortunate circumstance," she gasped, her heartbeat behaving in a most erratic fashion.

"I assure you it is," he said softly, "and if we were not in company, I would prove it to you."

CHAPTER 21

W hen Cassandra disappeared from sight, Laurence slowly gathered himself. He set aside his emotions and considered her last words to him. *And I, sir, had begun to think that you would make a tolerable husband, but I see that I was mistaken. We can have no more to say to each other and I will bid you good morning.* He felt his spirits lighten a touch. He had wounded her pride, but perhaps his position was not irredeemable.

Although part of him wished to immediately go to her and beg her forgiveness, he was shrewd enough not to give in to such an impulse. He had witnessed before how quickly her moods could change, and it might well be that she was already regretting her words as much as he regretted his, but he could not rely on it. A few days reflection would do her no harm, by which time Miss Thorpe's affairs would have been brought, he hoped, to a satisfactory conclusion in more ways than one, and perhaps Cassandra might view him in a more favourable light. If, that was, he had not mistaken her feelings.

He could not be in doubt of his own. His introduction to Cassandra had been extremely unconventional, but it had removed all the usual constraints that a more regular one would have imposed. She had not known who he was, nor had she cared. She had been neither flattering, coquettish nor dumbstruck, but had treated him very much as an equal, judging him on what she saw rather than what she knew. This had not changed during their subsequent meetings and although he would like to curb some of her impetuosity, he would not change her in any great measure but rather channel her energy. As mistress of both Westerby and his London house, she would act as hostess to the cream of society, his friends, and even politicians. He had an inkling that she would not be at all thrown but thrive in such an environment.

His feelings for her had made him unusually clumsy; she needed guidance, not recrimination, suggestions rather than commands, but most of all, she needed to be loved for who she was. He knew it without doubt, for he wanted the same thing. God knows he had enough faults. He could be reserved, proud, and uncompromising, but Cassandra would challenge him, argue with him, and laugh both at and with him, and there was nothing he wanted more. It would be far from satisfying to possess a wife who was no more than a decoration or there merely to minister to his comfort. What would they have to say to each other?

After a brief meeting with Alfred, he spent the morning finishing his painting in what had become his secret place, applying himself to the task with a trance-like fervour. When he returned to the house it was nearing three o'clock and a letter was awaiting him from Mr Lapworth.

Carteret,

Some men from the militia based in Lynn will be waiting at Grimston, some nine miles east of the town as soon as dark falls with a riding officer or two. I have been informed by your man that they will be following the old drover's road that passes that place and only hope he is as reliable as you believe, otherwise, I will be made to look a fool. I have asked to be informed of the outcome immediately and wish you will come to dinner and stay the night so that you may be with me when news is brought. That way I may have the pleasure of either shaking your hand or… well… merely shaking you. Bring Westerby with you as you intend to take him with you to Lynn in the morning to deal with the other matter.

I do beg, however, that you will be here no later than four so that you have ample time to change for dinner which will be served promptly at five.

Lapworth

Laurence could not help but smile at his summons. Mr Lapworth, whilst resigned, was clearly still put out. He pocketed the note and ran lightly up the stairs to request Salop to pack him an overnight bag.

"And will I be accompanying you, my lord?"

"No, you may enjoy a brief holiday."

"As you wish," the valet said unperturbed.

Laurence realised that he knew very little about his servant and said, "What will you do with your spare time, Salop?"

"When I am not engaged in keeping your wardrobe in good order, I like to indulge myself in a spot of reading, sir. Currently, I am making my way through the plays of Shakespeare."

"Oh?" Laurence said surprised. "Which one is entertaining you at present?"

"*Much Ado About Nothing*, my lord. I can already see the way it's going, but I shall enjoy seeing how it all resolves itself."

Laurence stared after the man as he disappeared into his dressing room and a soft laugh escaped him. He was ruminating over the likenesses between Beatrice and Cassandra as he made his way downstairs and hardly noticed when Miss Reynolds fell in step beside him.

"I am pleased to see you smiling, Lord Carteret," she said. "I hear you were most put out this morning."

"Really?" he said. "My sister's tongue wags too much."

"Oh, no, how can you say so?" the young lady said. "It was only her concern that you should be acting so out of character that made her confide in Mrs Pellow, and as I was also partaking of breakfast, I could not help but overhear. Neither of your sisters could understand it at all, but I did in a trice. I always thought Miss Fenton a trifle bold, but for her to use so flimsy an excuse to disturb you at so early an hour shows such a want of conduct that I am sure I do not marvel at your displeasure."

Laurence stiffened. "You are mistaken, Miss Reynolds. Miss Fenton's visit was prompted by completely selfless motives. Any displeasure I might have felt was not the result of her visit; she must always be welcome in my house, but from the circumstance of her being so foolish as to ride out on so inclement a morning."

"Oh." Miss Reynolds dropped her head bashfully before peeping up at him with a rueful expression in her pansy eyes. "I see. How like you to be so considerate. I fear I have also been foolish, but I beg you won't think too badly of me. It would cast me quite down, I assure you."

They had reached the bottom of the stairs and Laurence turned to her. "I have no idea why it should, Miss Reynolds, but comfort yourself with the knowledge that I shall not think badly of you."

"You are too good," she simpered.

Laurence repressed a feeling of faint amusement at her childish tactics and decided to end the tiresome game she was playing. He reconciled his conscience to his forthcoming brutality by the knowledge that a ruthless set down now, might teach her a much-needed lesson and prevent her from becoming a fully-fledged minx.

"Not at all," he said, "I shall not think of you at all."

She gasped, and he saw as much anger as humiliation in her eyes.

"Yes, it was very uncivil of me to say so, I know. Let me offer you some advice, Miss Reynolds. When next you set your sights on a gentleman, perhaps you should consider what you can offer him as well as what he can offer you. There are some who may be satisfied with a pretty face, but prettiness fades you know. You would do better to develop your character, form your own opinions, and then you may find companionship and secure both your future and your happiness."

She did not appear at all mollified, but flew back up the stairs, no doubt to lay down upon her bed with the headache. She rushed past Lord Malmsy on her way and did not return his greeting. He carried on down the stairs, raising an eyebrow at Laurence, but there was humour and intelligence in the gaze he bent upon him.

"Finally put her in her place, did you?"

Laurence grimaced. "It was not, perhaps, very well done of me."

Lord Malmsy clapped him on the shoulder. "Nonsense, my boy. I did suggest to Anne that we should send her home before we came here, but she would have it that Kitty was just the sort of girl you admired."

"Perhaps she was thinking of my calf love," he said.

Lord Malmsy chuckled. "Anne thinks she's awake upon every suit, but she's far and fair off there. A man's last love rarely bears any resemblance to his first. He'd be a numbskull if it did, and I'll say this for you, Carteret, you're not that."

Laurence drove Alfred in his curricle to Mr Lapworth's residence and listened attentively to his colourful account of his afternoon.

"Louisa is unusually perceptive," he said. "She immediately picked up that I had thought better of allowing Mr Gill to search the cellar and handled him with a deftness I could only admire."

"Am I to wish you happy, Alfred?"

He grinned. "You are premature. But I hope very

much that you will soon be able to offer me your felicitations."

"Should I be looking about me for a new steward?"

Alfred looked surprised. "Not at all. I will still need to support myself. I am not the man to live off my wife."

Laurence smiled. "No doubt it is very selfish of me, but I am very happy to hear it."

Mr Lapworth seemed a little on edge, but he greeted them congenially enough and became increasingly philosophical during dinner.

"Ah well," he said, "if it all comes to nought, I shall say I was acting in good faith. Everyone will think I was duped by my anonymous informer, of course, and that whilst our men were lying in wait, the rascals went another way and made good their escape, but I shall bear it as best I may."

Only a very small part of this pessimistic prediction came to pass, however. Shortly before midnight the butler came into the library where they had retired after dinner and gave a letter into Mr Lapworth's hands.

"An ostler from the inn at Grimston brought it, sir," he said. "He did not wait for a reply."

"Very well. That will be all." He read it swiftly. "Ha! They bungled it! Should have known they would! That's the problem with using part-time volunteers. What we needed was some dragoons; they'd have known what they were doing."

Laurence leaned forward, frowning. "You mean they got away?"

"They've got the cargo, but most of the men

escaped. One of the rogues fired and injured one of the riding officers, although not seriously. Panic ensued, but they caught the culprit, or at least the other riding officer did, a Mr Gill. It is he who wrote me this letter whilst they bound up both his colleague's wounds and those of the prisoner at the inn. Apparently, Mr Gill returned fire and shot the hand that held the gun, a nice piece of work if he meant it, but no doubt it was a lucky shot."

"Good for him," Alfred murmured.

"Then all is not lost, and your reputation is safe," Laurence said.

Mr Lapworth rose to his feet and stifled a yawn, coming forwards to shake Laurence's hand. "Very true. I don't know about you gentlemen, but that's enough excitement for one day, and I'm for bed."

Alfred looked pensively at his cousin. "Do you think he will talk to secure his freedom?"

"Unlikely, I think," Laurence said. "I suspect his life would not be worth a shilling on his release. How many smugglers have actually been committed over the years?"

"Few," Alfred admitted. "I suspect the assault will be the easier charge to prosecute."

"So do I," Laurence agreed. "From all I ever heard, juries have historically had a strange susceptibility to the most unlikely stories given out by smugglers. As the prisoner has not killed or seriously injured his man, he may hope to be transported. No doubt he will claim his gun went off accidentally. His wisest course, therefore, would be to keep mum and take his punishment."

Early the following afternoon they visited Mr

Rythorne. It seemed his funds did not run to a butler as a maid answered the door and let them into the hall. She took Laurence's card and went to see if her master was at home. Neither of them was surprised when she came back a few moments later and said that he was not. They were not deterred by this information, however, but merely walked past her down the corridor and entered the room she had emerged from.

They found themselves in a study. A man with thinning, red hair and pale skin sat behind a desk, a ledger open before him, but he was not working on it, rather he was staring into space. He started as they came into the room, shut the ledger, and pushed himself to his feet.

"I am not receiving visitors," he said, a tremor in his voice.

"I hate to disappoint you," Laurence said softly, "but you are quite mistaken. I believe you have met Mr Westerby once before?"

Mr Rythorne's eyes rested on Alfred for a moment and a flicker of recognition came into them. "Yes, I have met your steward before, my lord, and I told him then that Willow Tree Farm was not up for sale nor likely to be."

"A circumstance which Miss Thorpe was not, until recently, aware of," Alfred said, casting the man a look from under his brows.

Mr Rythorne became paler still. "I would not dream of bothering Miss Thorpe with business matters that she could not be expected to comprehend."

"No doubt it is inconvenient for you," Alfred said,

"but I am not so ignorant and have seen a copy of the lease."

A faint sheen of sweat glistened on the man's upper lip.

"It is a paltry rent, is it not?" he added.

Laurence sat down and crossed one leg over the other, allowing his cousin the floor. With his aquiline nose and sharp, focused eyes, Alfred reminded him of a hawk toying with its prey.

"It was the wish of Mr Tremlow that Mr Moore be allowed to rent the farm at so low a price," Mr Rythorne said.

"But you are no longer acting for Mr Tremlow," Alfred pointed out gently.

"There are circumstances which I could not easily explain to ladies of such delicate sensibility as Mrs Tremlow and Miss Thorpe as to why he did so, but I felt sure that as good Christians, they would wish him to continue there on the same terms if they knew the truth."

Alfred indicated a chair. "May I?"

"Of course," Mr Rythorne said sinking down into his own.

"I would be very interested to hear of these circumstances. You may, of course, be sure of my discretion. I would not like to shock Miss Thorpe, of course."

"Mr Moore is one of Mr Tremlow's father's bastards."

"Ah, his half-brother in fact," Alfred said. "I hope you do not mind me saying so, but he is not a very good farmer."

"No, he only had a smallholding before, but Mr

Tremlow said to leave him to his own devices, and he would learn soon enough."

Alfred rested his elbows on the arms of his chair and steepled his fingers. "I find it interesting that so shrewd a businessman should offer such charity, for I can call it nothing else, to his half-brother, especially when, from all I can discover, he was not at all kind to his wife." He smiled rather wolfishly. "One would almost think that he had another reason for his apparent benevolence."

Mr Rythorne's eyes narrowed warily. "I cannot imagine what it was."

"No?" Alfred said. "Let me put it to you, then, that Mr Tremlow had a somewhat wider vision, and realised that his properties, situated as they are, could bring him an extra and extremely profitable stream of income. It is of no use to prevaricate, Mr Rythorne, I have seen the book he recorded these profits in. In short, he was using them both to bring in liquor that did not pay tax at any port. And you, sir, have taken over that side of his business."

Mr Rythorne reached for the glass of wine that sat at his elbow, but his hand was shaking, and he knocked it over. It pooled on the table and then a rivulet snaked towards the ledger. As he produced a handkerchief and began to mop up the mess, Alfred stood, took one swift stride and plucked it from the table. Mr Rythorne's eyes lifted to his, but he said nothing. Alfred sat down again and began leisurely reading the columns of figures. Presently he raised his eyes.

"Your profit seems considerably less than Mr Tremlow's."

Mr Rythorne grimaced. "There is nothing

recorded in that ledger that I cannot explain away. There are no names, nothing to say where the money came from."

"As you say," Alfred said, turning another page. He tutted. "Ah, this, I think, is a record of your gambling. It makes depressing reading; so many losses."

Mr Rythorne poured himself another glass of wine and drank it down.

"You seem singularly unfortunate," Alfred continued. "I imagine you know by now that last night's cargo is at present sitting in the custom's house?"

The fight seemed to have gone out of the man and he nodded.

"And that one of the men was captured?"

"He will say nothing," Mr Rythorne said. "And even if he does, there is no proof. I have never put my name to anything."

"Not quite true," Laurence said, judging it time for him to intervene. He produced a letter from his inner pocket. "You put your name to this. It makes for interesting reading. You called Mr Tremlow back to Lynn on the very night he was murdered, and yet you said nothing of it to the coroner."

"Where did you find that?" Mr Rythorne said, his pallor now quite ghastly.

"Not where you searched for it, obviously," Laurence said.

"I did not do it!" Mr Rythorne said. He gave a bitter laugh. "If I could only turn back the clock, I would never have had anything to do with Mr Tremlow. It was he who introduced me to a private club where gambling was rife. I knew nothing of the smuggling for some years and only dealt with his legitimate business, but then I began to lose clients and lost a large sum to Mr Tremlow himself.

"It was the third year the farm's lease was up for renewal and as I had every year, I told him that he was losing money hand over fist by renting it at so low a rate and that it did not seem to me that Mr Moore had learned anything. It was then he drew me in. He wished me to take over the running of the operation; in return, he would write off my debt, and I would receive a percentage of the profits. Gambling had me firmly in its grip by then – it's a vile disease – and I agreed.

"Mr Tremlow dealt with the money, however. Jacob Turner, the captain of the vessel that brings in the goods, came to see me one day. He felt that Mr Tremlow was taking too much of the profits. He suggested that I bring him back to Lynn before he sailed on the next tide and that between us, we would try and persuade him to give us a fairer cut. Mr Tremlow was murdered by one of Turner's men before he got here."

He dropped his head in his hands. "I did not know what he had planned. It made me feel sick, but I could do nothing. There was no proof that led to him, only that letter which led to me. He claimed that he had it and said that as it was he who took the greater risk, so it was he should take the larger cut of the profits. He had me, or so I thought, in the palm of his hand." He gave a hysterical laugh. "He thought he was so clever, but by his perfidy, he halved the profits. He had some idea of frightening Mrs Tremlow into allowing us to still use Tremlow House, but I stood against him. That poor woman had borne enough already, and I was not so lost to all sense of honour as to take part in any such scheme and so I told him."

"I am surprised he did not also murder you," Laurence said.

"I'm sure he thought of it, but I told him I had given a letter to a friend, outlining all the details of the enterprise and those concerned in it, with instructions for it to be opened in the event of my death or disappearance."

"Did you do so?" Alfred asked.

Mr Rythorne shook his head. "No. There is no one I trust enough not to be overcome with curiosity and open it. Besides, I said it only as a precaution. It is I who have all the connections and make all the arrangements. I am too valuable to him to be easily replaced."

"Was it his ship that was taken off Hunstanton?" Alfred asked.

"Yes, but he and his main crew got away in a rowing boat. It will not be long before he has another, you may be sure."

"I think it will be better if you disappear before that happens, Mr Rythorne," Alfred said. "The lease on Willow Tree Farm will not be renewed, and Miss Thorpe's affairs are to be put in my hands."

He handed the man the letter from Louisa informing him of this. Mr Rythorne read it and opened a drawer. He pulled out a folder and pushed it across the desk. "It is all in there. You should perhaps know that Mr Moore is indeed Mr Tremlow's half-brother. His only part has been to turn a blind eye, hide the carts in one of his barns, and to look after the horses." He looked speculatively at Alfred. "You said you found Mr Tremlow's account book, did you also find the money? I have never been able to discover where he stashed it."

"No, a comprehensive search of the cellars turned up nothing apart from some damp and a rat."

"I am not surprised you found damp. Why he insisted on building the house over that creek, I will never know. It added considerable expense to the construction of the house. I have sometimes wondered…" he broke off and shook his head. "Never mind. I *will* disappear. Make a fresh start somewhere. It is only that letter that has kept me here so long. That and my lack of funds."

Laurence tore up the letter and threw the scraps into the fire. "The letter is disposed of, and perhaps, if you refrain from gambling, you may soon build up your funds and another business somewhere far from here. You have been foolish, Mr Rythorne, but I think you have been punished enough. You are no murderer, and you have at least looked after Miss Thorpe's other affairs well. I will bid you good day, sir, and good fortune."

CHAPTER 22

William drove the ladies to Lynn at a rather ponderous pace, the coach weighed down by four passengers inside and a quantity of luggage strapped to both the back and the roof, most of it, Mr Tremlow's things. Grace, liberated from her position as maid, chattered away in an excited style most of the way. By the time they arrived at the town, Emma's were the only pair of ears that weren't ringing, and all the carriage's occupants could have recited both Mr Cooper's strengths and his defects in their sleep. Nor were they left in any doubt that those few defects would soon be eradicated.

Mr Cooper was not one to put himself forward, but as Grace had already proven, he only needed a little nudge. He had more brawn than brains, but she was sure someone as well educated as her uncle would soon teach him a thing or two. She could wish he had more to say for himself but dealing with customers at the inn would soon loosen his tongue, she felt sure.

Wasn't he as handsome as he could be? He only needed a bit of smartening up and a haircut and she would be the envy of every maiden for miles around.

"And I know I need not worry for you anymore, Miss Cassandra," she said, taking her hand and beaming up at her a little mistily as they pulled up outside The Globe Inn where she was to catch her stage. "For you and Miss Louisa and Miss Thorpe go on so well together."

They waved her off with a sigh of relief but fond smiles on their lips. They had agreed that the Duke's Head would be their next stop and that Emma and Louisa would take some much-needed refreshment in the coffee room before visiting the second-hand clothing shop on High Street, whilst Cassandra had her meeting with Mr Penwith.

They were greeted by a very polite waiter, who on hearing that gentleman's name, immediately whisked Cassandra off to the private parlour he had hired.

"Shall I announce you, miss?" the young man said as he showed her the correct door.

"No, I thank you," she said, slipping a coin into his hand.

For some reason, she felt reluctant to enter the room, and she was aware of a slight feeling of nervousness. This was ridiculous as Mr Penwith was an old friend and she trusted him implicitly and yet, she had a feeling that whatever news he had for her, might turn her world upon its head. He had said it might make her reconsider her future, but there was only one future she wished to contemplate. Telling herself she was being foolish, she straightened her shoulders, opened the door, and walked into the room.

A thin man in his fifties, whose hair was still black as a raven's wing, stood, and with a welcoming smile that was reflected in his grey eyes, moved towards her with a swiftness that belied his age.

"My dear Miss Fenton," he said, taking one of her hands and holding it for a moment between both of his own. "How happy I am to see you in such good health."

He led her to a chair and helped her out of her pelisse. "Won't you sit down, ma'am? I took the liberty of ordering you a glass of ratafia. I felt sure you would stand in need of something after your journey. The roads about here are quite shocking."

Cassandra sat down and watched him lay her pelisse carefully over the back of another chair. He was an intelligent, efficient man, who possessed a gravity that suited his calling and inspired confidence in his clients, but he was not without humour. There was, Cassandra perceived, an air of expectation about him. She accepted the glass he offered her with a smile. "Mr Penwith, I am intrigued. There is something quite mysterious about you today."

His eyes twinkled. "You have always been astute, ma'am, very astute. I hope you do not mind me adding that you have also been known, on occasion, to be impulsive." A soft chuckle escaped him. "Do you remember when you were only eighteen, and Mr Green's hulking great sons neglected to mend the fence and the bull escaped? You were quite furious."

"I should think I was," she said. "I had already sent the materials to mend the fence and paid them to do it. And that bull ran into the road and nearly brought my horse down. It might have killed her!"

"How like you to be more concerned about your horse than yourself. Anyway, you somehow managed to get it onto the track to Mr Green's farm and drove it all the way there. And then, maddened by fright no doubt, it chased the boys around the yard until Mr Green came to their rescue and managed to get a rope around it, after which you dismounted, and took the broom to them, telling them that they were feckless, good for nothing idiots!"

"I believe I did," she said, laughing. "But how is it that you know the story so well?"

"It is still spoken of, along with a host of other incidents."

"Oh, dear," she said, smiling ruefully.

"You are spoken of with fondness by all concerned, I assure you." He became more serious. "But the point of my recollection is to assure you that not only will you be welcomed back by almost everyone in the district, but that there really was no need for you to flee as you did. If you had only come to me, or a dozen other households, you would have found succour, I assure you."

"It would have been infamous to have put either you, my tenants or my cousin in such a position," she protested, "never mind Mrs Fenton. She would not have been able to go anywhere and hold up her head. And you must remember that when I first left, which I admit I did in temper, I did not know the lengths my cousin would go to. The last thing I expected was him to send Mr Chubb after me. Do you know why he did it, Mr Penwith? I know you put it down to his autocratic disposition in your letter, but that does not seem to explain it fully. You also mentioned that you had managed to at least make my grandfather consider that we might not suit. Did he perhaps make some other provision for me than that I already know of?"

Mr Penwith crossed his legs and folded his hands in his lap. "I shall answer your last question first. He did. I was instructed not to tell you of it, however, until it became necessary for me to do so. He was so certain that Sir Francis would be a reasonable man that he added an extra clause to the will. If you were married within a year, he would receive an extra ten thousand pounds. If you were not, then the money would come to you to do with as you pleased."

"How could he have been so foolish?" Cassandra exclaimed. "No wonder my cousin was bringing more and more pressure to bear upon me." She gave an exasperated laugh. "And how unflattering. Did he think I was unmarriageable without a bribe?"

"Not at all," Mr Penwith said soothingly. "You were the one joy in his life, and he wished you to be settled at Darley. He knew how much you loved it. As for your cousin, his actions were not motivated by greed but by jealousy."

Mr Penwith's expression became grave. "I am about to tell you a tale that will seem like something out of a Gothic novel, but I assure you every word I speak will be the truth."

"I assure you that after everything that has happened to me recently, there is nothing you can tell me that will surprise me," she said dryly.

"We shall see," Mr Penwith said. "If I had not been involved in it, I would not believe it myself. What do you know of identical twins, Miss Fenton?"

"That they may be alike in features but quite

different in character," she said promptly. "And that once you know them, their expressions and mannerisms make it clear who is who. At least that is true of the only pair of identical twins I have met. Whether it is the general rule, I cannot say."

"Is there a rivalry between these twins you know? Is one jealous of the other?"

"No," Cassandra said. "Their natures are so different that it does not arise."

"Well, in the story I am about to tell you, the identical twins are sometimes similar in nature, but not always."

"You speak in riddles, Mr Penwith," Cassandra said. "Please speak plainly."

"Very well. Francis Fenton and his brother, Lucius Fenton were great friends, inseparable in fact, in their early years. They were very alike in temperament and went to school in Winchester where the family lived. Their father was a classics scholar and taught there. Both boys were bright and became trainee solicitors. Francis completed his apprenticeship, but Lucius began to struggle. He found it difficult to sleep and his behaviour became erratic. He began to think he was being watched and that people were talking about him behind his back.

"He returned to the family home and began to resent his brother and his parents. He became convinced that his brother had had all the advantages, that he was the better-loved son. When their father became ill, Lucius nursed him and supported his mother. He became much more himself. Francis eventually became an agent for Lord Finchwick, who had a large property in Jamaica and attained the position of overseer there soon after his father died. He took his mother and his brother with him and gave Lucius employment.

"All seemed well, but Lucius soon began to resent Francis again. If his twin disagreed with any of his actions, he flew into a rage and during one of these rages, he tried to strangle him. There had been other incidents of a less serious nature, but for Francis, this was the last straw, and he told his brother he would have to return to England. Lucius begged his forgiveness and became more and more withdrawn, and it became clear that he was not fit to travel alone.

"Francis and his mother brought Lucius to England and put him in a private asylum that they knew of not many miles outside Winchester. It is a small manor house and stands in its own sizeable but secure grounds. It was set up by a wealthy family whose son suffered from an imbalance of the mind.

"Regular reports were sent to Francis, and just before he returned to England to claim his inheritance, he received a letter saying that Lucius was much improved. He had not only taken over the exercise program for the handful of residents but was also writing plays for them to perform and had become a shining example for the humane and liberal treatment of those suffering from an imbalance of the mind.

"Francis was delighted, and on reaching England went with his mother to this private institution, hoping that he might be able to bring his brother with him to Darley."

Mr Penwith paused and took a sip of his wine.

Cassandra, who was hanging upon his every word as if she were at the play, begged him to continue.

"Lucius seemed happy to see his family, congratulated his brother on his inheritance, and showed a great deal of interest in all the details. He seemed reluctant to leave, however. He had become a figure of importance and was thought of very highly by both staff and patients. He told his brother to come back the next day alone when he'd had time to think it over. Francis duly returned and was shown into Lucius' room. He agreed to go and asked his brother to help him pack, but whilst he was bent over a drawer, Lucius hit Francis on the head and knocked him out. He stripped him of his raiment and donned it himself, dressing his brother in his own clothes and then started calling for help."

Cassandra gasped and put a hand to her mouth. Mr Penwith gave a mirthless smile. "I think you may have guessed the rest."

"Yes. The man we thought was Francis was Lucius. He was amiable at first, but our spats, my opposition to his wishes, caused him to betray himself. Oh, poor Mrs Fenton. I think that even she did not suspect at first, for it was only as the weeks went on that she became so nervous."

"You have it in a nutshell, Miss Fenton." He cleared his throat. "I do not wish to be indelicate, but I also suspect that his very real attraction to you may have contributed to his increasingly erratic behaviour. He did not want you for the money, you see, but because he wished to possess both you and everything that would have been his brother's. But as the weeks went on, his insecurities emerged, and he began to suspect that the servants were cheating him or loyal to you and so replaced them. He needed to feel in control of everything and everyone about him."

"But why did Mrs Fenton not say anything?"

"Who to?" Mr Penwith said gently. "She could not tell you for that would have been to put both of you in danger. You would have no doubt confronted Lucius, Miss Fenton, and that, I fear would have been disastrous as Mrs Fenton well knew. And you must also make some allowance for maternal instinct. Mrs Fenton still wished to protect both of her sons."

"Yes, I see that," Cassandra conceded.

"Mrs Fenton was as carefully watched as you were. The day you made your escape, your cousin had taken his mother shopping. I put it to you, Miss Fenton, is it natural when there are two women in the house, for a son with a new estate to manage, to take upon himself such a task?"

"Oh!" Cassandra exclaimed. "I have been so blind!"

"Not at all," Mr Penwith said. "How should you have suspected the truth?"

"The portrait!" she said suddenly. "The miniature the real Francis enclosed with his letter. When I knew my cousin better, I thought it a very poor depiction of him. Although the likeness was there, I felt that the artist had made him appear kindlier. I put it down to either flattery or poor execution! Mr Penwith, leave me in suspense no longer. How did you discover it all?"

Mr Penwith smiled. "One of the things I have always admired about you, Miss Fenton, is that you do not go into hysterics at the least provocation, but rather tackle a problem head-on."

"I know no other way," she said simply.

"You are Sir Thomas' granddaughter indeed." He took another sip of his wine. "You, I believe, received a letter from Mrs Fenton, which was delivered with your luggage."

"Yes, a few hastily scribbled lines and they unsettled me greatly; there seemed so much left unsaid. She said that I was right to go, that she was sorry not to have known me in happier circumstances, and that she regretted that she had not the courage to protect me as she should have. But I was left with the feeling that it was I who had not protected her as I should have. Of course, I understand her now."

"Her lines to you were hastily scribbled because she had written a much longer letter to me, explaining as best she could what she feared had happened. The courier brought it to my office immediately and left it there, but I had been called away and did not receive it until the following afternoon. I immediately posted down to the asylum. They had believed Lucius to have had a sudden relapse, which they put down to him being overwhelmed by his brother and mother's visit. They thought that he was suffering delusions and had kept him sedated for some weeks. Eventually, Francis stopped trying to convince them and took over his brother's role, hoping that his mother must eventually realise the truth."

"But how did you convince them?"

"That was not difficult. I explained that I was the family lawyer and showed them Mrs Fenton's letter. I then produced copies of the letters I had written to

Mr Francis Fenton and his replies. I also had the letters he had written to your father. Only Francis could have had any detailed knowledge of what they contained. Two men from the asylum accompanied us back to Darley and the scene that followed was not as painful as you might have imagined.

"Lucius was struggling with his new role, he had lost you, and he sensed his mother was afraid of him. When we all walked into the library, he looked at Francis and smiled quite gently. He got up and shook his hand and said that he could not do it, after all, and that his brother was the better man. Mrs Fenton, who had followed us in, then embraced Lucius and told him that she loved him. Some tears were shed, not least by Lucius. He returned to the asylum quite willingly and will remain there, I suspect, for the rest of his life."

Cassandra was surprised to discover a tear rolling down her cheek. She swiped it away saying, "Poor Lucius. To live a life so caged."

"It is regrettable of course," Mr Penwith said, "but he will be allowed to help his fellow residents when he can, he will know that he will not be able to do anything he should not when he is unwell, and he will not be forgotten."

"No, he must not be. Should I write to him, do you think? I see now that he could not help himself and I would not like him to feel any great guilt over his actions towards me."

"Knowing you as well as I do, I asked that question of his carers. But they were of the opinion that it would not be wise. They do not wish him to be exposed to anything that might cause him sadness or overexcite him."

"No, of course not," Cassandra said. "Not everything can be fixed, can it?"

Mr Penwith rose to his feet and smiled. "Most things can be, Miss Fenton, if there is a will, but not all things. Now, are you ready to meet the real Sir Francis and be reunited in happier circumstances with Mrs Fenton?"

Cassandra jumped to her feet. "Of course. At once, if you please."

Mr Penwith crossed the room and she realised there was a connecting door to another room. He opened it and said, "Miss Fenton is ready to meet you now."

Laurence set Alfred down at his tailors as he had decided he needed a new coat and Laurence proceeded to the Duke's Head alone. As he drove into the courtyard of the inn, he saw a carriage with baggage piled high and the footman from Tremlow House sitting on the box enjoying a mug of ale.

He frowned and said, "William, isn't it?"

"Yes, sir," he replied.

"Is Miss Fenton within?"

"Aye," he confirmed. "She has a meeting with someone."

"Might I enquire who she has a meeting with?"

"I couldn't say," the young man said.

Laurence swiftly jumped down and strode into the

inn. He found Mr Chubb waiting for him at the bottom of the stairs.

"Have you seen Miss Fenton?" he said curtly.

"I have," he said, adding portentously, "and she's not the only person who might be of some interest to you that I have seen. That's why I'm guarding the stairs."

"Be plain, man!" Laurence said, the sense of foreboding he had felt upon seeing the luggage strapped to the coach, growing.

"I saw Sir Francis Fenton go up these stairs some few minutes after Miss Fenton. Medium height, short brown hair, light brown eyes. Take the right landing and it's the third door on the left."

"Continue to guard the stairs," Laurence said through gritted teeth, already bounding up them two at a time.

He pushed open the door and was dismayed to find the room empty. But then he heard the low murmur of voices and saw that another door was slightly ajar. He rushed across the room and pushed it so hard that it slammed back against the wall. His eyes immediately found Cassandra. She was standing by a table, her hands in those of a gentleman of medium height.

"Let her go," he snapped, striding across the room and delivering a flush hit to the man's jaw. The man went down, and Laurence stood over him, his fists clenched. "Stay there if you know what is good for you."

A faint scream behind him made him turn his head, and he saw a middle-aged lady in a cap rise to her feet.

"How dare you, sir!"

A slender man dressed in black had been sitting with her and he also stood, his demeanour grave but the merest hint of amusement in his eyes.

"Lord Carteret, I presume?"

He felt a hand on his arm and the low, mellifluous voice he had come to love, say, "Let him up, Laurence. It is not what you think."

CHAPTER 23

The man on the floor rubbed his jaw. "That's quite a right you have there." He held up a hand, "Be a good sport and help me up, will you?"

This mild-mannered man with humorous brown eyes was not the ogre he had expected. He grasped his hand and pulled him to his feet.

"I apologise, sir," he said, his embarrassment making him sound stiff. "I had been led to believe that you were Sir Francis Fenton."

The man smiled ruefully. "I am Sir Francis Fenton. It was my twin brother Lucius masquerading as me who persecuted my cousin. But do not think too badly of him; he could not help himself."

"It is quite true," Cassandra said.

"I must thank you, Lord Carteret," Sir Francis said, "for taking such good care of Cassandra."

Mrs Fenton came forwards. "As must I. You have been so much the gentleman by all that Cassandra has told me, that I shall overlook what you have just done

313

to my son. However, you really should learn not to be so impetuous."

Laurence offered Mrs Fenton a brief bow, but it was Cassandra his eyes went to. Her eyes sparkled with happiness, and he thought he had never seen her look more beautiful.

"No doubt I am being stupid, but I must admit to being a trifle confused."

"It is a long story," Cassandra said. "And you deserve an explanation, but if you do not object, Laurence, I will come to you the day after tomorrow with the miniatures and explain everything. My cousin and I have much to discuss."

Laurence was left with no other option but to bow and withdraw. His descent of the stairs was much slower than his ascent had been, and a heavy frown marked his brow.

"I didn't expect you so soon," Mr Chubb said. "Where's Miss Fenton?"

"Stand down, Mr Chubb," Laurence said. "Sir Francis Fenton is no longer your or my concern."

Mr Chubb rapidly lost interest in Sir Francis as Laurence reached into the pocket of his greatcoat. He accepted his payment, saying, "It was a pleasure to do business with such a gentleman as you, Lord Carteret. I shall use this to help me set up as a respectable land-lord somewhere quiet."

"I am glad to hear it," Laurence said. "But not, I hope, in Norfolk."

When he went again into the yard, he saw Alfred handing Louisa into her coach.

"Good day, Miss Thorpe. Are you going on a long journey?"

"Oh no. I am merely carrying Mr Tremlow's old things to the clothes shop in High Street whilst Cassandra meets with Mr Penwith." She smiled confidingly at him. "I am quite agog to hear her news for he thought it might make her reconsider her future. I cannot imagine what it might be."

"You would miss her surely," Laurence said.

"I would, of course," Louisa said. "But she would never have been content to stay with me forever, you know."

Laurence allowed Alfred to drive them back to Westerby, not trusting himself to concentrate. When he told his cousin of what had occurred in the parlour at the inn, Alfred said, "It seems a very strange thing for this Lucius to do, but if Sir Francis said he could not help it, we must presume he is not quite right in his mind. There's no need for you to look so glum, old fellow. Do not tell me that the circumstance of Miss Fenton having such a relation has changed your feelings towards her?"

"Don't be such a clunch," Laurence said irritably.

Alfred was not the man to take umbrage at the uneven temper of a man in love. "Then I assume she is still giving you the cold shoulder."

"She did not give me the cold shoulder, on the contrary, she looked radiantly happy."

Alfred repressed a smile. "But that is good news, surely? Miss Fenton cannot have felt comfortable being estranged from her family."

"Did you hear what Miss Thorpe said, Alfred? Or were you too busy staring into her green eyes?"

Alfred laughed. "I am quite capable of doing both things, I assure you."

"I'm sorry, cousin," Laurence said wryly. "I am living in a state of uncertainty that I find exasperating, to say the least. If Mr Penwith considers that the news he brings may make Cassandra rethink her future, I can only put one interpretation upon that."

"Oh, here is a flight of fancy, indeed!" Alfred said cheerfully. "I didn't know you were capable of it."

"I am not," Laurence said dryly. "You know some of Cassandra's story, but you do not have all the facts."

"I don't need them to guess what is in your mind," Alfred said. "You saw her holding Sir Francis' hands, you saw a look of radiant happiness upon her face, and the thought that she might have fallen in love at first sight occurred to you."

"Sir Francis," Laurence said coldly, "is the man her grandfather wished her to marry. She admitted to me at our first meeting that she might have considered marrying him if only he had been a man of integrity. Furthermore, marrying him would allow her to return to the home and estate that she had poured all her energies into for years."

"How love can addle a man's brains," Alfred observed. "Mr Penwith may have considered that these facts might have made Miss Fenton consider her future, but he had not before met you and could not have known that her feelings had already been engaged by another. Did she tear a strip off you for knocking her cousin down?"

"No," Laurence acknowledged. "She merely laid a gentle hand upon my arm and told me all was not as it seemed."

"There you are, then," Alfred said. "Now if, and it

is a very big if, I admit, for I doubt many are capable of it, but if someone knocked you down, I imagine Miss Fenton would object, probably quite violently."

Laurence's lip curved up at one corner and his eyes grew distant as if he were picturing this unlikely event and thoroughly enjoying it.

"And has it occurred to you, cousin, that she may well have looked radiant *because* you had knocked him down? No doubt it is bloodthirsty of her, and I feel quite sorry for Sir Francis, however, I believe there are some females who might take such a savage action as a declaration of continued affection. Coming so soon after such a heated argument as I believe you to have had, I am sure it is quite understandable."

Laurence gave a dry laugh. "How is it, Alfred, that I was able to see clearly the path my friends' romances were taking, but my own is much more difficult to read."

"I believe it is often the case," Alfred replied.

"I do not think it is true of your case, however," Laurence said.

"Ah, but I am older and wiser than you."

"You have been led by the nose from the start," Laurence scoffed.

Alfred grinned. "Perhaps, but I went willingly."

Cassandra wrapped each of the framed miniatures in a handkerchief and carefully placed them into her reticule. She ran lightly down the stairs and went into the parlour to say goodbye to Louisa, finding her friend emerging from a passionate embrace, her colour much heightened and her eyes glowing.

"I am very happy for you both," she said, smiling.

"Thank you," Alfred said, straightening his rumpled cravat.

Louisa came forwards and embraced her friend.

"I am deliriously happy," she murmured.

"Will you both live here?" Cassandra asked.

"Alfred has offered the Moores a small cottage with a few acres of land on Lord Carteret's estate, and we thought we might live at Willow Tree Farm. It is nearer to Westerby. We are going to look at the house in a moment and make plans."

"I shall look forward to hearing them when I return from Westerby. Have you told Emma the news?"

"No, but I must do so immediately. She will live with us, of course. How she will enjoy helping us put it in some sort of order. I only hope it is not too ramshackle inside."

Cassandra turned and walked back into the hall, Louisa following close behind her. Her eye was drawn by the slate on the hall table. Six capitalised words had been written upon it in white chalk. I AM IN THE CELLAR. COME DOWN!

She picked it up and turned to show it to Louisa and Alfred.

"She went down there about twenty minutes ago after she had helped me dress," Cassandra said. "She wished to fetch the bed linen she had seen in one of the chests."

"She must have come back up but decided not to interrupt us," Louisa mused.

Cassandra slipped her reticule from her wrist and laid it on the table. "I doubt you would have noticed if she had come into the room."

She picked up one of the candles that were always kept there to light their way to bed. Alfred lit it and two more and they made their way as fast as they dared into the cellar. But when they reached the final room, there was no sign of Emma. One of the chests was open and the bed linen on the floor beside it.

Alfred was the first to reach it. "Good Lord!"

"What is it?" Louisa demanded.

"Come and see for yourself."

Louisa and Cassandra were soon at his side, and they stared, wide-eyed at the gaping hole in the bottom of the chest. They could just discern a set of steps leading into the darkness below.

"It had a false bottom," Alfred said, indicating the rectangular piece of wood that lifted on a hinge and now rested against the lid.

In a few moments, the darkness lightened, and they saw Emma, an oil lamp in her hand. She laughed and said, "I have found the treasure!"

Louisa gathered her skirts and Alfred grasped her arm firmly as she stepped into the chest and felt for the first step. He helped Cassandra next and soon they were all standing in a large cavern with an arching roof. A deep channel ran through the middle, but as the tide was low, only a benign trickle of water flowed through it.

Emma lifted her lamp, and they saw four smaller chests set against the wall. The lid of one of them was open and as they came closer, they saw that it was filled with leather drawstring bags. Emma grabbed

Louisa's hands and cupped them together, and then reached for one of the bags and poured a few golden guineas into her palms.

"There are one hundred guineas in every bag!"

Alfred smiled down at Louisa. "You may build your school, after all."

Cassandra drove herself in the gig, with Plackett as escort, sitting beside her rather than in the groom's seat. She had taken particular care with her appearance. Emma had curled her hair and although it was caught behind her head with a slender white ribbon woven through it, she had allowed several tresses to tumble over her shoulders and down her back. Her simple dress of white muslin was accompanied by a green spencer, the colour mirrored in the high crown of her bonnet, and a set of pearls were clasped about her throat.

"You look beautiful, Miss Cassandra," Plackett ventured.

"Thank you," she said.

"I take it you're not set on going back home any time soon, then."

"I hope very much to visit, of course, but I have no definite plans, you understand."

Plackett merely grinned and jumped down to help her out of the gig.

Laurence's butler came down the steps to greet her.

"Good afternoon, Needham," she said. "Are Lady Malmsy and Mrs Pellow at home?"

"I'm afraid not, Miss Fenton," he said. "Everyone has gone to the fair at Burnham Westgate, apart from his lordship that is."

"I had forgotten all about it," she said ruefully. "I know they particularly wished Lord Carteret to accompany them, but you said that he has not gone?"

"No, ma'am. He is awaiting you in the south drawing room."

She removed her bonnet and paused as they passed a mirror in the crimson saloon to pat a few stray curls into place. Needham gave no sign that he had noticed but patiently waited, his gaze averted. As she turned, she noticed one of the niches was empty. A soft chuckle escaped her.

"Is Thucydides keeping watch over the library?"

"I believe so, ma'am," the butler said. "He looks very well there."

As they approached the drawing room, she said, "Would you mind very much not announcing me, Needham?"

He inclined his head. "As you wish, Miss Fenton."

She paused with her fingers loosely clasping the door handle and drew in a deep breath, a small smile of anticipation trembling on her lips. Pushing the door gently open, she went in. Laurence stood at a window, gazing out at the Italian garden, but turned as she entered. He did not bow but stood staring at her for some moments, the rigid set of his jaw relaxing as he smiled gently. He spoke no word of greeting but walked slowly towards her.

Her breath caught as he stood much nearer than was polite and took a thick curling strand of her hair between his fingers. He lifted it to his lips. "I wanted to do this the first time I saw you."

"We are being as improper now as we were then," she said softly.

"I am about to be more improper still," he murmured, his lips finding the spot at the base of her neck where her pulse beat strongly.

She lifted an unsteady hand to his shoulder.

"I will exasperate you," she whispered. "Tease you, argue with you, perhaps embarrass you."

"I look forward to it," he said, lifting his head and looking deep into her eyes. His fingers traced the high line of her cheek before his palm curved around it. "I have been sleeping, Cassandra, but you have woken me from that slumber. Never do I feel so much alive as when you are near."

"It is the same for me," she said and pressed her lips to his.

His arms went around her waist, and he pulled her close, rubbing his lips teasingly against hers until she moaned softly, only then deepening their kiss. It was she who pulled her head back first, laughing shakily.

"Enough. I cannot think. I cannot breathe, and we have so much to say to each other, Laurence."

He reluctantly released her and led her to a sofa. They sat together, he with his arm around her waist, she with her head on his shoulder.

"First tell me that you will marry me."

She chuckled. "I am not so lost to all sense of propriety that I would have kissed you if I did not mean to wed you."

"I still wish to hear you say it."

She tilted her head back. "Yes, Laurence, I will

marry you. I did not mean those words I threw at you last time I was here. I regretted them almost instantly."

He smiled and stole another quick kiss. "As did I. I still had hope but then I saw you with your cousin and thought that perhaps your grandfather's wishes might take precedence over mine."

She raised her hand and brushed the hair from his brow. "When you strode into that room, your eyes blazing with anger and knocked poor Francis down, I knew that you still cared for me and felt fiercely exultant. That is shocking, I know. I should rather have been worried for my cousin."

His arm tightened about her. "I find nothing to object to in your response. I wish I had been as sure of your feelings. It was not until you walked into this room that I knew. You looked at me with such a mixture of love and hope that I could not be in doubt."

Nothing more was said for some time, but she eventually explained to him how Lucius had come to take Francis' place.

"The poor fellow," Laurence said. "Yet I find that I am grateful to him. If his brother had come first, I would never have met you and you might well have married him."

"No, I would not. I like Francis and am happy to know that Darley will be in safe hands and that Mrs Fenton may be easy once again, but my grandfather's wishes would not have forced me into a lukewarm marriage. He only wanted my happiness, and I have never felt happier than at this moment."

Laurence lowered his head as if to kiss her again,

but they heard Needham's voice, unusually loud outside the door.

"Can I bring you any refreshment, Lady Malmsy?"

"I am not deaf, Needham. Why on earth are you shouting? Some refreshment would be most welcome, bring whatever you think appropriate. You should know what we like by now."

By the time the door opened, Laurence had moved to a chair some way from the sofa. They both stood as Anne, Cecy, Lord Malmsy and Mr Pellow came in.

"You did very well not to come, Laurence," Anne said, stripping off her gloves. "It was a ramshackle affair and half of the promised acts were not there. Apparently, they are stuck in quagmires of mud somewhere up country."

She placed her gloves on the table and bent to pick up Cassandra's hat that lay discarded on the carpet. Her gaze swept the room and alighted on Cassandra.

"Good day, my dear. This is a very nice bonnet. You should take more care of it." She glanced from Laurence to Cassandra, noticed the distance between them and said, "I hope you two have not been arguing again. The children have been extremely fractious and whilst I can understand their disappointment, Kitty's bad temper is harder to forgive. Just when she might have made herself useful by amusing dear Phoebe, she positively snapped her nose off. I have never been more mistaken in a girl."

When everyone had greeted one another, Cecy said, "Have you finished the miniatures, Cassie? Only we are to go home tomorrow, and I did so wish to see them."

"As do I," Mr Pellow said.

"Do you think you will be able to tell them apart?" Lord Malmsy said. "In person, it is, of course, easy to distinguish the girls, but in a portrait and a miniature at that, I should think it will be impossible."

"Nonsense," Mr Pellow said. "I shall know my wife at a glance."

Cecy turned quite pink with pleasure.

"I will lay you a monkey you can't," Lord Malmsy said.

Mr Pellow held out his hand. "Done!"

"Please do not," Cassandra said perturbed. "I would not wish anyone to lose such a large sum due to my lack of competence."

"Do not disturb yourself," Anne said. "It is to be deplored, of course, but they cannot help themselves."

Cassandra shrugged, untied the strings of her reticule and pulled out the portraits. She laid them on a table still wrapped in their handkerchiefs.

"Very well. You come forward first Mr Pellow and choose one, but do not open it. Lord Malmsy will take the one that is remaining."

When they had done so, she said, "You may now unwrap the handkerchiefs."

"This is better by far than anything we saw at the fair," Cecy said in a breathless voice.

Both gentlemen intently examined their respective miniatures and then spoke at the same time.

"I think this one is yours."

The portraits swapped hands.

Lord Malmsy considered his and a wide smile

dawned. "Yes, that's my Anne. You are very skilled, Miss Fenton. Such crisp detailing, and the eyes, so expressive."

"Quite, quite," Mr Pellow said thoughtfully, evincing no great pleasure at winning such a large sum from his brother-in-law.

Not unnaturally, their wives demanded to see the portraits, but Mr Pellow said, "Wait a moment, if you please. We, who have the pleasure of seeing your lovely faces every day, must have known you. But even though Carteret is your brother, we rarely see him above two or three times a year. Malmsy, I bet you another monkey that he will not be able to tell the difference."

"Done," that gentleman said immediately. "Turn around, Carteret, whilst we lay them on the table."

"Certainly," he said.

"You may look now," Mr Pellow said.

Laurence came forwards and picked up one, replaced it, and picked up the other. Cassandra felt a prickle of nerves. His opinion was by far more important to her. He suddenly turned and took her hand, raising it to his lips. "My compliments, ma'am."

Even as she coloured, he held out one of the miniatures, "This is you, Anne." He then held out his other arm, "And this you, Cecy."

Both ladies rushed forwards and almost snatched them from his hands. The gentlemen strolled over and looked over their wives' shoulders. Mr Pellow dropped a kiss on his wife's head and said, "We are even, Malmsy."

"So we are," he said cheerfully.

Cassandra became embarrassed as she was

bombarded with compliments and was relieved to see Needham come into the room carrying a tray bearing glasses and a bottle of wine.

"Needham," Anne said, "Are you feeling unwell? First you shout and now you bring in the best glasses and if I am not much mistaken a very fine Madeira. Where is the tea?"

The butler merely smiled and left the room.

"Do you think he is becoming senile, Laurie?"

"Not at all," her brother said. "He is as sharp as ever he was."

"Never mind, now where was I, oh yes, as I was saying, Cassandra, I really think that your talent is remarkable— "

"Lord Carteret," she said quickly, searching her mind for some way in which she could deflect the attention away from herself, "did you not say you would show me your painting of the lake when it was finished?"

"So I did," he confirmed. He went to the corner of the room and removed a screen that had been placed there. An easel was revealed and the back of a canvas that measured about twenty inches by fifteen.

"Where have you been hiding away whilst you painted it?" Cecy asked. "I have several times sent someone to search for you, but you were nowhere to be found."

Laurence grinned. "Somewhere I knew I would not be disturbed. The cottage on the lake."

"But how could you paint the lake from the perspective you first sketched it when inside the cottage?" Anne asked.

"Because I did not paint the lake but a different

subject altogether. One that filled my thoughts so completely that I had no need to have it before me."

He turned the easel and the room fell silent. It was a portrait born of his imagination. It depicted Cassandra as he had often dreamed of her, and he now had the satisfaction of knowing that it was precisely how she looked after she had been kissed. Her eyes shone softly, her lips were slightly parted, and her hair streamed around her face and over her shoulders completely unbound.

"Superb," Lord Malmsy murmured. "It quite takes one's breath away."

"Indeed," Mr Pellow agreed.

"Oh," Cecy cried. "It is the most beautiful portrait I have ever seen."

Anne blinked and said, "My goodness. I see Needham knew what he was about after all."

Cassandra wiped away the sudden tears that sprang to her eyes and laughed. "Even in this, you had to get the better of me. You, who only paint landscapes, must outshine me on your first attempt at a portrait."

Laurence smiled lovingly at her. "Do not be dismayed, Cassandra, for you will be my only subject."

ALSO BY JENNY HAMBLY

Thank you for your support! I do hope you enjoyed
Carteret. If you would consider leaving a short review on
Amazon, I would be very grateful. I love to hear from my
readers and can be contacted at: jenny@jennyhambly.com

Other books by Jenny Hambly

Belle – Bachelor Brides 0

Rosalind – Bachelor Brides 1

Sophie – Bachelor Brides 2

Katherine – Bachelor Brides 3

Bachelor Brides Collection

Marianne - Miss Wolfraston's Ladies Book 1

Miss Hayes - Miss Wolfraston's Ladies Book2

Georgianna - Miss Wolfraston's Ladies Book 3

Miss Wolfraston's Ladies Collection

Allerdale - Confirmed Bachelor's Book 1

Bassington - Confirmed Bachelors Book 2

ABOUT THE AUTHOR

I love history and the Regency period in particular. I grew up on a diet of Jane Austen, Charlotte and Emily Bronte, and Georgette Heyer.

I like to think my characters, though flawed, are likeable, strong and true to the period.

I live by the sea in Plymouth, England, with my partner, Dave. I like reading, sailing, wine, getting up early to watch the sunrise in summer, and long quiet evenings by the wood burner in our cabin on the cliffs in Cornwall in winter.

ACKNOWLEDGMENTS

Thank you, Melanie Underwood, for being so reliable and efficient!

Thank you, Dave, for driving me all over the country on my research trips. Norfolk was a lovely surprise. I wonder where I will drag you next?

Made in United States
Orlando, FL
13 March 2022

15745534R00203